TWILIGHT

A NOVEL BY WILLIAM GAY

TWILIGHT

A NOVEL BY WILLIAM GAY

MacAdam/Cage

MacAdam/Cage
155 Sansome Street
Suite 550
San Francisco, CA 94104
www.macadamcage.com

Library of Congress Cataloging-in-Publication Data

Gay, William.
  Twilight : a novel / by William Gay.
    p. cm.
  ISBN-13: 978-1-59692-058-3 (alk. paper)
  ISBN-10: 1-59692-058-0 (alk. paper)
  1. Undertakers and undertaking–Fiction. 2. Funeral rites and
ceremonies–Fiction. 3. Southern States–Fiction. I. Title.
  PS3557.A985T86 2006
  813'.54–dc22

                                                    2006019865

Manufactured in the United States of America
10 9 8 7 6 5 4 3 2 1

Book and jacket design by Dorothy Carico Smith

The rest is silence.
William Shakespeare, *Hamlet*

᷍

How compliant are the dead. You can arrange them, like cut flowers.
Fenton Breece, 1951

BOOK ONE

❧

INTO THE TERRITORIES

The wagon came out of the sun with its attendant din of iron rims turning on flinty shale, its worn silvergray fired orange by the malefic light flaring behind it, the driver disdaining the road for the shortcut down the steep incline, erect now and sawing the lines, riding the brake onehanded until the wheels locked and skidded, then releasing it so that wagon and team and man moved in a constantly varying cacophony of shrieks and rattles and creaks and underlying it all the perpetual skirling of steel on stone.

Patton's store. A grinning man would halt the wagon with an upraised arm but it would not halt. When he noticed the quiltcovered cargo the wagon transported, he called, What you got there, Sandy?

The driver turned and spat and wiped his mouth and glanced back briefly but he didn't stay the wagon. Dead folks, he said. The wagon went on and vanished like some ghostwagon in the vaporous mist rising from the river.

Coming into Ackerman's Field the wagon and its curious freight accrued to itself a motley of children and barking dogs and a few dusty turtlebacked automobiles and such early risers as were stirring and possessed of enough curiosity to join the macabre parade to its ultimate end on the courthouse lawn.

Before he even stepped down from the wagon the man said, Get Sheriff Bellwether out here.

A fat man in overalls had approached the wagon. Bellwether's done been sent for, he said. Who all is it, Sandy?

The man pulled back the quilt covering with the faintest flourish, not unlike *a nightmare magician offering up for consideration some sleightofhand.*

Goddamn it, Sandy, that girl's half naked. Did you not have enough respect to cover her up?

The man they'd called Sandy spat. I ain't Fenton Breece, Hooper. All I undertook to do was bring em in. That's all the undertakin I aim to do. You want to handle em, then you cover em up.

The dead exhibited in the strawstrewn wagonbed. A man or the bloody remnants of one. A rawboned middleaged woman with one bare and dirty foot protruding from the makeshift shroud. A girl with hair the color and sheen of a bird's wing. About her throat an arrowhead tied to a leather thong, and the thong wound tightly into the bluelooking flesh. A boy of fourteen or fifteen and another younger yet and over all a welter of congealing blood. Aligned so and staring at the uncaring sky they are beyond any commiseration you might have for them and you'd be hard put to come up with a sin they might have committed enormous enough to have brought them to so shoddy an end.

The fat man in faded Duck Heads shuffled his feet awkwardly. Behind him the malign sun had burned away the last of the morning mist and the falsefront stores and tacky houses assembled themselves almost apologetically, dimensionless and makeshift props for the darker tableau that has played beyond the curtain.

There are some sorry son of a bitches in this world, the fat man said inadequately.

I believe about half of em are runnin wild in the Harrikin, Sandy said.

Who's runnin wild? Who done this mess, anyway?

God knows. Or more likely the devil. Old man Bookbinder got jumped by Granville Sutter and faced him down with a horse pistol. There's a Tyler boy lost in there wanderin around with a rifle and some story about a dead sister and Fenton Breece misburyin dead folks. Turned up at my house two or three o'clock in the morning half out of his head. Said we might ought to open some graves. I ain't much for graverobbin but after this I'd believe most anything.

Well, I'll be goddamned, the fat man said suddenly. I never noticed that. He pointed. A bloody mound of curly hair. A dog in there.

He brought out a taffycolored dog. Some breed of terrier. The dog's eyes were open and its distended tongue as purple as a chow's. Strangest of all, the dog's ears had been pierced and it wore a gaudy pair of dimestore earrings.

Well, I'll be damned. I don't believe I ever seen a dog wearin earbobs.

Reckon why whoever it was killed the dog anyway?

I've thought about that some, Sandy said. I believe it was just all there was left to kill.

They came up through the stand of cypress that shrouded the graveyard, the pickup hidden off the road in a chertpit clotted with inkblot bowers of honeysuckle. There were two of them, a young woman and a gangling youth who appeared to be younger still. A leaden rain out of the first slow days of winter had begun some time after midnight and the cypresses wept as they passed beneath them, the tools the pair slung along in their hands refracting away such light as there was and the pair pausing momentarily when the first milkwhite stones rose bleakly out of the dark. Behind and below them the church loomed, a pale outraged shape, no more, and only the impotent dead kept its watch.

The girl moved ahead amongst the gravestones with a sense of purpose but the boy hung back as if he'd had second thoughts or had other places to be. She turned a flashlight on and off again immediately though in truth she hadn't needed it.

Here, she said. This one here.

Yeah, the boy said. Rain ran out of his hair and down his face. His clothing was already soaked and you could hear the water in his boots as he walked. This is crazy as shit, he said.

This seemed so selfevident she didn't even reply. He drove the spade into the earth mounded atop the grave and leaning his weight into the work began to remound the earth in a pile next the grave. She seated herself on a gravestone and crossing her legs at the ankles and shielding her lighter from the rain with her body lit a cigarette and smoked and watched this curious midnight shift at work. A car passed once below them snaking the curves, the lit cypresses rearing out of the windy rain and subsiding and there was a fragment of girl's laughter and a flung bottle broke on macadam. Gone in a roar of gutted mufflers and dark fell final and absolute and she could hear his breathing and the steady implacable work of the spade. She was on her third cigarette when metal scraped on metal and when it did, something she couldn't put a name to twisted in her like a knife.

The scraping ceased. Bring me the light, he said.

Come and get it.

Goddamn, can't you do anything?

I don't want to see. Come and get it.

Silence. The soft sough of the windy rain in the trees. He said something indecipherable and clambered up out of the grave all gummed with mud and his claycovered boots outsized and clownish and crossed between the stones, a grotesque figure halfcomic here in this township of the dead. He wordlessly took the light and descended again into the grave. When the spade struck the casket this time she stopped her ears with the flat of her hands but she could still hear the wrench when the lid came free.

Nothing for some time. Then he came up to the gravestone and hunkered there in the rain. There was a ragged sound to his breathing but she couldn't tell if he was crying or just out of breath.

What we thought?

Yes. Worse. The son of a bitch—

She leant forward abruptly and stopped his mouth hard with the palm of her hand and they just sat there, his dark face like rainwashed stone and his wide frightened eyes burning palely out of the dark.

❧

On the last mild morning of an impending winter and on what was one of the last peaceful days of his life, Fenton Breece came out of his undertaking establishment and stood for a moment on the edge of his manicured lawn just breathing deeply the morning air. He looked about and there was reassurance in all he saw on this December morning in the year of our Lord nineteen-fifty-one. Past the glass sign that told in gothic script BREECE FUNERAL HOME he could see the intersection of Oak and Maple, and on opposing corners there were three churches. The Centre Church of Christ, the Cumberland Presbyterian, the First Methodist. He had stood so as a child with his father's hand clasping his own and he had no reason to doubt it would always be so.

The trees had bared and even as he stood listening to the distant sounds of commerce from the town a few last gold maple leaves drifted with the breeze. Winter was coming. He exulted in this knowledge, there was something warm and comforting about it. He'd live in his own cozy rooms, venturing out only when he had to, as comfortable as Badger from *Wind in the Willows*. He'd see few people, and most of them would not see him back, business was always good in the winter, old folks were always going to sleep and just not waking up.

Here in this land of Duck Head overalls and felt hats he was a model of sartorial elegance. He wore a fawncolored topcoat over a tan gabardine suit with a matching vest buttoned over his wellfed belly and an offwhite shirt with a green tie of iridescent watermarked silk. He wore a brown Stetson with a rolled brim and a flat crown, and he carried an umbrella though there was no cloud in sight.

He looked at his watch. It was time for his morning coffee break. He figured he'd take it at the Bellystretcher Café this morning, and he leisurely ambled that way. Townfolk he met nodded formally to him. Sometimes if they were women who appealed to him in some way and whose death he anticipated with relish he'd tip the Stetson and watch their eyes skitter away to somewhere else and they'd hurriedly walk on.

Folks were always doing that. Their eyes would sidle away to study intently something they hadn't noticed a moment before. They had been known to cross the street to avoid meeting him. Some loathsome bird. His penguinlike waddle, some dark and unlovely bird of paradise. He'd smile his one-size-fits-all smile. That's all right, he would think. Laugh at me while you can. The last laugh is mine, for it is my stainless steel table you will lie on. The water that flushes away your blood and offal and the last perspiration you ever perspired will be charged to my bill. We'll see how you like it then when there's no one left in the round world to snigger to.

At the Bellystretcher he seated himself next to a pair of oldtimers in overalls and denim jumpers and ordered his coffee. He nodded to the two men and they gave him back little nods so distant as to barely qualify as greetings. A fierce anger perpetually ached in him but he'd learned to bank it. The living are capable of revenge the dead cannot exact. He just went back to sugaring his coffee.

He had a horror of people but he'd learned to control this too. All he had to do was imagine them naked and dead on his table with the pump humming their blood away and he'd be able to hold his own.

But on this morning one of the old men would not let him be. He kept sniffing the air ostentatiously and nudging the other oldtimer in the ribs, and after awhile he said, Somethin sure does smell sweet.

The other nodded. Flowers damn sure in bloom somewhere, he said.

Breece pretended he didn't hear him.

The man said, Somebody sure does smell good in here.

Breece turned to face him. He dreamed the old man's face ashen and slackjawed, the rheumy eyes dry and staring.

Well, it's obvious it's not you, he said conversationally. You smell like cow shit and Sloan's liniment.

It took all he had to say it. He commenced drinking his coffee though it was so hot it almost scalded his throat. The man next rose with his coffee and moved a few stools down. Breece finished his coffee and set the cup down hard. He laid too much money on the counter and rose and went out. The door closed behind him and the small bell chimed once and ceased.

You best leave him alone, Shorty, one of the men called. He ain't just right in the head. One of these days he's going to pull out a sawedoff shotgun about a yard long and put you to sleep. Then he'll drag you by the hair of the head up the street to his parlor and embalm your dead ass.

Hell, I didn't do nothin, Shorty said. The truth shall set you free. He did smell good. Put me in mind of an old gal off Tom's Creek I used to go with.

It rained for four more nights and Tyler and his sister opened as many graves. These were nights of cold winter drizzles and sullen heavens with no one about and they felt perhaps rightly that the dark belonged to them. She seemed possessed by this folly. He'd begun to think her mad. Had begun to accept that this madness had infected him as well. For they both by now moved in a peculiar detachment from reality. A sort of outraged disbelief that such things could be.

She didn't go to work. He didn't know if she'd quit her job and he didn't ask. He didn't know if she slept during the day or whether she'd reached some curious state of grace in which she was sustained not by food and sleep but by the fixation that drove her. He would lie up and sleep in a dreamless state of exhaustion and awaken in the same position he'd held when sleep took him. He would have expected nightmares but then he came to suspect he was getting his full quota of them during his waking hours and that no more were allotted. His hands were raw with bleeding blisters from the shovel and his fingers felt permanently cupped to fit its handle.

Each day he swore was the last. Each night they'd be abroad with the tools in the bed of the old truck. It was a wide world with no shortage of graveyards, and he began to think of the earth as ripe and fecund with the dead, stick a spade anywhere and you'd strike a corpse. Nor was it lost upon him that they were wresting secrets from the millennia. Burial is sacred. It is secret. When the lid is sealed, it is for all time. For all time. The earth with its cargo of dead shuttles through the black dusty void while empires rise out of nothingness, others fade into the same. Days clock into night and back again and the seasons cycle their endless repetition while the dead repose with their clasped hands and their dreamless sleep and it is all the same to them.

A cold detachment had seized him. He was wrenching open the forbidden with a crowbar and each atrocity he was uncovering seemed worse than the last. An old man in a shirt and tie and a gray suitcoat and no more. He was buried a eunuch though he'd not been one in life. A woman who had been buried with these missing or other similar genitals between her thighs. As if he'd alter these helpless folk to his liking. Or was yet some mad geneticist burying his mistakes and starting anew.

Some of the caskets had garbage in them. He recorded all these minutiae with a spacey disbelief. Coke bottles, candy wrappers, half an apple, old newspapers, emptied ashtrays. The ultimate garbage disposal. Someone had just swept up the trash and disposed of it forevermore.

There was a body with no coffin at all laid a foot or so beneath the earth in windings of stained bedsheet. An old woman shared her resting place with a young man who'd had his throat straightrazored, and he lay humped athwart her thighs as they lay arm in arm in eternal debauchery.

At first she had refused but now she was looking too. Cataloguing these forbidden exhibits. From a carnival freakshow wended here from the windy reaches of dementia praecox. He hadn't known there were perversions this dark, souls this twisted.

≫

What do you think? Corrie asked.

I think he's one sick son of a bitch.

We know that. I mean what else do you think?

I think he's fixing to be sicker.

She sat studying him. By the yellow light her eyes were depthless and opaque. He had never known what she was thinking.

What do you think we ought to do? she asked.

Do? Put his sorry ass away. Tell the law and let them open the graves themselves. Put him away forever in some crazyhouse. They'd have to.

You think they would?

I know they would. What would you do with him? There's supposed to be respect for the dead. It's the way we evolved or something. It's genetic. This man here…he wouldn't cull anything. He'd do *anything*.

He's rich.

I don't care how rich he is. Rich is no good here. All these dead people's folks…we just opened up a few of the graves. There's still worse covered up. Somebody's husband or son would kill the sorry son of a bitch. It's more than the craziness. The sick stuff. It's contempt, just emptying the trashcan into somebody's casket before you close it and haul it to the graveyard. It's beneath contempt. Somebody'll kill him.

He'll hire a team of sharp Nashville lawyers, she said. There'll be some publicity about it. He might even lose his license or whatever you have to have to operate. They'll send him to talk to some psychiatrist for a while; then they'll say he's cured, and he'll be back at the same old stand. We've got to get him ourselves. We've got to get more evidence.

He thought she'd taken leave of her senses. More? What more do we need? There's enough now for a lynch mob and enough left over to tar and feather him. Anyway, what's all this *we* mess? It's not our job. Let the law or somebody dig up a few more graves. There's your more.

The law. Seems like we never had much luck with the law. Daddy never did.

Bootleggers hardly ever do. It's an occupational hazard.

Well. You know so much about it. I doubt a bootlegger's son would, either. Anyway, don't start on Daddy. He's dead and gone and you hated him anyway.

I never hated him.

You hated him because he beat you. You hated me because he never hit me.

No. That's the one thing I was grateful for. If he had ever beat you, I'd have had to fight back. Or kill him. The way it was, I could take it and go on. Anyway, it doesn't matter. Like you say, he's dead and gone.

I never understood how you did that. How you just took it and went on, as you say.

Because it all balanced out. Because I knew something that he didn't know.

What?

I knew he was going to die and I'd still be alive.

She was silent for a time studying him. She shook her head. You've got a hell of a way of looking at things, she finally said. But let's get back to Fenton Breece. I've been thinking about this, and I know how to make him pay where it'll hurt him the worst. In the pocketbook.

How long have you been thinking about this?

I guess from the minute you saw him hauling that vault back to the funeral home that was supposed to be in Daddy's grave. From the time I seen the way he done Daddy when he was past doing anything to help himself.

Tyler was wishing he'd kept his mouth shut. This is crazy and you know it, and whatever you've got in mind, you can include me out.

This time it's not that easy for you You can't be included out of a family. It's not that easy. Once you're in one, you're in it for life. You can't turn away from blood. Will you help me?

No. Not only no but hell no. This mess is too crazy for me.

The first time Fenton Breece saw Corrie Tyler had been in the spring of that year. She was walking past the café as he had his nine o'clock coffee. She was wearing a tight black skirt, and he was watching the side-to-side movement of her hips when the man next to him said, I wouldn't kick that out of bed.

Breece turned on the off-chance the man might be speaking to him, but he wasn't. He was talking to the man on the other stool. Unless there was more room on the floor, he added.

Who is that, anyway? the man two stools down asked.

Old Moose Tyler's daughter. Don't know who she got her looks from, but she damn sure never got em from Moose.

Breece watched her out of sight. He felt the weight of eyes and when he turned the man was watching him with sardonic amusement, as if he had looked not at Breece but into him and read his thoughts. Breece flushed and looked away.

A bootlegger's daughter, he had thought. White trash who had probably done it with every man in town save him. He remembered a phrase his mother had used long ago in some old cautionary fable. He had forgotten the fable and disregarded the caution but the phrase was with him still: anybody's dog who wants to go hunting. It seemed applicable here.

But back at his desk he closed his eyes and let her body drift in his mind like the remnant of a dream that will not fade. He had already decided to learn what there was to know about her.

He found she worked in the garment factory, and he used to cruise by sometimes in the afternoons and watch for her coming out of the plant. She drove an old primerspotted pickup truck that seemed held together with baling wire and blind luck. She never came out in the groups of girls that strung across the parking lot laughing and talking. She didn't seem to have any friends. He was encouraged by this. Half a dozen times he had intended to pick her up. He had his lines meticulously rehearsed, but when he saw her the spit would dry up in his mouth and the carefully chosen words roil like leaves in the wind.

The day he finally did speak to her he was in the white Lincoln. It was the first warm day in May and he had the top down. The Lincoln had a beautiful red interior it still held that newcar smell of money and he thought that would get her if all else failed. His cheeks were shiny and freshly shaved and he was redolent of some special pheronomic aftershave he'd mailordered from California that was supposed to be made from the glands of male hogs and possess aphrodisiac properties. He was wearing one of the new seethrough nylon shirts that were just beginning to catch on, and he didn't see how he could fail.

Apparently the truck wouldn't start, for she had the hood aloft and was standing hipslung before it staring into the engine.

He stopped the Lincoln.

Car trouble? he called. Can I help?

She turned and glanced briefly at him. Her face was harried and irritated. I was just about to send for you, she said. I believe this thing is deader than hell.

I'm not mechanically inclined, but I can give you a ride somewhere, he said. He was listening to his own calm voice say these things, and he was thinking: Mechanically inclined. That wasn't half bad.

If it's not too much trouble, she said. She turned toward him again.

The voice he could manage, but he couldn't make his eyes behave. They kept darting about as if they had independent wills of their own. One wanted to go up, the other down. They'd lock onto her sharp breasts, then drop to her crotch, then back up to the breasts, and he thought if he could just grasp his eyes with his hands and point them into her face he'd be all right, but he could not.

It's a little ways out there, she said. Where I have to go. My brother's the only one who can keep this thing running.

That's fine, that's fine, he told her crotch, and she fell silent watching him. She shook her head and looked away toward town. She didn't make any move to get into the car.

He reached across and opened the door on the passenger side. Just jump right in here, he told her. It took an enormous effort to raise his eyes to the level where her navel would be could he have seen it.

I guess I'll just walk, she said. She turned and struck out for the street.

He was cranking the car. Wait a minute, he called in confusion. He didn't know if he was coming on too hard or too easy. He'd had it and thrown it all away. He slipped the car into gear and followed a little way behind her, riding the brake.

Come on and get in, he called. I'll take you wherever you want to go.

She just waved him away onehanded and didn't look back.

We could drive over to Columbia for dinner, he called, and sure enough his eyes dropped to the tight denim between her legs and he could have clawed his eyes from their bloody sockets.

Fuck off, she said.

He just stared. What? What?

You heard me.

No, I didn't. Say it again.

You sick bastard.

This time she kept on walking and he didn't follow. He just sat in the white Lincoln watching her form diminish down the street. He kept thinking about how she'd looked. The way her eyes had snapped and the way her fall of straight blonde hair had tossed when she said Fuck off.

Sooner or later, he promised himself. One way or another.

❧

It is told by Squire Robnett at the Bellystretcher Café:

I never cared for undertakers in general and Fenton Breece in particular. There was just always something about him. I done some work for him out there when he was buildin that mansion he built, but times was hard and I'd of worked for Hitler if he'd of been hirin.

Whatever it was, he was born with it because I knowed him when he was a boy, and he was just as peculiar then as he is now. Fenton was a rich kid, and that's when I first begun to suspect rich ain't all it's made out to be.

Fenton's daddy was a undertaker, too, but they had plenty of money besides. That's one reason why I never understood him takin up undertakin. Why not medicine, or the law? Now I don't know if you choose your trade or the trade chooses you, but at the very least you've got to have an inclination for it. I've always believed that Fenton just liked foolin around with dead folks.

He just didn't fit in. Didn't or couldn't. He used to get dead animals off the side of the road and play like he was embalmin em. Cut em up and see what they was made out of. If he couldn't find none and the mood was on him he took to killin em hisself. Strangle em. There for a while he was hell on the neighborhood cat population.

He's got that smarmy act down pat, but a act is all it is. You know that hangdog sorrowful look that he can turn on and off. But the truth is he just don't give a shit. He ain't got no respect for the dead. I was workin out there at his place buildin a rock wall around what he called his duck pond when one of these fellers works for him drove up in a flatbed truck with a casket strapped to the back. It was some feller that had died off from here, and they hauled him back to be buried with his folks. You would have thought he would take it on into town to the funeral home, but he didn't. It set right out there in the boilin sun all day. Like a piece of machinery or a load of lumber or somethin while he was prissin around settin out peonies and box elders.

What I'm sayin is that it ain't that he's a undertaker. Undertakin's just a job, like anything else. It's him. There's just somethin about him that makes your skin kindly crawl, like turnin over a rotten plank and seein one of them slick brown centipedes. I never wanted him pawin over any kin of mine, and that's why when my sister passed away we took her to Ackerman's Field. And that's why when I kick off, the arrangements is done made for a feller in Memphis to cremate my ass and spread the ashes in them hills back of Allens Creek, back in the Harrikin where I was raised. I sleep a little better ever night knowin he won't ever lay them soft white hands on me.

❧

Here was wealth beyond measure. Beyond even Tyler's powers of comprehension. Set on the gently rolling slopes of grass, the house might have been the counting house of some wicked ruler living in exile. Or yet an evil magician with spells cast on the rightful heirs, legions of familiars to do his bidding.

Scarcely five years old, already the house is part of the folklore of the region. There is conjecture as to just how many miles of electrical wire, how many miles of copper tubing. So far does the hot water travel there must be an auxiliary water heater to maintain Breece's chosen temperature. The glittering bricks came wrapped five to the bundle and woe to the mason who marred one in the laying. The tile came from Italy, the light fixtures from France. The bay windows are roofed with braised copper, and the workmen who installed it spoke no language the local workers could understand. Some kind of Chinese gobbledygook, they said.

There was even an interior decorator imported from Memphis who talked with a slight lisp and whose airy hand gestures were of great interest to local craftsmen. Just to listen to that son of a bitch talk, you'd think the only thing on God's green earth that mattered was winder curtains, one of them said. He could talk about drapers till you never wanted to hear about drapers again. This decorator's vision of the house clashed with Breece's and he left in a snit, pressing upon Breece in parting a slip of paper whereon was written the name of the builder of a Beale Street whorehouse.

The house had started out vaguely Georgian but ended up with a

decided bent for the grotesquely opulent. Gables and peaked roofs and tur-
rets had been added seemingly by Breece's whim or a coin toss so that the
house came to resemble the temple of some old king overthrown solely
because of his sorry taste.

Tyler had been watching the house all day, and so far nothing at all had
happened save the movement of light and shadow and he was about ready
to give it up when Breece came out of the house and got into a silvergray
Cadillac hearse and drove away toward town. Tyler sat for a time waiting
to see if there was to be further movement but he didn't expect any and he
was proven right. He came out of the spinney of sassafras he'd been concealed in and wended his way down the slope to the house.

For a time he just wandered around the outside of the house staring
upward. He felt a deeprooted contempt for Breece but at the same time he
couldn't help being impressed by the sheer size of the house. Breece had
simply outdone himself here, and Tyler wondered at the number of unoc-
cupied rooms and the number of caskets sold and crying kids and widow
women it had taken to accomplish this.

He didn't know what he was looking for. Or where to look. Something
he could hold in his hand, something incriminating. The gun still warm
and smoking, the dagger with a drop the color of claret forming at its tip.

In a land where folks seldom even locked their doors Breece was an
anomaly: there was no way in save stoning out a window, and his desire for
evidence fell short of that. He tried every door, but they were all locked,
and there was no key hidden about that he could find. He looked under
mats that lied welcome, in flower urns, and ultimately decided that the
only keys existing rode in Breece's pocket.

He came on around the house, wandering through curious oriental-
looking hedges he didn't have a name for and strange dwarf twisted trees
and to a covered carport laid in flagstone where sat a Lincoln convertible
with the top up. The car gleamed and the flagstones were still damp and he
guessed Breece had been washing it; he hadn't been able to see this side of

the house from the slope.

The hearse made so little noise it was almost too late when he saw it. He couldn't believe it was already back. Breece must have only gone to the mailbox. Sunlight off its lustrous surface caught his eye and it was already wending its way up the curving drive past marble fountains and the stone eyes of arcane statuary and he looked about wildly for somewhere to flee to: the woods were too far away and the way to them open territory.

At the end of the stone floor opposite the house was a garage or shop but he had no doubt it was locked and no time to try for it anyway and he had barely made the cover of the far side of it when he heard the Cadillac's tires hissing smoothly on the concrete drive. He sat crouched against the glittering brick wall fearing he'd left some spoor, triggered some crafty snare that would show evidence of trespass.

He heard the no-nonsense click of the hearse's door closing, footsteps crossing the flagstones. He grew bolder and chanced a look.

Breece was standing behind the Lincoln, a tan leather briefcase by his side. He had a set of keys in his hand, unlocking the trunk lid. He raised it and set the briefcase carefully inside and slammed the lid. He stood for a moment as if abstracted by some new notion, then strode purposefully to the back door of the house and withdrew yet another set of keys and unlocked the door of the house and went inside and pulled the door to after him.

Tyler didn't plan his next move or even think about it. There was just something in the careful way Breece had stowed away the briefcase. If Tyler had thought about it, he wouldn't have done it, but the keys were still in the trunk of the Lincoln, and in an instant he had darted across the carport and wrenched up the trunk lid and seized the briefcase. He was already fleeing with it when the door of the house opened and the undertaker came down the steps.

Tyler was running full tilt up the grassy slope toward the line of trees with the briefcase swinging choppily along and his shirt blown out cartoonlike behind him like some halfcrazed and ill-dressed commuter chasing a fleeing train. He was holding his breath and expecting the crack of a gun and buckshot snarling about him like angry hornets but all that came was a hoarse cry like the cry of some wounded animal hopelessly snared, a strangled ululating shriek of outrage or despair.

Once he reached the cover of trees he kept on going, crashing through brush with saplings whipping past him and his breath coming ragged, and when he thought how ludicrous the picture of portly Fenton Breece leaping brush and fallen trees was he stopped and sat on a stump to catch his breath.

He listened intently but all was silence save the hammering of his heart against his ribcage. He sat for a time staring at the briefcase. He had to see what manner of beast he had here. There was a businesslike lock on the strap but he didn't even try forcing it. He just took out his pocketknife and cut the strap and looked inside.

Papers. He leafed hurriedly through them, glancing occasionally at the woods. Invoices, bills of lading, receipts. Copies of orders placed with various firms for chemicals, caskets, clothing. Curious the trades men follow. Beneath the sheaf of papers lay a flat zippered pouch of the sort businesses use to carry deposits to the bank. His heart sank. A sack of goddamn money, he thought. I take a chance on getting shot and get chased through the woods by a fat undertaker and all I've done is prove I'm a thief.

He unzipped it with trepidation.

The first thing he saw was a pair of lavender silk panties. They were discolored up one side and hip with a faded rustbrown stain that had long soaked into the very texture of the fabric and appeared very old. He didn't even want to know what it was or how it came to be there. He laid them aside and stared at them in a kind of appalled wonder.

Here was more. A rubberbanded stack of glossy black-and-white photographs. He slipped off the rubber band to rifle hastily through them.

He dropped them suddenly as if they'd seared his hand. Or he'd been handling one of those clever medieval boxes with their springloaded needles cunningly hidden and tipped with curare. He felt infected, poison freezing his nerve and brain.

The photographs had scattered, some face up. He stared at them in fascinated revulsion. They were all of nude women. Some young, some old. Some pretty, some not. They were arranged in grotesque configurations they'd probably not aspired to in life and they were all unmistakably dead. Legs spread flagrantly, some grouped in mimicry of various acts of sexual congress. Their faces painted in carmine smiles. Their weary eyes, their sagging flesh. He'd used some sort of timer with the camera, for here was Breece himself, nude and gross and grinning, capering gleefully among the painted dead.

He picked the photographs up carefully by their edges and replaced the rubber band and just sat holding them. What to do with them. These trading cards from beyond the river Styx, picture postcards mailed from Hell.

❧

She took the underwear up delicately by its unstained hem. Laid it aside.

Where do you suppose he got them?

He shrugged and took a sip of his coffee. Why might be a better question.

Well, you certainly outdid yourself. I suppose you know what this means. We've got the son of a bitch. We've got him in a way nobody's had him before, and it's going to cost him.

I'll tell you what, Corrie. You've got him. Not me. I want nothing whatever to do with him. I don't want to talk to him, to see him, to ever hear his voice. I don't even want to know he's in this world. I've seen some sorry things, but Jesus.

I do. I want to watch his face when I tell him.

He didn't say anything. There didn't seem to be anything to say. She was studying the pictures clinically, one at a time, laying them aside.

Watching her face by the lamplight, he thought she looked somehow fevered, her rapt eyes fired by something akin to religious frenzy. Sister of some secret sect, perusing its dark devotional. Prayers offered to a horned deity squatting just beyond the rim of firelight. Watching her so he was touched with pity. She'd come up hard. A childhood that passed with an eye's blinking. Stepping over sleeping drunks on the way to school. With girlhood came the whistles and catcalls on the schoolyard. Hey, Corrie, how about a piece of that? You've done it with everybody else, how about me? He'd fought over her and he remembered the coppery bright taste of blood in his mouth. She tried to be like everybody else. To be one of the freshfaced town girls with their air of entitled confidence. She wore the same kind of clothes the other girls wore but somehow without the right flair, and ultimately all her efforts underlined the fact that she was just another piece of the puzzle that did not quite fit.

Why are you looking at me like that?

I was thinking I've known you all my life, and yet I don't know you at all.

There's nothing to know. I get up, I work, I do the housework. I cook, I go to bed. Then tomorrow I get up and do the same thing over again.

He didn't answer.

I don't know you. I don't know where you go when you're wandering around. What you think. No one's ever known what you think. You get what you think out of a book. It's like you hardly ever talk and when you do it's in some foreign language. Some language nobody even speaks. But one thing you can know about me is that I'm going to shove the knife in Fenton Breece and twist it. That's the main thing about me right now.

I wish you'd forget about Fenton Breece. He's like that card on the wall, the invisible listener at every conversation, the guest at every meal.

You may develop a taste for him. He's going to put us on Easy Street.

This is absolutely crazy as shit. There is just no way he's going to smile and start counting hundred-dollar bills into your hand. Just no way.

Hellfire, Kenneth, what can he do? Run to the law? There's nothing he can do but pay up. Try to put yourself in his shoes.

I don't want in his shoes, Tyler said. And if I was I'd cut my throat.

≫

During the last few years of his life Tyler's father would reach a certain stage of drunkenness during which he used to sit and watch Tyler with a peculiar speculation, as if he'd see what manner of beast this was he'd sired. Tyler walked a narrow line those years; it didn't take much to set the old man off.

When Tyler was twelve or thirteen he took to sleeping in the attic. It was quieter up there, and quiet was at a premium, for the house was oft-times full of drunks by turns convivial and quarrelsome. There were two doors between the attic and the ground floor and on one of these Tyler had installed a lock he'd come by. He liked the slope of the dark oaken rafters over his iron bed, and there was a window you could open to the weathers in the spring and summer. This window faced the back of the house and looked out upon a stony field sloping toward the cedared horizon. There was a hiding place in the boxing over the door for books he chanced upon. The old man possessed an enormous contempt for the written word and those who would decipher it.

That year the old man fell to beating him when the notion struck him, and it struck him more often as time drew on. Young Tyler grew wary and careful and watchful as a cat. All his movements seemed provisional and subject to change at a moment's notice; he seemed always poised for flight.

A schoolteacher who'd befriended him came once to visit. She sat for a time under the malevolent gaze of the old man, glancing about with nervous skittery eyes. She never came back. You better quit hangin around them goddamn schoolteachers, he said, wiping a hand across his mouth. Grayyellow stubble flecked with ambeer and spittle. Washedout blue eyes veined with meanness. You won't amount to a goddamned thing.

It was a summer of storms that year. Lightning walked the ridges all that July and August and conjured out of the night in strobic configuration stormbent trees writhing in the windy rain. Images of heightened reality rendered instantly out of the flickering night then snatched so instantly back into the absolute darkness they seemed never to have existed at all.

After the old man beat him he'd flee into these windtossed nights. Something in all this chaos seemed to find its counterpart in his own chaotic heart and he'd turn a face stained with blood and tears into the remote heavens and defy the lightning to take him, to char his heart and boil the blood hammering in his veins and seize and short the circuits in his head but this was not to be. Once he followed a light through sheets of windy rain, and in the riverbottom a lightningstruck pine burned like a solitary candle flaring down the night. Set there like a sign to read could he but decipher it. Then he quit crying altogether and took the beatings he couldn't escape with a kind of stoic and sullen outrage.

In his fourteenth year he heard the old man's step on the stair and snapped the thumbbolt. The steps ceased and there was no sound anywhere save the whippoorwills measuring out the dark. He was holding his breath and waiting for the steps to start their descent when the old man's shoulder abruptly slammed against the door.

He was sitting on the cot with his back against the wall and his arms laced around his knees. He figured the lock to hold. The lock did, but on the third stroke of the old man's shoulder the top hinge gave and the very door itself toppled into the room with the old man athwart it like some demented carpetrider and Tyler was out the window and gone. He went hand over hand down a trellis crept with ivy with the ivy tearing away in handfuls and the trellis itself tilting away from the wall like a toppling ladder, and he jumped the last few feet and was up and gone into the cedars.

The wind that night was out of the south and warm and balmy and there was a smell of freshly turned loam on it. From the sanctity of farther woods whippoorwills were calling each to each and he walked on toward them.

This time he just kept on walking, as if the boundaries of his world had suddenly dissolved and the landscape before him become limitless. He crossed thin dark woods with light falling in broken shards about him and owls calling inquiringly and when the woods ended fallow fields began so white in the starlight they appeared ghostfields. He went on in a straight line, steering by the stars. Through a cornfield so dry with ancient autumns he moved steadily in a conspiratorial whispering of cornblades and finally out of anything at all attended by men and he guessed he was in the edge of the Harrikin. He came to a creek or river and waded into it. When his feet lost the bottom he drifted downstream awhile then dogpaddled to the far side. He climbed a bank strung with honeysuckle slick black in the moonlight and through such a heady reek of their blossoms he seemed drunk on them and he staggered on.

Daylight found him where he'd never been. He went down a bloodred ravine cut out of clay by old floodwaters and came out in a field with the tilted ghosts of old cornstalks leached thin and fragile as ancient parchment. The sun came smoking up out of the mist and hung above the black treeline and it was almost instantly hot. After a while his clothes began to steam. Below him an abandoned farmhouse and fallen barn and fences gone to kudzu and wild roses. There was no sign of life in all that he surveyed, then he looked upward and a hawk wheeled against a flawless void and it glittered in the sun like some sinister contrivance of flesh and chrome.

He wandered aimlessly about the farm, his mind reconstructing old lives. Old long-silent voices told him tales. Beseeched him to remember them and carry them back to the world they'd lost. Folks were born here, grew old here. Died here, for he found tilting tablets of stone and sunken oblong declivities in the earth beneath the sawbriars and orange bells of cowitch. Old rooms papered with newsprint and flour paste, and he'd wander the house reading this surreal mural of old news as if it had something to tell him.

He felt remote, utterly alone. With the cool earth against his back he awoke sometime in his second night and he could feel the earth wheeling on its mitred course through eternity. Here the sky was clear and so strewn with stars there seemed no darkness between them but simply a vast phantasmagoria of light. Weak with hunger, he watched loom out of the night strange gaudy constellations like great wheels rolling toward him and turning endless in the void as if here in the Harrikin even the heavens were ancient and strange. They seemed to alter night to night as if the universe itself was still in flux. Once a shower of falling stars that seemed to have fallen prey to some celestial epidemic but instead of them showering around him he felt the pull of the earth fall away from his back and he became weightless, rising toward their streaking light like ofttold tales of souls raptured upward.

On the third day he came upon an apple orchard reverting to wildness. Most of the trees were dead, black twisted trees like the skeletons of profoundly deformed beasts. Yet one was thick with fistsize summer apples. The earth beneath strewn with them and the drone of bees and the musk of apples everywhere. They were sweetly tart and full of winy juice and he wanted nothing better. He seemed to have reached some curious point where he wanted nothing at all save the fall of night and the configurations of the stars to study as if he'd decipher some message there. Some sign.

On the third or fourth night in a dream or vision an old man came to him who would lead him out of this blighted waste. He'd been sent, he said, he couldn't say by whom. The old man's flesh had wasted away on his bones and beneath the faded chambray shirt he wore his arms were thin and fragile as sticks. In times past he'd been shackled in irons, hands and feet. He wore them yet but the chains had been sawn away, they were just heavy bracelets at the ankles and wrists with the sawn links appended like fey adornments.

Tyler had a fire going he kept feeding sticks and balls of grass. He on one side of the fire and the old man at the other like ancients at council.

Somewhere in the night foxhounds bayed then passed in a hollow below them and the wind brought voices or ghostvoices of men. He shook his head and told the old man he guessed he'd find his own way out. He couldn't be beholden to another. In order to survive in this world and then make a life in it he had to do this on his own. At last he lay back and slept with his head pillowed on an arm. He awoke once in the night and raised up and looked through the smoke of the dying fire and he was alone.

The next day his sister and a schoolteacher named Phelan and a hunter they'd hired as guide named Tippydo found him and took him home. It didn't seem to matter. All things and all places had come to seem transitory at best and he seemed to have arrived at some idea of where he fit or did not fit into the scheme of things.

The old man was contrite. He grasped Tippydo's hand and pressed into it a twenty-dollar bill. Twin tears crept down his pouched cheeks, etching paths of cleanness out of the grime. He'd never do it again. Wouldn't have done it then but for bad whiskey. There seemed little whiskey that was good that year for soon he was at it again. He seemed in a constant state of anger which Tyler seemed to bring into focus.

By the time he died Tyler could have whipped him instead, but he never did it. He never hit him, never cursed him, just did his best to stay out of his way. Honoring some biblical restraint of parental honor.

Already he was groping for a way to live, to accommodate himself to the world or it to him. He felt that if he fell upon his father with murder in his heart that he had proven irrevocably that he and the old man had the selfsame cankered blood in both their hearts and if this was so all was lost.

The day the old man died he was standing on the stairs to the attic. He'd stopped a minute to rest and catch his breath, and then he'd come on and batter at the door. Tyler imagined the door charring beneath his ceaseless tirade of invective. Against Tyler, against the uncaring God who'd let such twisted fruit of his loins thrive.

The way Tyler always imagined it, God had been sitting before the fireplace with his feet propped up on the hearth. Or maybe just on midair—God could do that. He was reading an old hymnbook or maybe a seed catalog. Listening with one ear and trying to concentrate on his reading. Finally after years and years of this just getting totally fed up and throwing his book against the wall of Heaven and turning and fixing the old man with his fierce eye. God's eyes flickered with electric blue light and the old man's heart exploded in a torrent of black blood and corruption and he just dropped like a stone, dead before his body touched the stairs, and God went back to his seed catalog.

For the first week after the briefcase disappeared from the trunk of his Lincoln, Fenton Breece lived on tenterhooks, waiting for the other shoe to fall. Dark visions haunted him waking and sleeping. The faceless burglar in an alley or a stone culvert hurriedly slashing open the briefcase and dumping out its spare contents, expecting money or who knew what but certainly not expecting the neat stack of photographs. Riffling through them, an act of sacrilege. A greasy thumbprint perhaps on the pale bloom of a breast. A thin fingernail of ice traced the nape of Breece's neck and down his spine.

I've just got to *do* something, he thought in his brisk businesslike manner. But there wasn't anything to do.

Then in a few days a measure of reason returned. No one had called him. Nothing sinister in the mail, the sky had not fallen. At length he began to see the faceless thief glancing at the rubberbanded photographs in disgust and tossing them away in a ditch. Mud, debris, shards of broken glass, and clotted leaves hid them modestly from prying eyes. Yellow water opaque with mud sent them turning dreamily, pale washedout ghosts of themselves, toward the muddy sanctity of the Tennessee River.

The woman behind the desk had an officious manner and carefully coiffed bluelooking hair. She seemed to have appraised the girl by some abstract standard she kept in her head and found her wanting.

Mr. Breece is not in right now, she said.

I reckon I'll just wait then, the girl said.

It may be a good while, the woman said.

Then I reckon I've got a good while to wait, the girl said. She crossed the narrow office and seated herself in a contoured yellow chair. She took up a magazine and sat staring at it though she could have told you no word that it said. She could hear the woman shuffling papers importantly about. After a while the woman cleared her throat.

What was it about?

It was about me seeing Fenton Breece, she said. She went back to her magazine.

He may not be in for a while. Perhaps I could help you.

You couldn't unless you're Fenton Breece, and I don't believe you are.

After a while the outer door opened and Breece himself came in. He was wet and coldlooking and beyond him rain fell slantwise in the wind. She hadn't known it had begun to rain. Breece folded his umbrella and stood it in the wastebasket to drain. Messy out, he said brightly. A pale hand to the smooth bird's wing of his hair.

A lady to see you, the woman said grudgingly.

Breece turned, and for an instant recognition and something other flickered in his eyes. Then nothing. He glanced back at the woman behind the desk. He looked at his watch.

You can go any time, Mrs. Cothron, he said. My office is back here, he told the girl. He pointed down a narrow hall. She got up and followed him.

She sat primly on the edge of an armchair. Worn purse clutched both-handed in her lap. Her eyes on Breece's face were fierce and intent and unwavering, and they made him nervous.

You buried my father, she began.

He nodded unctuously. He couldn't wonder what this was about. He remembered the girl, and he remembered the old man, but he couldn't fathom what she wanted unless someone else was dead. He kept glancing at the purse, and he couldn't remember if it had all been paid or not. Maybe she owed him money.

Mann Tyler, she said. He had an insurance. We paid for an eight-hundred-dollar steel vault to go over his casket, and it's not there anymore.

The room was very quiet. She could hear rain at the window. Breece got up and crossed the room. He peered down the hall and closed the door. He went back and sat down. His hands placed together atop the desk formed an arch. He was watching her, and she could see sick fear rise up in his eyes.

Just not there, she went on. And that's not all. He's buried without all the clothes we bought for him, and he's been…mutilated.

She just watched him. A tic pulsed at the corner of one bulging eye like something monstrous stirring beneath a thin veneer of flesh.

Absurd on the face of it. I'm a reputable businessman; no one has ever questioned my professional ethics. My work is exemplary, a matter of pride to me, and you are treading on dangerous legal ground if you intend to accuse me of misconduct.

Misconduct, she said. Her mouth twisted with the taste of the word. She had leant forward, elbows on knees. She smiled slightly. From the street the faint sound of a car door closing, an engine starting up. The blue-haired lady drove away. Breece was staring past the girl's shoulder through the window to the street.

Dangerous ground indeed, he murmured. A matter to be taken up with my counsel. But for the sake of discussion, just speaking hypothetically, suppose that such things were true. How would you come to know of it?

We dug him up, she said.

You what?

We dug him up. We had reason to suspect something was wrong about his burial, and we were proved right. Then just to be sure we dug up several more. I forget how many. I don't even want to think about the things we found. No one would expect to find the things we did, not in a thousand years.

Graverobbers. Vandals digging up graves and committing atrocities. Desecrating the corpses. I've often heard of such things but I never expected to find it in the town I live in.

I've heard of them myself. But none where these vandals took pictures of you and a bunch of naked dead women and then hid them in the trunk of your car. Why do you reckon they did that?

His eyes darted away. They were a hard glassy blue, slick as wet marbles. The open-shut eyes of a doll. The hands were pale, fleshy spiders, the fingers meshing endlessly. One hand trembled violently, and he stayed it with the other. She thought he might weep.

My car was vandalized. So it was you that did that.

I bet you ran straight to the law, too. I bet there's an all-points bulletin out about those pictures.

What do you want?

You're finished. You don't begin to suspect how finished you are. When all these people hear about what you've done to their folks, they're just going to mob you. They'd hang you, but you won't last that long. They'll tear you apart like a pack of dogs.

What do you want?

I want the things you done to my daddy made right. I want him buried with the decency you expect your folks to be put away with. I want that waterproof vault we paid for around his casket.

Breece was nodding. Head bobbing metronomically. Of course, he said. If you aren't satisfied, I'll do anything I can to satisfy you.

I'm a hell of a way from satisfied.

Of course, I'll refund your money. No question about that. I could even give you a liberal sum for what they call, ah, punitive damages.

And what would you expect in return for that?

He was silent for a long moment. The pictures, of course, he finally said. I'd have to have them back. They're subject to misunderstanding, a delicate subject, part of an experiment you wouldn't understand.

I expect you're right about that. I was wondering about the panties. Are they part of the experiment, too?

He flushed a deep crimson. I'd want your agreement to remain silent. I'd have to have that in writing; I trust you have been circumspect so far. Again, I'm trying to avoid misunderstanding. I have a position in the community, a reputation to maintain.

I want fifteen thousand dollars. That's nothing to you, pocket change. I could ask for a lot more, and you'd have to pay it, but I'm not going to be greedy. All I want is the money you cheated us out of and a fair amount for the grief you've caused us.

Whatever you call it, it's extortion. Blackmail. Both of them are against the law.

She shrugged. All right. We both go before the grand jury and tell our stories. We'll see how it all comes out when they dig up a grave or two.

I don't keep that kind of cash around. I'd have to make a withdrawal.

Then make it. You're getting a bargain and you know it.

I can have it for you in a day or two. I may have to convert some bonds into cash.

Then you'd best be converting. You don't get the pictures, or the panties, until I've got the money in my hand. We'll be waiting on you.

She rose. She was halfway to the door when he made some curious strangled noise. She turned. He was watching her. He shrugged helplessly. You must think me terrible, he said.

She didn't have an answer for that. She went out and pulled the door to behind her. She went down the hall and through the office and so into the street. She stood for a moment letting the rain wash over her. A cold wind smelling of trees, the wet streets, woodsmoke. She looked up and let the rain course down her cheeks. The rain felt cold. Clean.

He sat unmoving while the day drew on, and still he sat with dusk gathering at the windows, and ultimate dark fell unnoticed with the rain fading to just a persistent murmur at the glass, and he didn't turn on a light. The dark suited him very well and soothed the seething turmoil of his mind.

What to do. Options presented themselves only to be discarded and alternates sought. Nothing seemed feasible. The dread thought of the retribution she'd spoken of left him weak and clammy with cold sweat. He closed his eyes. Tried to clear his mind, to force order onto the chaos of his thoughts. He imagined his mind a slate, an eraser moving methodically across it. Then what had been at the bottom of his mind all along surfaced, like a rotten log in a swamp brought up by its own putrescent gases. A headline from last summer's newspaper: LOCAL MAN INDICTED FOR MURDER. A measure of peace returned to him. A feeling of self-confidence, of being in good hands.

Granville Sutter, he thought.

❦

Early in June of that year Lorene Conkle came out of the drugstore and Sutter was there the way she had known he would be. He was leant against a brick wall with a toothpick cocked up out of the corner of his mouth. When she walked past him, he unleant himself, elaborately casual, and followed her as if he'd been going that way all along and was just waiting for the notion to strike him.

The drygoods store then. She'd look up from whatever garment she was fingering and glance covertly through the glass, and there he'd be, this time leant against the column that supported the striped awning. A tall, gangling man with the false appearance of sleepy indolence. Warped and twisted by the bad glass as if this glass had the property of character analysis and showed the world what you were like inside your skin. He caught her looking and just looked levelly back, and she dropped her eyes.

Was it something I could help you with? the clerk asked. He had approached silently behind her and startled her. A prissy little man with an oldmaidish air about him.

She seemed to make up her mind about something. She laid the gown carefully atop the pile. I reckon not right now, she said. I may be back later.

Sutter wasn't watching her now. When she stopped in front of him he was looking off toward the railroad track where the train was uncoupling boxcars. He seemed finally to notice her and turned toward her. High cheekbones with the leathery brown skin pulled taut over them. A blade of a nose broken once and healed slightly askew so that the face looked different from side angles, a face with two different profiles. The eyes were brown and flecked in their depths with gold so they looked almost amber.

I want you to stop watchin me.

Then don't stand in front of me. Folks don't always get what they want. It's people in Hell cryin pitiful for Eskimo Pies, but they ain't handin none out. It's a free country, and I can watch who I want to.

You been followin me, too. And this is not the first time you done it. I seen you parked across the street from my house a few days ago.

I was just visitin a feller lives down there. Besides, you don't even know I'm followin you. You in a drygoods store. That's a public place. I might have had in mind to buy me a set of drawers or a pair of socks or somethin.

I want you to let me be. And my husband Clyde, too. I hadn't said anything to Clyde, and I don't want to go to the law. It's been too much about trials and lawyers already. I don't want no part of it. If I ever mention it to Clyde, he'd have to talk to you, and you don't want Clyde ahold of you.

You know who I am, don't you?

Yes.

Why don't you just mention it to Clyde? He might not even want ahold of me.

You just let it be. Clyde couldn't help bein on that jury, and he couldn't help votin what he knew was right. What does it matter anyway? You got out of it, didn't you?

It took a year out of my life. Two trials. I'd of been acquitted the first time if your old man hadn't been bound and determined to send me to Brushy Mountain. Eleven votin not guilty and he had to hang the jury.

Yeah. Eleven people afraid you'd burn them out like you did old Mrs. Todd. Clyde wasn't afraid of you.

You think I burnt that old woman's house?

I know good and well you did. And so does everbody else. What you can't buy off you scare to death with threats.

You come down mighty hard on me, Sutter said. You believe too much of what you hear. I'm just like everbody else. I had a old daddy and a old mama, and I come up hard the way everbody else did around here. You think you're better'n me, don't you?

He had leant his face to hers, and she backed away. Her expression was a mixture of anger and contempt.

Cause your old man works in a drugstore, he went on. Wears a little white apron and mixes up pills and nerve tonic and shit all day behind a counter. Yes, ma'am, no, ma'am. I reckon you think your shit don't stink.

You watch your nasty mouth with me or I will go to the law. I swear I will. Such law as there is in this town. And yes, I do think I'm better than you. Not because of my husband but because I mind my own business. I don't burn people's houses in the middle of the night or steal from them or poison their livestock.

Aww, you just got me all wrong. You was to get to know me better you wouldn't be so down on me. Hell, catch me right and I'm a likeable sort of feller. You right nice lookin. A little long in the tooth maybe, but you're holdin up all right. Me and you just might get together sometime.

She just stared at him utterly aghast, as if such a bizarre circumstance was beyond her powers of comprehension.

Sutter was fumbling in the bib pocket of his overalls. He withdrew a worn leather wallet secured by a clasp chain. He opened it and for a surreal moment she thought he was trying to give her money, for what she couldn't say.

Here, he was saying. I keep tryin to tell you I'm like everbody else. I was a innocent babe the same as you. Now this here's my first-grade picture.

He was pressing upon her a photograph, and in a moment of confusion she took it from his hand and stared at it.

A fairhaired child of five or so stood facing the camera. Perhaps it was even Sutter. His arms were upraised, and each hand was clasped by a disembodied adult hand, one large and one more diminutive. The woods he stood in were sundrenched, and the child was squinting into the sun or the eye of the camera. He was naked and superimposed over his genitals was an enormous drooping penis that reached nigh to his ankles. A great bull's scrotum. His stomach was covered with a thicket of dark pubic hair.

She dropped the picture as though it had seared her hand and whirled away, her face gone pale with embarrassment and anger. She walked blindly away.

Course it's growed a inch or two since then, he called after her. Sutter was retrieving the picture where it had fluttered to the sidewalk. Can't lose this, he mused to himself. My old mama toted this in her pocketbook till the day she died.

So long, widow Conkle, he called to her departing back.

She didn't even halt. I'm not a widow, she said.

Not yet, Sutter said.

That stopped her. She turned and raised a hand to shade her eyes and just stared at him.

Granville Sutter lived in a tiny house he'd built himself. Two miniature rooms, a kitchen and the front room he slept in. Most nights. Other nights he slept wherever he might be when night fell on him. The house was painted white with green shutters and trim, and it looked like a little fairy-tale cottage or a house in a fabled wood where a gnome might live. It had a neat cobblestone walk curving toward the blacktop and a great walnut tree on the south side in whose shade he could be found on warm days taking his leisure, sitting on one Coke crate with his feet propped on another and his back leant against the trunk, watching the infrequent traffic with heavylidded eyes, the cars dropping off the grade toward the river and the Lick Creek community and ultimately the edge of the Har-rikin. Sometimes a wagon creaking along behind plodding horses until the man would snap the lines and say, Come up there, and the horses would step out smartly, their shoes ringing on the macadam until they passed the house. If there were children, they would turn and stare back at this figure of nightmare dread who'd been used to scare them into behaving, but the adults would generally keep their eyes straight ahead as if something of enormous interest were about to appear around a curve in the road. Fig-uring perhaps it was best not to attract his attention, wary mouse easing past a drowsing cat. If you don't look, he's not real.

This particular gnome had estimated the time of Conkle's arrival to within fifteen minutes. He thought: She told him at work, but he ain't about to leave work. He'll work on till five so as not to piss off old man Wipp or jeopardize his cushy job, and then he'll jump in the car and head out here.

Sutter was sitting on a Coke crate with a rifle across his lap, and he had a polishing rag in his hand, and when a car passed he'd take a swipe or two at the stock, but it didn't need it.

Conkle was driving that year a dark green '47 Studebaker, the model that looked almost the same front or back, and when the car hove into view Sutter smiled a tight little smile to himself; it had looked for a moment as if Conkle were coming at him sixty miles an hour in reverse.

The Studebaker was still fairly rocking on its springs when Conkle leapt out and slammed the door and came striding around the car. Conkle had been in a bad fire once and his face was scarred slick and plasticlooking over his cheek and forehead and these scars were white as dead flesh against his livid face. You son of a bitch, he was saying. You've finally done it this time. He was already coming up the walk, he still had his druggist's apron on and he looked slightly ridiculous.

There was a robin singing somewhere in the top branches of the walnut. Sutter was listening to it instead of Conkle when he drew the rifle to his shoulder and took aim.

Conkle saw the rifle and Sutter's intent simultaneously and he threw up his hands as if to bat away lead with bare flesh.

Sutter shot him in the left temple and the right side of his head exploded in a pink mist of blood and bonemeal and he was flung backward and fell limp and ragged as if he'd been stuffed with sawdust. The robin hushed. It had grown very still. The echo of the rifleshot came waving back across the river bottom.

Sutter approached and with the rifle at a loose present arms bent over and stared into Conkle's face. The eyes were open, and Sutter leant further to study these eyes as if he might see the soul fleeing out them in ectoplasmic spiral or death rise up in them like a face at a window but he didn't see anything at all.

He went into the house and put the rifle away. He came back out with a tow sack. He grasped Conkle's hair and raised the head and onehanded spread the sack beneath it and released the head and it hit the cobblestones with a soft plop. The scar on Conkle's forehead angled up into the hairline, and the hair that grew there was fine and thin.

Sutter grasped him by one leg and pulled but the other leg splayed out and kept hanging, and, breathing hard and cursing Sutter leant and took up the other foot. Conkle's ankles were thin and he wore winecolored socks with clocks on them, they didn't say what time; Sutter guessed they'd run down. He had to keep replacing the sack under Conkle's head.

To get him into the front room he had to prop the screendoor wide and drag him through. He left him by the door. Conkle was studying the ceiling with a look of bemused whimsy.

He went back out with a bucket of water and a broom and dumped the water on the bloody stones and scoured hard with the bristles of the broom and threw rinsewater. He repeated it a time or two until he was satisfied.

He went back in and sat across the room on an old carseat that served him as davenport and studied the body critically as if it were some new piece of furniture he'd come by and wasn't sure where to place. After a while he got up and took the heavy iron firepoker from behind the wood heater and laid it in Conkle's right hand. He studied the effect. He smiled onecornered to himself and leant and moved the firepoker right hand to left.

There was a long zigzag crack in the plastered courthouse ceiling, and Sutter spent a lot of time staring at it as if somehow he were above these dull proceedings. The hard back of the oak chair against the base of his skull. Smoking wasn't permitted, and he worried a small slice of tobacco in his jaw and swallowed the juice while the prosecution went on around him. All this ceremony. All these legalities. He paid it little mind.

The crack in the ceiling became a canyon grown with hemlock and cedar, and he was scrambling down its stony sides toward an ultimate abyss. He came out on a rocky outcropping and lay flat on his stomach on the warm stone and looked down and past the tops of trees so far away they looked like mockups of trees. A river crept like a winding silver thread drawn amongst the rocks.

Then the crack was Flint Creek, where he'd grown up long ago, and he was wandering down it in the warm June sun of youth with a rolled fishline in his pocket just looking for the right cane to cut. A world incredibly green and saturated with sun and scented with the riotous spring growth.

Sutter's lawyer was named Wiggins. He wasn't very good, but he was cheap, and Sutter didn't figure he needed one anyway and had hired him simply as a matter of form. Wiggins wore plaid sportcoats of an almost audible hue, neckties with pictures of mallards flying south on them, and he had the soft indefinable manner of a professional drunk. He always seemed slightly harried, as if he'd like to get all this over with and retire somewhere behind closed doors with a bottle.

Early in the defense he spoke eloquently of the sanctity of the home. Of man's God-given right to defend it. Then he put Sutter on the stand.

Sutter told his tale in a dry, emotionless voice and sat calmly awaiting cross-examination. Without saying so directly he had managed to leave the impression that the whole thing had started as an altercation over Conkle's wife.

The state prosecutor that year was a young man named Schieweiler. He was extracted from the Swiss who'd settled Ackerman's Field. He had intense, slightly protuberant eyes and no political debts to pay, and he adhered to a straight and narrow path. He had a great deal of difficulty understanding the fear folks in Centre had for Sutter. He was an earnest young man appalled by the story Sutter had told after laying his hand on the Holy Bible. He sensed a miscarriage of justice in the making here, and he was determined to head it off.

Mr. Sutter, in your long and varied life have you ever previously had occasion to shoot someone who was attacking you with a firepoker?

Sutter seemed to study awhile. I reckon not, he said. I don't recall it. But if I did, I ain't on trial for it here.

No. But bear with me. If you had, I think you would see a pattern begin to emerge. A man shot in the head with a high-caliber rifle would be flung backward. Perhaps he would lie on his back with his arms flung wide, the palms of his hands upwards, the way Mr. Conkle was found. What is really remarkable is that the poker, with an unerring homing instinct, would defy the laws of gravity and physics and follow the man across the room and come to rest in his palm. Do you have any explanation for this?

No, I don't. I never went very far in school. I can't explain the world to you. Things happen one way, they happen another. I reckon he was hangin onto the poker and then he opened his hand up.

Mr. Conkle was righthanded, yet the poker came to rest on his left palm. How do you explain this lapse of your judgment?

Objection.

Sustained.

I'll rephrase it. Do you know of any reason why a righthanded man would attack you with a weapon in his left hand?

Sutter cleared his throat. He grinned at the jury. Maybe he was just spottin me a few points, he said.

The judge leaned from his oaken bench. Answer the question put to you, Mr. Sutter. And one more example of facetiousness and you will be in contempt of this court.

I didn't know whathanded he was. All I seen was a firepoker comin at me. I never thought it would come any easier lefthanded than any other. It was a goodsize poker and wouldn't feel too good whatever hand you got hit with.

It's common knowledge there was bad blood between the two of you. Mr. Conkle had the misfortune to stand by his convictions, a character trait that probably amuses you. What is it with you, Mr. Sutter? Do you think you can kill the whole world? Slaughter a long line of jurors who vote their consciences? Can you silence them all? Do you have access to that many firepokers? You'd have to hire assistants in your war against order. You're a busy man, Mr. Sutter. All those widows to create, homes to burn, land to salt. I've been checking on you, Mr. Sutter. That's the way you've lived your entire life.

Wiggins was objecting vehemently. The defendant is not on trial for his entire life, he told the judge. Only a particular segment of it.

Confine yourself to the matter at hand, the judge told Schieweiler. The jury is instructed to disregard the prosecutor's remarks, he added.

Is it not a fact that you addressed Mrs. Conkle as 'widow' just prior to her husband's shooting?

Don't pop your bug eyes at me, Schieweiler, Sutter said. I don't know what you want from me. All I was doin was defendin myself. I come and got the law myself; I never tried to hide nothin. Why would I lay a poker in the wrong hand and then call the law?

I don't know, Mr. Sutter. I'm here to try to extract the truth from you, not psychoanalyze you. Did you call her 'widow Conkle' or not?

No. I swear to God I did not.

When the trial was over and Sutter acquitted, Schieweiler still could not let it be. He followed Sutter to the courthouse steps in a rage he didn't even try to conceal.

You may think this is over, Mr. Sutter, but I can assure you that it is not. I'm going back to Nashville, and there is going to be an investigation of this case and this tainted jury from the top to the bottom. I'm going to get you for something if it's only spitting on the sidewalk.

You just a bad loser, Sutter said. He grinned like a Cheshire cat. Small yellow canary feathers about his jaws.

Your day is drawing to a close. You can intimidate these people with threats, but you can't intimidate me.

Sutter was fumbling about his overalls pockets. He held an imaginary pencil poised over an imaginary pad. Now what did you say your street address was? I might want to drop in on you some night. I'm over in Ackerman's Field ever now and then.

꙳

The first cold spell of winter has routed the old men from their habitual benches on the courthouse lawn, and the warm stove in Sam Long's store has drawn them as a magnet attracts iron filings.

What always got me about him was the way he could just slide out of anything. Killin, burnin, sellin whiskey. He sold bootleg whiskey out of the front door of his house for fifteen year and never even got arrested. They used to worry old man Moose Tyler to death raidin him and finally did send him up to Brushy Mountain for a year or two.

Yeah. And killin folks. He told me one time, said, it's more people than Fenton Breece can bury somebody. Everbody knowed he killed Clyde Conkle in cold blood, but he never drawed a day for it. They let him walk. You take old man Bookbinder up in the Harrikin. His wife took up with one of them Hankins boys and run off and sent Hankins back to get a bedstead or somethin. Bookbinder was goin to run him off, and he wouldn't run. They took to scufflin and Hankins got killed. They stuck a stamp on Bookbinder and mailed him straight to the penitentiary. He done ten year. I guess he never had none of Sutter's luck.

꙳

It was the middle of the night when Breece knocked but almost immediately the tiny door-within-a-door opened and a goldflecked eye was regarding him.

Whoever sent for you lied, Sutter said. I'm still alive and kickin.

Breece guessed this was Sutter's idea of a joke. He wasn't amused. I need to talk to you on business, he said. Let me in. It's cold out here.

The door opened. Sutter was fully dressed, as if he slept in his clothes or he slept not at all. The room was dark save a warm orange glow from the woodstove.

Turn the lights on. I can't see where I am.

You in my front room and you ain't been here thirty seconds and you done givin me orders.

Breece wandered around in the halfdark and finally seated himself in a bentwood rocker by the fire and spread his hands to the warmth of the heater. He seemed ill at ease, someone who must soon be off.

Turning colder, he said awkwardly.

What can I say? It's December. But I could of stuck my head out the door and told that. You didn't have to drive all the way out here to give me a weather report.

Like I told you, it's business.

If it's whiskey business, you're shit out of luck. They cleaned me out last week. The fuckin revenuers. I'm under indictment again. Out on bond. The son of a bitches just won't let me be here lately. Somebody's got it in for me. I've paid these goddamned local laws enough money to buy a farm in Georgia and the niggers to work it and not a word of warning do I get. They didn't even fool with the county. You know what they done? A nigger come walkin up out of the woods and I sold him a pint. He shoved it in his hip pocket and walked back down in that holler. A nigger in woreout overalls and bustedout shoes, and I thought he'd been down there diggin sang or somethin. Then when the feds came in a big black car with their warrants, there set the son of a bitch right in the front seat wearin a suit of clothes and a necktie. The front seat. Black as the ace of spades. The slick son of a bitches. Who'd of thought they'd send a nigger?

Breece's eyes had adjusted to the halflight from the open hearth, and by it he was covertly studying Sutter's face. Sutter wouldn't have noticed anyway. He seemed to be abstractedly talking out of a store of rage he'd laid by and a hot but unfocused anger burned in his eyes.

It was the first time they had ever talked face to face and Breece divined in a moment of dizzy revelation something about Sutter that no one had noticed before. Why, he is mad, Breece thought. He's not what people say about him at all. He's not just mean as a snake or eccentric or independent. He's as mad as a hatter, and I don't know how they've let him go so long.

What is it you want, anyway?

Someone has something that belongs to me, and I'm being black-mailed. I've got to have it back, and I think you're the man to get it for me.

Sutter was rolling a cigarette. Who is it?

Well, there's two of them in together, I think. A brother and a sister named Tyler. The girl is the one who actually approached me about the money, but I know for a fact the young man is the one who stole the article out of my car. That's what I want back, and I'm willing to pay for it.

The article.

Yes.

Say I try to do it for you. Do I get to know what the article is, or do I just wander around finding things that look like they might have belonged to you?

Of course, you'll know what it is.

Then let me in on it.

All right. Some photographs were taken of myself and a…young lady. They are potentially very damaging. The photographs are of a very incriminating…a very intimate nature. The young woman is connected politically, and they are threatening to go to her husband if I don't pay them fifteen thousand dollars. I've been in a quandary. If anything goes wrong, my position in this community will be ruined.

This story was so monumentally absurd that Sutter did not even take offense at being lied to. He was even a little impressed. The idea of Fenton

Breece doing things of an intimate nature to a politically connected young woman while someone else took potentially incriminating photographs was so far beyond the realm of probability that he permitted himself a small smile.

Of course, we both know that's bullshit, he pressed on. But it's your business what you done and what specie of animal you done it with. Pictures then. And you want em back. If they're as bad as you say, why don't you just give them the fifteen thousand dollars. That's chickenfeed to you. What do you think, I'm goin to do it cheaper? I ain't no bargain basement, ain't runnin no sales.

Breece was silent for a time. He seemed unused to speech, as if he'd gone too long without the companionship of the living. He studied a bit and then he said, I flatter myself that I know something of human nature. I can read people. If it were simply a matter of the fifteen thousand dollars, I'd pay it and be done with it. However...there was something in the Tyler woman's eyes. It was clear she means to ruin me. She'll take the money and then want more. Or perhaps they've already had copies of the pictures made and she'll show them about anyway. There was a vindictiveness in her face. Utter viciousness.

This utter viciousness, where do you reckon it came from? Wait a minute. I'm gettin an insight into human nature. Let me guess. You was doin things of an intimate nature to this Tyler gal, and then your attention wandered to this gal who was politically connected, and the Tyler gal got pissed and aims to run you out of the undertakin business.

It's not necessary to ridicule me.

Then quit actin like I'm a goddamn fool. Quit jerkin me around and get on with it. Make me an offer or get the hell out of here.

Very well. I'll give you the money. All fifteen thousand dollars, half now and the rest when I have the pictures. I'm sure you could use a sum of money like that in your...legal difficulties. I've had no experience in that area, but I'm sure that would buy several lawyers.

Judges is what I'm shoppin for. And why are you goin roundabout like this if she offered to sell you the pictures straight out?

I told you. She wants to ruin me.

Sutter had an actual insight of his own then into human nature. He gave Breece an acute look. It's not just the pictures, he said. They've got some kind of a deathlock on you and you want it off. You want me to kill them.

No, no, certainly not. I can't condone murder, hire murder done.

Sure you can. You just don't want to know about it. You don't even want to say it. You keep dancin all around it. You want me to do it for you.

You must be aware that you have a certain reputation. Your words would carry more weight than mine. Perhaps violence wouldn't be necessary. Perhaps you could just talk to them.

Perhaps I could.

Breece was hesitant. How many…how many people have you killed?

You don't owe me for them.

Will you tell me that if I tell you something of my own past?

What is this, you show me yours and I show you mine? I don't care about your past. And whatever I done, I done it because it was what I had to do at the time and it's yesterday's news anyhow.

I'm aware you killed Conkle. I could hardly have avoided knowing that. Breece hesitated, studying Sutter warily. But this was business, and money had been promised. He didn't have it on him, and that weighed in his favor.

You killed Conkle and laid a poker in his hand so you could claim self-defense. But Conkle was righthanded and you put the poker in the left hand. How smart was that?

In the warm halflight Sutter was smiling. I knowed he was righthanded.

Say you did? Then why did you mess up?

Sutter's voice grew confidential, conspiratorial. I'll let you in on a little secret. I didn't mess up. I did it on purpose.

Why would you do a thing like that?

I don't know. For sport, maybe.

For sport? What the hell kind of an answer is that?

For sport, you know what sport is, don't you. Anyway, I done it. And I'd not have even as sorry a piece of shit as you thinkin I didn't know whether a man I was about to kill was righthanded or lefthanded.

Well. I was just curious. I killed someone myself once, while I was still in college. I killed a whore in Memphis.

Sutter just gave him a quick glance of dismissal as if murdered Memphis whores did not quite meet whatever arcane criteria he judged peers by. He leant and spit into the fire and rose and laid another stick of wood in the sparking coals.

I killed her with a Pop-Cola bottle.

This evinced some small interest. I expect that would do it, Sutter allowed.

Breece fell silent. Perhaps wandering down the alleys and byways of his curious past. Other whores, other bottles.

What'd she do, take your money and run out on you and you busted her head with it?

Oh, it wasn't anything like that. She took to bleeding. You never saw so much blood. The bedclothes were soaked, white sheets with great crimson centers, like flowers...the bottle broke something loose inside her, punctured her in there somewhere, and all the blood ran out of her.

Inside? Sutter wondered, then he stared at Breece as comprehension came over him. I don't want to hear anymore of this perverted shit, he said. You just keep anymore stories you got about Pop-Cola bottles to yourself.

Breece just sat bemusedly, hands laced across his corpulent belly. He seemed to be intently inspecting the shine of his shoes. After a time, he said, Did it ever occur to you that we're a lot alike?

Not hardly.

We're both to a great degree involved with death. You in your way, I in mine. It's only natural that a person as intimately associated with death as I am would think quite a lot about it. There's a poem I've remembered that seems to best sum it up. Do you want to hear it?

Why, hell yes, Sutter said. I believe it's been a day or two since I've had anybody in here quotin rhymes at me.

It's by Auden, W. H. Auden. Are you familiar with Auden?

Sutter leaned and spat into the coals again. Seems like I knowed him when he lived over on Jack's Branch, he said.

> *As poets have mournfully sung,*
> *Death takes the innocent young,*
> *The rolling-in-money,*
> *The screamingly-funny,*
> *And those who are very well hung.*

Sutter watched him with something approaching disbelief. This mad quoter of poetry, nightmare minister to the dead so far beyond the pale light could never fall on him.

Did you find it amusing?

Let me get this straight. You want the pictures and you want it hushed up. This threat to your social standin removed. Is that about it?

Breece thought it over for a moment. Yes, that's what I want. What I really want is for everything to be back like it was before they stole my pictures.

He thought some more. He was aware that things could never really return to the way they were, for Sutter knew about it now, but he had already done some thinking about that. When the time came, he could take care of that himself.

Give me the money.

I'll have to get it from the bank. I don't carry that kind of money around. I'm not a fool.

Sutter let that pass. Tomorrow, then.

Breece rose. He stood awkwardly a moment as if about to proffer a hand to seal this bargain, then thought better of it and made ready to leave.

I've kept you up long enough, he said. The money will be ready tomorrow.

When Breece was gone, Sutter closed the hearth door and turned down the damper and lay back on the bed still fully clothed with his hands clasped behind his head and stared at the ceiling and thought about the money. Fifteen thousand, but it could be readily turned into more. If Breece wanted the pictures desperately at fifteen, he would want them only a little less desperately at twenty. Perhaps twenty-five.

But it was more than the money. Something in his life that had been without form was taking shape. A dark, cauled shape that stood to the side and watched him with hooded, expressionless eyes. In some curious way he intuited that all his life previous had simply been a rehearsal for this.

By three o'clock Tyler had the roof of de Vries's store painted and was cleaning out his brushes with gasoline. His hands and clothes were so smeared with red ochre he looked like the survivor of some terrible highway calamity. He wiped gasoline out of the brushes and stored them in the old milkcrate in the back of the truck and while he was loading the ladders, de Vries came out. De Vries crossed the alley and stood on tiptoes against the building on the other side the better to see his own roof. Then he came back to where Tyler was.

You done me a good job, he said.

Well. It's painted, anyway.

De Vries had taken out his wallet and was carefully thumbing through bills. He took out a sheaf of them and counted money into Tyler's hand. He held a five poised in midair as if in momentary indecision, then laid it atop the others and put away his wallet.

That's five more than we agreed.

You did me a good job. No accidents. You stayed with it and got done in good time. You're a careful worker. Last time I had it done Clarence Treadway done it drunk, and he dropped a paintbrush loaded with bright red paint right on the hood of Clyde Tookie Bell's car, and Clyde was drivin a white Buick that year.

You hear of anybody else wants anything done, try to get word to me. I'll try most anything once.

I sure will. I'll get you some work.

I better get on home then.

He started toward the truck parked in the mouth of the alley but something in de Vries's manner or in his face made him hesitate.

De Vries cleared his throat. Hold on a minute, he called.

Tyler waited.

It's a feller been hangin around out front waitin for you to get done. He figured you was up on top and said tell you he wanted to see you. He knowed you was down, I guess he'd done be back here.

Who is it?

Do you know Granville Sutter?

I just know of him.

If you know of him, then you know he's got a bad name.

What does he want with me? Did he say?

No, he didn't, and I didn't ask. Didn't figure it was any of my business, and Granville would of let me know that right quick anyhow. Reason I told you back here, I figured if you wanted to give him the slip, you wouldn't have to go around front. You could just head up the alley there.

Well, I don't mind talking to him. I never stepped on his toes that I know of. He may need some work done.

De Vries's look said that this was not a strong likelihood. Any work Sutter needs doin you'd be well advised to pass on, he said. If he didn't do nothing else, he'd figure a way to beat you out of your money. But you suit yourself on that.

I'll talk to him.

There was an empty bench against the front of the store, but Sutter was hunkered against the brick wall waiting with the calm patience of the country folk you used to see sitting about the town square. This bench was usually filled with loiterers or old men settling world affairs, but Sutter's mere presence seemed to have cleared it. Tyler approached him, and for no reason he could name, there was a tight empty feeling in the pit of his stomach. Something in Sutter's remote eyes told him that this was the knock on the door at midnight, the telegram slid under the door in the dead of night.

You looking for me? I'm Tyler.

I know who you are. You old Moose's boy. You don't look much like him. Old Moose was heavy and built right close to the ground. You kinda rangy. Must of took after your mama's side of the family.

Tyler didn't say anything.

Sutter dropped his cigarette. Ground it out with a conscientious foot.

Or who knows, he shrugged. Maybe you do look like your daddy. Names and blood don't always go arm in arm.

Tyler was momentarily off balance. He stood studying Sutter as if measuring his size against his own. Finally he said, You might ought to watch your mouth. Anyway, I don't reckon you been hanging around here waiting to talk to me about my daddy.

As a matter of fact, I ain't. Let's take a walk, Tyler.

He started off toward the railroad tracks and after a moment's hesitation Tyler fell in beside him. He was torn between curiosity about Sutter's purpose and the desire to just walk away. More's the fool he didn't, Tyler thought, but the moment when he could have just walked off down the road and made this never be had passed and it would not come again. Somehow this all felt preordained and out of control, as if someone was behind the curtains mimicking voices and controlling the strings. As if for all the years of his life he and Sutter had been passing and repassing in the dark and now here they were face to face in God's own daylight and there was nothing for it.

 They walked past the drygoods store down toward the railroad track. Poolroom loungers watched them pass with curiosity. Mentor and protégé, perhaps, warlock and aspiring wizard. People they met seemed to defer to Sutter, to give him more room than was necessary for his passage. Grimes's carlot. Grimes's cars sat forlorn and lustreless under the leaden sky, and the pennants strung on wires snapped and fluttered in the stiff wind.

Sutter didn't talk for a time. He built himself a careful cigarette as he walked and lit it and just strolled on with Tyler a pace or so behind. He never glanced back to see if Tyler was following.

The barbershop was the last building on Main Street, and the street ended here in a series of steps down to ground level. Past the gravel parking lot, dully gleaming railroad tracks curved away into blue distance, and an open boxcar sat sidetracked with two blacks on a flatbed truck unloading chemical wood into it.

Sutter sat on the top step awhile studying the blacks as if this were some job he was charged with overseeing and listening to the rhythmic hollow boom of cordwood slamming against the boxcar wall.

I asked around about you, he said. When the feller told me what he told me. Everbody had a good word for you. Good worker. Honest. Sharp in school. I hadn't of knowed better, I might even of believed some of it.

Tyler was confused. What fellow told you what? I don't know what you're talking about.

The feller whose property you stole. He wants it back. I studied about you last night, Tyler. Went to sleep thinkin about you. I kept askin myself, what's a boy who's sharp in school and honest as old Abe Lincoln doin tryin to blackmail Fenton Breece out of fifteen thousand dollars? I kept wonderin if you thought it was that easy. If it wasn't no more trouble than that to make fifteen thousand dollars, everbody would be doin it. Everbody would be drivin Cadillacs. Factories would shut down. Farms would grow up in blackjack scrubs and folks would just be blackmailin one another.

Of all the things Sutter might have wanted with him this was the last thing Tyler expected, and for an instant he was almost dizzy with shock. He wished himself fleeing along the railroad tracks. All this over and forgotten or never been.

Course a man can get the bigeye thinkin about all that money. I can understand that. That's why we can get this mess straightened out right here at the start and make it easy on everbody. All he wants is the pictures back. He's willin to forget the rest of it, the blackmailin charge, the theft, just to get his property back. There might even be a small piece of money, call it a finder's fee, say five hundred dollars, when you lay them in my hand.

Apprentice blackmailer though he was, even Tyler knew something about this did not quite ring right. He knew it was more than the pictures. Breece and Sutter knew it as well, for the pictures were only symbols for the dark perversions of the waiting graves: the graves lay ticking like timebombs, untold numbers of them, dividing insanely like the malignant cells of an embryonic cancer. The pictures didn't mean anything.

I'd like to help you out, Tyler said. Lord knows I could use five hundred dollars. I just don't know what you're talking about. Pictures of what?

Sutter was quiet for a time. He seemed to be studying the cordwood haulers. They had the truck unloaded now and had jumped down from the bed. Tyler could smell the hot winy odor of curing wood. The sun had descended further and what he could see of the world lay half in shadow, half in thin light splayed out across the houses clustered on the hillside across from town.

He chose to ignore Tyler's last words, as if they were so ludicrous they didn't deserve comment or perhaps his acknowledgment might lend them a credibility they didn't deserve.

Course I took into consideration maybe it wasn't all your doin. Maybe you just easy led, and I ought to went to her to begin with. But I believe a man's accountable for the actions of his womenfolks, don't you?

No, Tyler said. I don't believe one person can be responsible for another person's life. We're on our own.

Sutter shrugged. Still, I figured man to man between me and you would be better. We ought to be able to come to terms. What it is, you don't quite see the whole picture. You're lookin at it, but you're not seein all the details. You've got some idea about Fenton Breece and you're judgin me by him. Fat and soft and very likely some specie of queer. Let's get it straight right now that me and him ain't nothin alike. Right? If we was, he wouldn't have me agentin for him to begin with. He'd of just took care of it hisself.

What's he paying you?

I won't lie to you. He's payin me plenty. Because he's got a lot to lose and because he thinks I can stop up the holes where it's spillin out. And make no mistake about it, Tyler, I can. I'm the fix-it man, and you're the problem I been hired to fix.

I don't have them, Tyler said.

Maybe not. But you know where they live. Whatever you have to do, you better get your mind right to do it. Because I'm not foolin around, and I don't want no mistake about it. If you have to talk to her, you better let her know I'm dead serious.

Tyler didn't say anything. The cordwood truck had gone, and a cool blue dusk lay over the railroad yard. Across the tracks where happenstantial shanties spilled yellow light, three young blacks strolled toward town, and a woman's voice, faintly ridiculing, called something after them.

I got to get on, Tyler said. He'd thought he was able to handle whatever befell him but this was something new. Something far outside the borders, and he could feel a panicky fear like cold waters rising about him. He didn't know how deep they were and he didn't know if he could swim in them. Anywhere seemed preferable to here but when he made to go

Sutter's hand on his arm stayed him.

Not just yet, Sutter said.

The hand tightened on Tyler's biceps, then moved away.

None of this means anything, Tyler said. It's all just a waste of time. If I went to the law, it would all be out the window anyway.

If, Sutter said contemptuously. If a frog had a glass ass, he'd only jump one time and bust like a dropped teacup. We both know you're not goin to the law. If you did, there'd go your big money. Which is gone anyway, you've kissed it goodbye and never knowed it. And on top of that, graverobbin and foolin with corpses ain't never been too highly thought of in this part of the country.

We never robbed any graves.

Sutter shrugged. You got your story, Breece has got his. He's prepared to swear in a court of law that he caught you and your sister diggin up graves and doin stuff to the bodies. Desecratin em, he called it. I guess the first tale told is the one that gets listened to.

I got to get on. I have to think what to do.

Then while you're at it, think about this: I'll do what I have to do. It's a hell of a lot of money, and it would move me pretty far down the line, and it looks like I need to be there. All these son of a bitches. Push and push and keep on and I've had about all I want of it. I'm goin to lay some folks out to cool if I have to, and I don't particularly care who. But what I want you to think about is the worst thing that can happen. You know when somethin bad happens, how folks kind of console one another? They say, well, it could of been worse. This or that could of happened. Well, not this time. Believe it. I am absolutely the worst thing that can happen to you.

I just don't know.

You better know. If you don't, ask around about me. I don't carry no references, but folks'll tell you. And you better let me know somethin one way or another by tomorrow night. If you don't, it'll be on your head.

What will?

Whatever happens. Whatever it takes. It's enough that you know that Fenton Breece ain't the only man can bury the dead, and the grave ain't the only place to put em.

Tyler rose to leave, and this time Sutter made no move to stop him. He just sat unmoving, letting night take him and sinking into darkness as if he kept some obscure watch against whatever of dread might be approaching the town.

Tyler went woodenly back up the street. His mind wouldn't work. Everything seemed jammed, overloaded. He went past closed and shuttered stores, a lit café where shards of brittle music fell about him and diminished with his passage. A voice called Tyler after him, but he didn't heed it. Where a neon sign blinked BILLIARDS he went through a paintscaled door and down a halflit stair to where smoke drifted in the glow of fluorescent lights strung over pool tables and where there was a loud clanging of pinball machines and a hubbub of human voices. He bought a Coke at the counter and went to a long bench anchored alongside the wall and sat drinking and watching a pill game in progress.

Hey, Tyler, a man called Woodenhead yelled at him. Want to play some pill?

I got to get home here in a minute.

Draw me a couple of pills then. I need a change of luck, and you the luckiest fucker about pill I ever seen.

Tyler shook the canister and spilled out two red wooden pills onto his palm. He looked at the numbers on them. Not tonight. The four and the twelve. He passed them to Woodenhead. Sorry, he said.

Woodenhead looked at them. Grimaced. Goddamn, Tyler. I meant from bad to better. I could of went to worse myself.

Damn, there's old T-Texas Tyler, another sang out. He fell to studying Tyler's carminesmeared clothes. Hell, he's been in a terrible wreck. Was anybody killed in it besides you, Tyler?

Oh, he's just got ahold of one with the rag on, Woodenhead said. Hell,

Tyler, if you couldn't of waited a day or two, the least you could of done was take your britches off.

Tyler just grinned weakly and didn't say anything. There was something reassuring about this ribald camaraderie, but he knew he must be off. He drained the Coke and set the bottle aside, and so into the night.

When the last streetlight stood vigil against the night and the highway dropped and curved sharply, he was thinking about Sutter as he rounded the curve and was suddenly hurled into absolute and inexplicable darkness. Reflexively he locked the truck down in a caterwauling wail of protesting rubber and ceased in the middle of the road with his hands clamped whiteknuckled to the steering wheel. Faroff and faint headlights were wending toward him, and he felt for the light switch. He hadn't even remembered to turn on the headlights.

❧

I'm going to the law, he said.

No, you're not. That would be the end of it. The money and everything. This is our last chance to get away from here.

It's not mine.

He's bluffing. Trying to scare us. Looks like he did you, too.

You didn't hear him, Tyler said. But she was implacable as stone. His words rolled hollowly out, and her hardened face just turned them back to him and they began to sound craven even to his own ears.

Think what it would be like, Kenneth. Us somewhere else, some city, Nashville or Memphis maybe. With all that money, thousands and thousands of dollars. Dressing fine, driving a fine new car. Doing what we please. And the law won't help. Daddy always said the law was like two people fighting over a blanket on a cold night. The one that's the biggest and the strongest winds up with most of the cover. And the last time I looked that wasn't you.

Give me the pictures.

What are you going to do with them?

Hide them. Just in case.

She went out of the room. When she came back in, she laid them on the table. He took from his pocket a square he'd cut from a canvas tarp, and he wrapped the pictures carefully and taped them and slid them into a Prince Albert tobacco tin.

She watched him wordlessly. He finished and rose and just as wordlessly went out into the night.

⤜

He was sitting at the bottom of the basement stairs in the courthouse drinking a dope when a deputy came through a side door with a sheaf of warrants in his hand. He went past Tyler without speaking and stood for a moment before a door marked SHERIFF'S OFFICE fumbling out keys. He unlocked the door and went in. He was in there for a few minutes. When he came back out, he didn't have the warrants and Tyler was still there. He'd finished the dope and sat holding the empty bottle as if he didn't quite know what to do with it.

You want something?

I wanted to see the sheriff.

He ain't in.

I figured that by the door being locked, Tyler said. The deputy stood waiting as if there might be more forthcoming, but there was not.

What did you want with the sheriff? The deputy was a small stoop-shouldered man with fiery red hair and a long, aquiline nose, and his eyes veered warily as if he didn't know whether to suck up to you or push you around.

I wanted to talk to him, Tyler said.

I'm a duly sworn deputy sheriff, the deputy sheriff said. If it's got anything to do with breakin the law or enforcin the law, then you can take it up with me.

When do you reckon he'll be back?

He'll come when he comes, the deputy said. He ain't responsible to me. You through with that bottle, it needs to go back upstairs by the dopebox where it belongs.

It was a good half hour before the high sheriff came, and when he did the deputy was with him. They stood before the door unlocking it, and Tyler wondered vaguely what there was to steal. The world was all locked doors. Watchdogs, KEEP OFF signs. As he turned the key, the deputy nodded toward Tyler. Him, he said.

Uh-huh, the sheriff said.

They went in and Tyler sat a few minutes longer debating whether to stay or leave. He'd about decided to leave when the door opened halfway and the deputy's head poked out.

He'll see you now, he said.

Tyler rose and went in. The sheriff was seated behind his desk with his palms laid flat on it. He was a big man. He wore pressed khakis, and his shirtsleeves were folded back a neat turn. He was dark, and his hair was brilliantined back into ornate and intricate waves. He wore a thin mustache of the sort favored by certain movie stars of the nineteen-forties and he was considered to be something of a ladies' man.

Something I can help you with, young feller?

I hope so. I don't know, but I thought I'd ask and see.

Take a chair there. To begin with, who are you?

I know him now, the deputy said. I told you I thought I knew who he was. That's old Moose Tyler's boy.

Uh-huh. What can I do for you, Moose Tyler's boy?

Now that he'd come this far, he didn't know what to say without saying too much. It seemed to him that with the mention of his father's name a line had been drawn with him on one side and them on the other.

He'd lived too long on the outskirts of the enemies' camp to ever dine at their table.

My sister and I have been having some trouble with Granville Sutter. He's done a lot of talking about what he's going to do. He's threatened to rape my sister and kill both of us.

The sheriff was watching him, deceptively casual. How'd you happen to wind up on the wrong side of Sutter?

Well, it sort of come up about my sister.

The deputy laughed. I'll just bet it come up about his sister, he said. He turned to the sheriff. He's got a hell of a nicelookin sister.

Hush up, Harlan. You want to elaborate on this business about your sister, Tyler?

He tried to go out with her, and she wouldn't go. He didn't want to take no for an answer. He slapped her around some and threatened to shoot us.

Where do you fit into this?

What?

Why's he threatening you?

Hellfire. I don't know. Because I took up for her, I guess.

Uh-huh. Listen close to me, Tyler. I'm going to explain something to you. You're young and you ain't been around and you've got a lot to learn. You take a man wants something real bad and don't get it, he's likely to say some things he don't mean. Sort of in the heat of the moment, you might say. When he cools down a bit, it'll all be forgot. Likely he's done forgot it, and you worrying yourself to death about it.

And that's it? You're not going to do anything? Talk to him, or anything?

The law's a funny thing, Tyler. It requires that a crime be committed before a man's arrested for it. If we arrested everybody that thought about doing something illegal, there wouldn't be jails to hold em. And if everybody Granville Sutter threatened to kill wound up dead, Fenton Breece would have to hire him a couple of helpers and put on another shift. If

Sutter roughed her up like you say and she swears out a warrant for assault, that's another matter. But she'll have to do it. You can't do it for her.

But then if she did, you'd have to serve the warrant and arrest him? He'd be in jail?

Till he made bond. Which knowin Granville would be somewhere in the neighborhood of fifteen minutes. And then he would be madder than hell. Which you wouldn't want. My advice to you would be to let bygones be bygones.

Whiskey, the deputy said suddenly.

What? the sheriff asked.

This has got to do with whiskey or I miss my guess. This boy here's got into it with Granville over whiskey the same as his daddy did. Probably set up back there in one of them hollers in the edge of the Harrikin and Sutter's got wind of it. Man go prowlin around back in there, no tellin what he's liable to find.

Tyler had risen. Unnoticed, his chair toppled sidewise against the wainscoting and fell. His face was white with anger.

I ought not to have come here, he said. He was staring down into the sheriff's face. The face was bland and almost politely inquisitive. I knew better all along and by God I came here anyway.

You watch your mouth, boy. Anybody cusses in my office I kind of take it they're cussing me, and nobody cusses me.

Tyler went out without speaking and left the door ajar. The deputy's voice said, Wouldn't mind takin little sister a round myself.

He went on in a kind of cold, detached rage up the stairs and into the failing winter light. Dusk was falling, and a purple mist seemed to be seeping up out of the earth itself and obscuring the town. Buildings looked blueblack and dimensionless. He stood for a moment looking back down the stairs; then he shoved his hands in his pockets and hunched his shoulders and went on.

❧

Two stone lions stood sentinel at the gate of the house, but they were chipped and weathered and their ancient eyes were blind. They might have guarded some city long sacked and forgotten: the house they actually watched was subtly going to seed, and the gate itself canted on one twisted hinge.

Tyler went up the cracked concrete sidewalk. A plaster mother duck and six plaster ducklings wended their way singlefile through the sere winter weeds, but like the lions they were weathered and blind and seemed to have lost their way.

He went up the steps to the gloom of the porch. Somewhere behind the curtain windows a light glowed, and he could hear soft jazz playing within the house. He rapped on the storm door, then opened it and knocked on the peeling white door. He waited awhile and knocked again. After a time he could hear soft footfalls, and a porchlight came on over his head. The door opened.

Kenneth?

Hello, Mr. Phelan.

A pair of limpid eyes behind the thick lenses of reading glasses. A thin scholarlylooking man in a white shirt and a blue necktie. Phelan's cheeks were slick and freshly shaven, and he smelled of Lilac Vegetal. His hand clutched a thin leatherbound volume a forefinger marked his place in.

I thought you were in Knoxville, Kenneth.

Well. No. Not yet.

If you wanted to talk to me about it, this is not really a good time for me. Could you come back tomorrow, perhaps in the afternoon?

I did want to talk to you, but not about that. I need some advice about something. Could I come in for a few minutes?

Well. Sure, I guess so. Come on in, Kenneth. He ushered Tyler into a neardark room and made no move to turn on the lights. The room was warm. A gas furnace burned with a soft hissing sound and a thin blue flame. A door opened off this room to what Tyler remembered was the kitchen, and Phelan kept glancing nervously toward it. There was a warm spicy smell of Italian food cooking.

If I've come at a bad time—

Oh, no, not a bit of it. Well, to tell you the truth, I was just having a guest over for dinner.

I'll just be getting on.

Stay a few minutes as long as you're here. I was just surprised to see you. I'd assumed you'd gone to east Tennessee.

The kitchen door filled with a shadowy form. A heavyset girl in a white dress. A girl Tyler remembered from school. A junior then. A semi-pretty girl with soft uncertain eyes. At length a name floated into his memory to match the face: Retha Ellison.

Phelan became agitated. There was a curious mixture of humility and defiance in his face. Suddenly it all made a kind of sense to Tyler. Phelan laid a hand on Tyler's arm.

Kenneth, you remember Retha.

Yes. Hello, Retha.

Hello, Kenneth. How have you been?

Just fine. The grip on his arm had tightened and seemed to be moving him gently toward the door. Tyler felt that for days folks had been taking him by the arm and guiding him places he did not want to go on his own. The anger that Phelan's kind, familiar face had dissipated returned, seethed just beneath the surface. He jerked his arm hard, and Phelan's indecisive hand fluttered away.

I guess I'd better get on, Tyler said. He wondered what madness had driven him here to begin with. What advice Phelan could possibly have given him. All these myriad differences between the world he was discovering and the world he'd been taught. There was nothing in Yeats or Eliot or Browning to cover this: had the situation been reversed, Phelan would probably have been coming to him for advice. He wondered how Eliot would have fared against the look in Sutter's dead eyes.

Well, Kenneth, if you must, then I suppose you must. Tomorrow night, then?

I doubt it.

It wasn't anything urgent, then?

No. No, it wasn't anything much. I'll let you get back to your guest.

Ushered in, ushered out. The hand was at his elbow again as if he were blind or halfwitted and must be forever shown the way.

I'm sorry you have to rush away into the night. But we'll do it another time. I just had Retha over for some tutoring and we decided to have a bite to eat. You know how things are.

He smiled a quick nervous smile and gave Tyler a conspiratorial wink. Tyler looked away. Beyond the limits of the porchlight the streets lay already dark and slicklooking and empty.

Yeah, Tyler said uncertainly, as if the way things were would forever be a mystery to him.

Phelan waved an arm goodbye. His hand still clutched the book, and he looked down at it as if he had forgotten it.

Tyler started down the steps. What are you going to read to her?

Pardon me?

Browning, I'll bet. You're going to read her Browning, aren't you?

For a moment Phelan's face was empty and dead. You were never a petty person, Kenneth, he said. I wouldn't start at this late date. You don't have the flair for it, and it doesn't become you.

Goodbye, Mr. Phelan. He went on, but at the gate he turned and looked as though he might say something further, but Phelan had already gone back inside and closed the door. He stood for a moment in the line between light and dark as if he didn't quite know where to go or what to do.

Well, he thought. We tried the law and we tried the Poet's Literary Tea Society. I guess I do it my damn self.

Sutter was sitting under the walnut tree with the Coke crate cocked against it when the county car pulled into the drive and stopped. A deputy got out and crossed the yard and squatted before him like some great ungainly bird. He didn't speak.

Ezell, Sutter said after a time.

Part of Ezell's jaw had been shot away and surgically reconstructed and the plastic surgery hadn't taken properly so that he looked like a partially healed escapee from some mad scientist's laboratory.

I heard something you'd maybe be interested in, he finally said. There was a curious vibration to his voice, his disfigured jaw lent it the residual hum of some stringed instrument strummed gently and laid aside.

Sutter was paring his nails with a switchblade knife. He did this in silence a time. Then he said, Well, are you going to tell me, or are we playin guessin games? You'd give some kind of a hint might make it easier. Just somethin to let me know what general area it pertains to.

You remember that state prosecutor you got into it with at your trial? Schieweiler, from over at Ackerman's Field? He's trying to get you a new trial, and get it moved out of the county. Maybe at Ackerman's Field.

Hellfire. They can't try me again on that. They done tried me on it. It done got thowed out.

Well. They claimin jury tamperin. Perjury too, what I hear.

Jury tamperin? I never tampered with a one of them son of a bitches. Never had to. They was already scared shitless.

I just told you what come down. Like I always do. He's workin with Sheriff Bellwether, over at Ackerman's Field.

Sutter took out a bag of Country Gentleman and rolled himself a cigarette. He lit it. I appreciate you warnin me, Ezell, he said, his voice slightly furred from the smoke.

Ezell was silent a time. Finally he said, I'm takin a chance just tellin you. It'll be my ass they ever catch me out here.

Well. I said I appreciated it.

Still the deputy sat. Sutter was tempted to just wait him out, to see would he sit hunkered there while darkness fell and be there still when dawn broke, his Adam's apple bobbing every time he swallowed.

Was there somethin else?

Well, Ezell buzzed. Last time you gave me a little somethin.

Sutter took out his wallet. Peered inside. Just how little was this somethin I give you?

Last time you give me forty.

If I did it must of been good news, Sutter said. This only qualifies for twenty. Hell, by all rights you ought to be payin me.

Ezell rose and took the proffered bill. By some sleight of hand it disappeared into his khaki pocket. Just whatever, he said. I'm always lookin out for you.

He crossed the yard to the car and got in. Lifted a hand farewell and drove away. Sutter went on sitting. Everbody's always lookin out for me, he said. He thought of Schieweiler. His bulging earnest eyes. Of Bellwether, the sheriff who wasn't for sale. An anger that would not dissipate seethed somewhere inside his chest.

All these son of a bitches, he said aloud.

❧

His old mama died in the madhouse, you know. Died huntin a butcher knife she swore she'd hid and couldn't find. She'd get up in the mornin and hunt all day like a man puttin in a day's work. She'd'a hunted all night if they hadn't of strapped her in.

They've always told that when Granville was a boy he woke up one time in the middle of the night and she was settin on the side of the bed watchin him and she was holdin a butcher knife. Said she was watchin him, but it was like she wasn't really seein him. He laid awake the balance of the night waitin to see what she'd do, then he took to sleepin in the woods or in the barn. Just wherever. She'd set up all night like she was studyin about somethin. They took to hidin all the knives.

Then finally she tried to kill old Squire Sutter. They kept her locked up awhile, and when she got to be more than they could handle, they put her in the crazyhouse. They was funny folks, them Sutters. The last time Granville even seen his mama was the day they come and hauled her off, and if he ever regretted not seein her before she died, he never said so.

Then later on when the old man took sick and got down, I heard he was bad off and went down there. That old man was in a hell of a shape. He hadn't been took care of. He hadn't been shaved or washed since God knows when, and with Granville doing the cookin, no telling what he'd been eatin. If anything.

Granville was grown then and about ready to leave the nest. He already had that look in his eyes. That look like he's lookin not just at you but right on through you to whatever you're standin in front of. He was settin on the front porch, I never heard tell of anybody catchin him workin. I told him I heard his daddy was bad off. Asked if they'd had the doctor out there. He said there wadn't any need for a doctor nosin around his business. The way he said it, I could tell he meant me, too. Hell, I wadn't nosin around. I always liked the old squire, even if he was funny turned. I told him they didn't have one, his daddy would likely die. He just looked at me. Well, he said, if he lives, he lives. If he dies, he dies.

I left and I didn't know what to do. He put me on a spot. I knowed I ort to send a doctor, and I'd always worry about it if I didn't, but at the same time Granville was goin to hold it against me, and somewhere down the line I'd have cause to remember it.

I sent old Doc Powers down there. That was before Pierce ever come here. Paid him out of my own pocket to go, but when he did Sutter was already dead. Granville was on the wing then, and there wadn't nobody left to call him back. I knowed right then that Sutter was always goin to make people feel that if they done the right thing, like anybody would, a ticket was goin to be made on it, and sooner or later they'd have to pay it. I don't like to feel like that myself, so I've steered clear of him.

And never regretted the loss of his company.

❧

All day doves cried close to the house and all day Corrie moved in an impending sense of dread. Long a believer in signs and portents she felt this was one of the worst and signified a death in the family. Why don't he come on? she wondered. She did everything about the house she could think of, and then she cooked his supper.

The day drew on. She went out once to look up the road to see if the truck was coming. She stood in the packed earth yard. A hand to shade her eyes. Wanly pretty, slightly harried. Her shadow was long before her. She stood gazing up the road in an attitude of listening, but there was nothing to hear, nor did she see the truck. She waited for a moment in seeming uncertainty, and then she went back in.

The house had seemed empty since the old man died. His ghost hovered yet in dark corners; the air seemed forever resonant with his voice. Once she'd forgotten and set his place for supper. Before twilight she went about the house turning on lights, dispelling shadows though light still lay redly at the western windows. He didn't come and he didn't come. She went out again to listen for the truck, but there was nothing. Even the doves had fallen silent. Nothing she could name drew her eyes to the hillside. Black slashes of inkblack trees against a mottled red sky. An angular shadow, one among other less substantial shadows, moved as if in some curious way the weight of her eyes had given it life or at least the kinetic semblance of it, and it rose from where it had been crouching there in the twilight and ambled down the slope toward her. She stood motionless and mute. A hand to her mouth. When she saw the rifle, there was a moment not of apprehension but of relief, for she thought: a hunter. When the figure reached the fence it didn't come around to the gate like anyone else would have done but simply stepped across it as if to show what he thought of fences and the folks who'd built them. He carried the rifle aloft across his chest like one fording deep waters, and when the light struck his face, she saw then it was Sutter. As with a terrible inevitability she'd known it had to be.

Hidy, he said.

She didn't say anything. He skirted a planter made of an old cartire turned wrong side out and its edge scalloped and sat on the edge of the porch.

I been waitin up there, he said. I been kinda holdin off thinkin he'd come, but I don't think he's goin to. He may have left plumb out. He may be across the Alabama line by now. He sat idly tapping the stock of his rifle against a booted foot. Just a weary traveler taking brief respite from the road. Soon to be off again.

Then you ain't seen him?

Not today, Little Sister. But I was supposed to. Ain't you goin to ask me in to supper?

No. I don't know what you're doin here in the first place. Kenneth'll run you off when he gets in.

Kenneth couldn't run water through a garden hose. And nobody's runnin me anywhere. Not today. I come here on business, and I ain't leavin till it's finished.

He had risen and stepped onto the edge of the porch. In the failing light his face was all angular shadows and, with the skin drawn tight, seemed composed solely of the skull beneath it and out the wells of dark the yellowflecked eyes as compassionless as a cat's.

Let's go in, he said. He would grasp her arm but she jerked away and whirled as if she'd slap him then thought better of it. She went through the door fast and tried to slam it on him, but he kicked it hard with her shoulder against it and she fetched up on the front room floor with her head against a toppled end table and a ringing in her ears. She wiped her forehead with a hand and the hand came away bloody.

It would save time, Sutter said, if we just cut through the front part and go right to the end. The front part is where I ask for the pictures and you tell me you don't know what I'm talkin about. None of that is in question. I know you got em. You tried to blackmail Fenton Breece with em, and he sent me to get em back. Now come up with em before you do somethin to put me in a bad mood.

She was on her hands and knees. The pattern on the linoleum floor went in and out of focus. Geometric white tiles. A single drop of blood dropped off her nose and splattered into a crimson star.

You can kiss my ass, she said.

Temptin as that offer is, I'm goin to have to let it slide. Maybe later. I hardly ever mix business with pleasure.

She looked up at him. His face was stony and remote.

Let's have em, he said. Where are they?

Where you'll never find them.

Well, we'll see. But then I got a ace in the hole. I got you to show me.

He leant over her and grasped her hair and pulled her to her feet. He twisted his fist in her hair and pulled her head back. His face was very close to her own. He was detached, and there was nothing at all of life in the emptylooking eyes. They might have been shards of agate flecked with iron ore.

He slapped her. She had begun to cry. He'll kill you, she said.

It's been tried before, he said. By better men than he is. I figured you for a harder case than this. Folks into blackmailin and extortion need a harder shell than what you've showed.

You ought to know.

He released her hair. She settled back to the floor. Her head drooped.

She sat with her legs folded beneath her.

Get over on that couch and set, Sutter said. I'm goin to look around a bit. Don't get up. Don't even think about slippin out that door. If you do, I'll hear you and I'll drop you in the front yard like I was killin hogs. Do you believe me?

She didn't reply, but she believed him anyway.

He began in the front room. He emptied out drawers, checked their bottomsides, pored over their contents. He took the backs off picture frames and looked behind them. From time to time he glanced sharply at her. She wondered where Tyler was; she'd wish he'd come and then she'd hope he didn't. She sat trying to think. She didn't know what to do. She'd been holding something of an intricate design, and it had collapsed in her hands, and she didn't know where the pieces went. It was dark outside. The windows had gone opaque and all they showed her was the reflection of the room.

Be putting this shit up, he told her. I don't want this place lookin like it was turned wrong side out. He wandered into the kitchen.

She got up listlessly and began to store away papers in the drawers. She could hear him in the kitchen opening and closing doors. When she had the room tidied up, she looked toward the kitchen door and he was standing there watching her speculatively.

What's them pictures show, anyway? he asked.

Just dead folks.

Dead folks? Why's he wantin pictures of dead people so bad?

She shook her head mutely. There was no way to explain even if she had wanted to.

Is he screwin dead women or what?

She didn't reply. She wondered idly if it had been the money Breece was paying him or just a perverse desire to see the pictures that had set him in motion.

He crossed the room toward her. Maybe you got em on you.

I ain't, though. I'm not that stupid.

It might be fun to look.

How much is he paying you, anyway?

Sutter considered a moment. A thousand dollars, he said.

They're worth a lot more than that. Me and Kenneth'll give you five thousand and all you got to do is leave us alone.

He just looked at her.

Half, then.

It's a hard fact that half of nothin is nothin, too. That's what you've got and what you're goin to wind up with.

He grasped her shirt, a hand to each side of her collar. When he yanked buttons spun off and she stood with the shirt hanging open. When she made to hold it together, he slapped her. He unpocketed the knife and pressed a button on its mother-of-pearl side, and the blade snicked out. He slid the blade between her breasts, dull side in. Let's see what's under here, he said. When he pulled the knife outward, the narrow edge of cold steel sliced the strap between the brassiere cups. He uncovered her breasts, studied them clinically. No pictures here, he said. Nothin here but titties.

She was crying. You're going to pay for this, you son of a bitch.

She could hear the truck laboring up the hill. He heard it too, stood in an attitude of listening, the knife still clenched in his fist. A moment later and the walls moved with the shadows of treebranches, the fence, sliding along the wall like illusory images propelled by some enormous wind.

He got a gun in that truck?

I don't know what he's got.

You holler and I swear I'll kill you. I'll cut your throat, then hide behind the door and cut his.

Crazy, she said, so softly she might have been talking about herself.

Footsteps crossed the porch, and the door opened. Tyler stood for a moment framed darkly against the paler dark outside. He held a thermos bottle in one hand; a toolbelt dangled from the other. His eyes grew wide and seemed to take in the whole room at once. His mouth opened but he didn't say anything.

Everything looked harsh and surreal: What he saw was Sutter standing slightly behind her holding her left arm twisted between her shoulder blades. The blade of the knife lay across her throat. She was attempting to hold the shirt closed but her right breast was exposed. She had her eyes clenched shut, and her face was twisted in pain.

I don't believe you thought I was serious, Sutter said.

He released the girl and stepped away from her. He closed and pocketed the knife. Fix them clothes, he told the girl. He grinned at Tyler. She can't keep her clothes on. Somethin about me affects women that way. She'd'a had mine off, you hadn't of showed up when you did.

Sooner or later I am fixing to kill you, Tyler said. If you don't kill me first. You had no business going after my sister any such chickenshit way as this. You already told me. I thought you'd be man enough to come after me.

Sutter shrugged. Whatever works, he said.

He watched intent form in Tyler's eyes, and when Tyler threw the thermos he sidestepped and heard it smash against the wall somewhere behind him. When Tyler came for him he just feinted left and slammed Tyler in the side of the head with his fist. Tyler staggered and swung the toolbelt hard but Sutter caught it onehanded and jerked and when Tyler came stumbling into range Sutter drove a fist into Tyler's abdomen and the boy's breath exploded outward in a harsh whoosh and he sat down hard and rolled over. By the time he got up Sutter was sitting on the couch with the rifle across his lap. Now get out the memory box and let's look at them old family pictures, he said.

I don't have them, Tyler said. Someone's keeping them for me.

Sure they are. You just handed them over for somebody to keep a few days. You think I just fell off the haywagon? Shit, Tyler, you can do better than that.

I went to the law with them. Sheriff Odel's got them. I told them the whole thing, and they're going to be looking for you. You better not touch my sister again.

Fact is, I know you went to the law. But you went with some cock-and-bull story about me and your sister. Odel done talked to me about it. We had a laugh and a little drink, and he left thinking you was either a trouble-maker or kind of light in the head. A blackmailer runnin to the law is one of the stupider things I ever heard of.

There is just no way you can get away with this.

Watch me. We're in the process of me getting away with it right now.

Tyler was silent a time. He glanced at his sister. Don't tell him, she said, but she wouldn't meet his eyes.

They're in the truck, Tyler said at length.

Sutter rose from the couch. We'll see if they are, he said. You go first. Little Sister stays with me. I've got a knife on her, and you try anything even approachin what you done awhile ago, she gets another slit cut in a place where she's got no use for one.

The truck sat facing the house. Tyler was wishing he'd left it pointed outward bound. A cool wind was looping up through the pines. They sighed softly. A three-quarter moon the color of bone hung suspended over them, and the truck gleamed dully.

Where in the truck?

They're taped under the dash. If you want them, you'll have to get them out.

Not in a million fuckin years.

Tyler opened the truck door and lay back across the seat. Hands behind his head and fumbling under the dashboard. A myriad of wires here. He felt the tobacco can ducttaped behind the radio.

Hell, it's gone, he said.

Involuntarily Sutter leant forward as if he'd look too. Tyler kicked him in the chest as hard as he could with both booted feet and before Sutter struck the ground he was immediately scrambling to get under the steering wheel. He was already cranking the truck when Sutter dropped the rifle and went stumbling backward and fell. Get the hell in here, Tyler was yelling. Move it.

She jumped in and sat holding the door handle. When the engine caught Tyler popped the clutch and spun it backward in the gravel not knowing or caring where Sutter was or even if he was under the wheels. He slammed the shift lever into low and went sidewise out of the driveway with the rear wheels fishtailing onto the road. Shut the door, he said, but she just sat there. She seemed not to know where she was. She was very pale. He glanced back once, but he didn't see Sutter, which was just as well, for there was an explosion behind them, and both windshields erupted in flying pellets of safety glass. What the hell do we do now? he asked aloud, but he was already doing all there was to do. Get down, he told her. Shut that door and lay down in the seat. She slid obediently down in the seat but left the door flopping and when Tyler reached an arm across her to close it they were already going too fast for the curve.

He was trying to correct the skid the truck was in but the rear tires were already schoolhopping along on the packed chert when there was a dull boom and a tire went and the truck spun with the windshield opening an elongated frieze of fleeing trees and inexplicably the house itself sliding toward the edge of the world. The truck was riding eerily sideways on the embankment with brush whipping the rocker panels and headlights lost in the halfgrown pines they were riding over. He was afraid to break the truck's momentum by slowing and he had some halfcrazed idea he might get back on the road where the curve ended if he could just keep the truck from flipping. The right side of the truck was topmost and it kept defying gravity and bouncing playfully upward then returning to the ground again. Her weight had slid against him and the door kept banging. If he'd continued downward he might have made it but where his course intersected the road he cut right and when he did the right side of the truck lifted and would not settle back. It stood eerily balanced for a moment like a carnival trickrider then rolled upward and over in a cacophony of rending metal and breaking glass and the grating shriek of steel sliding across stone. She'd slid away from him when the truck rolled and when it slid again she was gone.

The truck righted pointed downhill with headlights cocked into the onrushing trees that were just a whirlpool of light he was driving into. He was in the floorboard when the truck slammed into a tree and ceased in a final outrage of breaking glass and he was out immediately to find her. His next thought was for the cover of the trees, he wanted it desperately.

He could not feel anything broken but something had peeled the skin from his shin and he was bleeding into his boot. All the while he was feeling for broken bones he was looking wildly about for her and he could hear brush popping somewhere and he knew that Sutter was already coming at a run.

A white body strewn on the homemade road they'd constructed. He leapt deadfalls of broken pine skinned bonewhite in the moonlight to where she was sprawled and caught her up under the armpits and dragged her toward the truck. She seemed slack and unwilled as a sack of grain and he kept talking to her but she didn't answer.

At the truck he dragged the rifle from behind the seat. He untaped the Prince Albert can from beneath the dash. His hands were shaking and it seemed to take him forever. Something kept dripping out of the truck and onto the leaves, drip, drip, some vital fluid, his truck was bleeding to death. He shoved the can in his hip pocket and caught her up again and started for the woods. All the breath he had was just a ragged sob in his throat. He won't shoot, he was thinking; he don't know for sure where the pictures are. To show what he'd learned of Sutter the moon rode from behind a skiff of ragged clouds and a bullet thocked solidly to earth, sending chunks of dirt skittering away across the girl, and another sang off somewhere in the treebranches.

He'd stopped stockstill, mindless of the bullets, just staring at her. She lay with her head pillowed facedown on her breast. Arms outflung defenselessly. As if the world was coming at her at a blinding rate of speed and she'd thrown up her hands to thwart it. All he could see was the dishwater blonde of the back of her head and when he gently righted it it moved without resistance like something moving underwater. Her eyes were open with the exposed whites rolled upward and he could see the dark freckles against her colorless face and her pale breasts bared without shame and her hair all caught with leaves and sticks like some luckless soul drowned and beached here by a receding tide.

He'd begun to cry. Keening some inarticulate grief over her broken body. All the cruel things said and done, the kind ones saved for later. Could I but do it over.

He lowered her head gently and closed her eyes and took up the gun. He'd thought when he made the woods he might lie up in the brush and kill Sutter but the light was chancy at best and what he wanted most right now was to hear her voice, for things to be the way they had been scant minutes before with her weight against his shoulder but the clockhands would not roll backward. What he needed was distance. There was a hellhound on the trail and when the dark sanctuary of trees swallowed him he just kept on going.

❧

Yet sometime past midnight he came cautiously back through the timber again, and the field was alive with activity. He watched with an almost dispassionate bemusement varicolored lights flickering like spirit lamps, dark folk moving about the field. Disembodied voices almost surreal in this clockless hour drifted to him without clarity or coherence. The staccato static of a scanner like a dispassionate chorus commenting on the depths his life had fallen to. An ambulance backed out onto the roadway and tires slewed on gravel and it sped off toward town. He waited for a siren but there was none forthcoming. It vanished in silence and he sat watching its lights wind up into the hills. A bitter grief lay in him like a stone.

Another vehicle backed around and its headlights swept the field and ceased and he could see black figures moving about in the light. A wrecker with its revolving strobe. A figure at the wrecker was paying out cable across the field toward Tyler's truck.

He sat getting his courage up. His story straight. At length he rose and started to enter the field and then he stopped. There was a dread familiarity about one of the figures. The angular unmistakable shape of Sutter. Shouting something back from where Tyler's truck sat canted against the tree. Instructions, directions, who knew? Overseeing all this perhaps. The world had turned strange and seemed to proceed without logic, or any logic he could follow. Even as he watched the cable tautened and the wrecker backed further into the field to provide more slack, and Sutter hooked the cable and shouted. Once more the cable grew tight and the creaking winch slowly drew Tyler's wrecked truck back into the field.

He hunkered at the edge of the wood and watched this shabby tableau. A wind stirred, clashed in the drying leaves. Leaves drifted about him but he did not notice. The wrecker was leaving with the pickup, climbing the steep embankment to the roadbed, its lights canted upward briefly limning moving trees then the clouds absorbed them and there was only a faint glow like some celestial light flaring behind them and the wrecker cut into the road with the headlights clearing out its path. Other engines cranked; all this seemed to be drawing to a close. One by one the other cars followed the wrecker like mourners in a funeral procession. Then the field lay dark and revenantial and silent and there came the cry of an owl.

Still he sat. He seemed to have nowhere else to be, no one in all the world to talk to. The image of the ambulance lights wending upward over the horizon of dark hills would not fade, it seemed to have seared itself onto his retinas. A lifetime ago she strolled up the roadbed toward the school bus, books clutched defensively against her breasts, her face already closed against the anticipated catcalls and whistles. A lifetime ago she led him to the first-grade door and released his hand and consigned him to life. Little sister Death, commended to Fenton Breece.

❧

The house sat in the haunted glade. Fairytale cottage, gingerbread house, but where is the playful troll? The warlock seems not about. Somewhere about his rounds perhaps. A pale ribbon of nighcolorless smoke rose plumb from the flue and dissipated in the windless air.

Tyler pillowed his face against the polished walnut and squeezed the trigger. A windowlight went and he heard glass fall somewhere inside. He waited. A rifle barrel might appear at a shotout window. A warping face appear like a face from a nightmare. He profoundly hoped it would. He just lay there with the sun warm on his back shooting out window glasses. Playing X and O with the six-pane windows. When at length he was bored with this he reloaded the rifle and with it yoked across his shoulders he went off down the slope toward the house.

No soul about. The room still held a vestigial heat though the fire had burned down and the heater when he laid a palm to it was only warm. He looked about. The room was neat and austere. Yesterday's dishes washed and put away on the drainboard. Cot carefully made.

He opened the door and looked into the stove. A bed of coals waxed and waned in their delicate cauls of ash. Suddenly he wrenched the heater over. It toppled on its side in a hail of falling stovepipes and drifting soot. He scattered the coals with a foot. The linoleum darkened, then bubbled beneath them. He piled on the neat chintz window curtains, torn pages from old farm magazines, whatever seemed combustible. He knelt and blew his fire. A flame flickered, caught, a thin cutting edge of fire.

He went out.

⫸

Most of the morning Sutter was hid out by the Tyler place waiting for something to happen. The law to return, the boy to turn up. He'd had time to alter the scene in the field to some degree by calling the law himself and he wasn't overly worried about the local law but Tyler might have it in his head to make it to the state or to Bellwether and he had to have the pictures before that happened. But this morning nothing happened at all. The place seemed vacant, abandoned, a dreamlike place where no one lived anymore.

He went down and searched some more. He didn't find anything. Memorabilia, relics, the castoff souvenirs of life. They seemed to have possessed precious little worth keeping. He went out and hunkered in the yard watching the road and thinking while he smoked a cigarette. If I was a rabbit, he thought, and a fox jumped out of the bushes on me, which way would I run? Would I stick to the road where there was other rabbits, or would I head for the deep pineys? In his heart, he knew. A rabbit would cut for the deep pineys every time. And if the rabbit had any idea of making it to Ackerman's Field, the shortest way was across the Harrikin. If the rabbit was fool enough to chance it. He stood up. There seemed little point in rushing in blind. He'd ask around a bit.

By midday he was in Patton's store. He was eating cheese and crackers and drinking a dope when a man said with a patently spurious air of concern, Shore sorry to hear about your house, Granville. Did you manage to save anything?

Do what? he asked in a spray of cheese and crackers.

Did you manage to get any of your stuff out of the fire?

I'm a son of a bitch, he said. He slammed the bottle down on the dopebox and went out.

It was true what the man had said. He crouched before the quaking ashes. The day had turned chill and he held his hands outstretched for the warmth. He just sat staring mutely at all that was left of his home as if his mind would not quite accept it.

Rabbit my ass, he said at length.

He thought of a rabbit he'd run down and caught as a boy, hemming it in the tall grass. Its soft fur shrouding the delicate bone, its eyes almost confused with fear, its fierce little heart hammering against his cupped hands.

❧

The deputy carefully laid the warrant back on the high sheriff's desk. He shifted his weight in the folding chair. He cleared his throat.

I'm supposed to serve that?

The sheriff finished paring his nails and put away the penknife. Well, it's a state warrant. I figured you still planned on drawin your pay the fifteenth. Christmas comin on and all.

Hell, he'll go right through the roof. You know he shot it out with Radio Atkinson that time. Run him plumb off.

Then he'll just have to go, Odel said. If you hang up your badge and retire, then somebody else'll just have to go. He's goin through the roof all the same.

Yeah, but I won't have to see it.

Suit yourself.

You want to ride out there with me?

About as much as I want acute appendicitis.

The deputy drove out the Riverside Road. He drove slowly, taking in all the scenery. The day was very bright and he felt it just might be the last of his life. All this he might never see again. Sweet scrub blackjack. Beer cans and Coke bottles and windblown candywrappers pressed like dubious gifts onto the honeysuckle. Shotgun shanties with folk sitting about their leaning porches taking their ease. They seemed in no immediate peril. No warrants for Granville Sutter riding like malignant melanoma in their breast pockets. Before he reached Sutter's gingerbread house he braked the car and checked the load in his revolver and placed it on the seat between his legs.

Piss on it, he said aloud. Let's go get the big mean son of a bitch.

But the gingerbread house was gone. In its place mounded gray ashes. He couldn't believe his luck. It was one of those miracles when the gods pity and spare you that only happens once in a life. He kept looking about the still empty woods and back at the ashes. He approached them. There was yet a faint and fugitive warmth.

He sat in silence. The day had perceptibly brightened. All the sound there was was the car idling and the faroff calling of a mourning dove.

Gone like a bigassed bird, he breathed. He looked across the folded dreamlike horizons to the far blue timber of the Harrikin.

If you drove out the Riverside Road through the flatlands and crossed the high trestle bridge over Little Buffalo, then went on past the alluvial riverbottoms to where the earth begins to rise in a series of folds that become hills and hollows and sheer limestone bluffs, and if you kept roughly parallel to the river at some indeterminate point, you would be in the Harrikin. The road would fade to a ghostroad, the timber would thicken, the earth begin to climb in ascending hills. You would begin to come upon abandoned farms whose acreage bore only the faint spectral traces of tillage. Fallen houses with their broken ridgepoles and blind windows and windscattered shakes that are home now only to the foxes and dirtdaubers and the weathers. Tiny gray crackerbox shacks with dark, doorless apertures and tin roofs skewered with rusted stovepipes. Landscaped by the winds with the fallen leaves of decades. A series of them like a housing development brought to fruition by the profoundly impoverished. The roads meander and cross each other. They deadend and vanish. There are occasionally the ruins of houses where no road ever existed, once occupied by folk who had no need for anything wider than a footpath.

Once this land was privately owned. Now it is owned by companies or conglomerates of companies in Atlanta, Chicago, New York. By people who have never seen it, are perhaps unaware even of its existence.

It was bought up in blocks by other companies in the first days of the previous century for next to nothing. It was rich in phosphate, in iron ore. There were boom times for a while. A town sprang up virtually overnight. Originally it was the county seat of Overton County, though the Harrikin itself extends over into two other adjoining counties. A railroad bisects it, but the track is unused, as are the roads, and honeysuckle and kudzu cover its rails with impunity. There was a company store, a jail, a post office. Graveyards, one black, one white. Flush times. The heads of these companies grew very rich. The miners subsisted. They made enough for their families to survive. Those with other inclinations made enough to support the whiskeymerchants and whores and cardsharks who had materialized the first payday by some intuition of money approaching magic and these selfsame cardsharks and whores when the mines were shut down vanished like rats scuttling down capsizing decks.

The earth was sunk with vertical shafts, with horizontal tunnels. Great pits were eaten to the surface with pick and shovel and machinery, and some of this machinery is there yet, rusting back into the earth.

When the mines closed and the railroad shut down the town died and the money quit, the people left like the Maya abandoning their cities to build other cities, and all that remained were the few families who'd refused to sell their land and itinerant squatters staking dubious claim to what no one else wanted and misanthropic misfits who felt some perverse kinship with this deserted, tortured land. Some of these folk did not, in a sense, exist. They paid no taxes, were listed on no courthouse rolls. They owned no Social Security numbers, having neither applied for nor received anything from the federal government, in fact only vaguely aware of its existence, its distant machinations only rumored to them. Census taking in the Harrikin was haphazard at best. There were folks born here with no birth certificate to show they were alive, folks buried with no papers to show they were dead.

The Harrikin grew wild. Trees sprouted up through the works of man. Kudzu and wild grapevines climbed the machinery until ultimately these machines seemed some curious hybrid of earth and steel. Roads faded and the woods took them until there was nothing to show that wheels or hooves or feet had ever passed here. Brush and honeysuckle obscured the sunken shafts, and horses or whatever trod here might abruptly have what they'd taken for solid earth suddenly vanish beneath their feet. Livestock wander into the Harrikin and are seen no more. Hunters have vanished as well, folks who thought they knew the woods lose their sense of direction in these woods, even compasses go fey and unreliable.

It was called the Harrikin long before the thirties when the tornado cut a swath through it. Folks called the tornado a harrikin, a hurricane, one fierce storm the same to them as another. This one came up through Alabama in 1933 and set down in the Harrikin as if it had had its ticket punched for there all along. It ripped away the roof of the old Perrie mansion that had stood since the eighteen-forties, and lesser houses it reduced to kindling wood or just whisked off to somewhere else. It snapped off trees and hurled them into hollows like flung jackstraws, and when it was gone the Harrikin was more of a maze than ever. Roads and paths were blocked, streams dammed and rerouted. The woods were full of deadfalls. Most of the folk who'd been dispossessed, and some who hadn't, moved on somewhere else. The Harrikin was becoming a symbol for ill luck.

A time would come within twenty-five years when all this would be changed. When timber began to thin the companies who owned these half-forgotten properties realized their potential, and paper companies bought the timber and ravaged the land again and planted pine seedlings, and the Harrikin did not exist anymore.

But all this was not yet. When Tyler fled and Sutter pursued him, this was the closest thing to a wilderness there was, and there was really no thought of going anywhere else, and as these fugitives, mentor and protégé, fled from a world that still adhered to form and order they were fleeing not only geographically but chronologically, for they were fleeing into the past.

Don't he never sleep?
Davis Grubb, *The Night of the Hunter*, 1953

⤜

The rest indeed is silence.
Cormac McCarthy, *Suttree*, 1979

BOOK TWO

BEYOND THE PALE

A spring came out of a rocky hillside, and rusted steel pipes virid with moss had been driven back into the rocks. There was a tin cup affixed to a cutoff sprout but Tyler drank from his cupped hands then washed his face in the cold water. All he could hear was the rushing water and the air was heady with the scent of peppermint.

He had come up a rainwashed gully through a clutter of floodleft debris, old bottomless buckets and washtubs and mudclogged cartires worn out so finally there were booted holes in them. The gully ascended in a tangle of blackberry briars and leveled out into a walnut grove, and he could see the back of a house. Whitewashed, respectable, middle-class. He moved to the cover of a shed and skirted a rotting grape arbor with gray deadlooking vines and past a curious machine from which wires appended to poles led to the house. He scaled a sedgecovered slope into the sun and went on to the summit and lay in the warm grass watching the house. Somewhere off in the distance a tardy cock crowed daybreak.

After a while a heavyset woman came out of the house carrying a dishpan. He judged her to be middleaged. She went purposefully up the roadway to a gardenspot and stooped and began to gather turnip greens.

He didn't think there was anyone else about: there was no stock to see after, and the place seemed to be going to seed, as if there were no husband about to keep it in repair. He decided to chance it; he didn't figure he really had a choice anyway. He went around the back side of the ridge and down to the shed again and up the back steps of the house. The door was ajar as if in standing invitation to whoever might chance by. There was only a screendoor, and that was unlatched.

A cool, serried gloom smelling of years, decay. The sun was faint and heatless through dirtspecked glass. He was in a storeroom stacked nigh to the ceiling with boxes and boxes of what looked like old farm magazines, seed catalogs, newspapers. Cases of empty fruitjars. He was looking for a larder or a kitchen, and this wasn't it. He went cautiously out.

Into a hall smelling of lemon oil and floor wax. Doors stood open, and he peered in to see if there was anyone else about. A bedroom with a cherry fourposter bed. A picture in a heavy oval frame. From it a young couple stared at him across time with vaguely accusing eyes.

The kitchen had a window above the sink, and it gave him a view of the yard but not the garden, and he figured he better hurry. In a cupboard there was a stack of brown paper bags folded and laid up for reuse, and he took one and began to search for food. Under a cloth on the table he found the remains of breakfast. Here was provender beyond his expectations: biscuits and leftover sausage patties and a pint jar of what appeared to be strawberry preserves. He dumped the sausages and bread into the bag and turned to look for more. In a piesafe he found a loaf of homebaked bread and two beautifully browned pies. He slid one carefully into the bag, cradling it so as not to crush it, and turned about and stood a moment as if in indecision and then took the other one as well. He found a tin can half-full of ground coffee and took that and was already at the door and out-ward bound when the thought of the strawberry preserves struck him. He'd read once it was bad practice to shop on an empty stomach and so was forewarned. The strawberry preserves were his undoing. When he had them in the bag and had turned to leave, there were heavy footsteps. A shadow darkened the room. There was only one door out of the kitchen, and the heavyset woman was standing in it staring at him with eyes huge with surprise.

Well, if you ain't the beat, she said. Sneakthievin in broad daylight.

Tyler was gripping the bag bothhanded and ready should she give him leeway through the door, but she was standing in it with the dishpan of greens on her hip, and there was not room to get past her.

What've you been up to, you thievin little scoundrel? What've you got in that sack?

Just food, Tyler said. What was left from breakfast mainly.

Well, if you don't take the ribbon. I reckon you was just too proud to knock on the door and ask for somethin to eat. You don't seem too qualmy about sneakin in the back door and helpin yourself, though.

I didn't want anyone to know I'd been here, Tyler said. There's a man lookin for me, and I'd just as soon he didn't know which way I'm going.

I'll just bet there's a man lookin for you, the woman said. It'd be my guess he wears a badge and got a paper in his pocket with your name on it.

No, not the law. This man aims to kill me. I'm looking for the law, going to find Sheriff Bellwether.

Well, he ain't in my kitchen, she said. Her eye had wandered to the piesafe. The telltale door ajar. Her eyes narrowed. And if you been in them apple pies I baked for the church social, I aim to kill you myself. Them was as fine a apple pies as I ever made, and they wadn't made for the likes of you.

She made a tentative step or two toward the piesafe, and when she did Tyler made a run for the outside world. He made the door but not through it for she had anticipated him and stepped back and slammed him with a heavy hip into the door frame then bonged his head hard with the dishpan.

God*damn,* he said.

Blaspheme in this kitchen again and I'll lay this pan upside your head a little harder, she said. Now you set right there a minute.

She stepped across him through the door, and he heard another door abruptly open and as abruptly close and she was back with an enormous shotgun breeched down and she was fitting a shell in the chamber. The gun was nigh as long as Tyler was tall and its elongated barrel was lustreless and crept with brown lichens of rust.

Now let's see what all you've helped yourself to, she said. Dump that poke out.

Tyler's miserable chattel aligned on the kitchen floor. The pies had been illy used. He'd fallen on them and one was broken into two sections and the other was crushed flat on one side and dripping apple juice. She just looked at them in silence. After a time she slowly raised the barrel until it was pointing into Tyler's face.

Now mister, she said, you fix them pies.

Do what?

Man oughtn't to break nothing he can't fix. Fix em like they was.

Hellfire, he said. I can't fix them. You can't fix pies. They're broken. Anyway, you did it. You pushed me down on them.

He'd fallen into the hands of a madwoman here. Someone too long alone who dwelt in a surreal realm where the punishment for piethievery was death by shotgunning and the alchemy by which crushed pies were made whole was commonplace.

He shrugged helplessly. I'll pay you for them.

A wisp of irongray hair curled over one eye. She blew it away. She still held the gun trained on him, and she was watching him with fey cunning.

If you got money, then how come you sneakin in my back door sackin things up?

I told you. There's a man looking for me, and I don't want him to know where I am. He'll probably be around here asking questions, and the less you know, the less you can tell him.

What makes you think I'd tell him anything atall?

You'd tell him all right. He's clever. He'd find out.

Where you from, anyway?

He didn't know why he lied, but he did. He just did it instinctively. Shipp's Bend, he said. Over on the other side of Centre.

I know where Shipp's Bend is. You got a name? And this feller after you, he wouldn't be named Tyler, would he? Man from over on Lick Creek?

What makes you think that?

She didn't answer immediately, but she lowered the gun.

All the meanness around is one reason I always been in the Harrikin. Now I reckon you've tracked it in here. You hear about that girl getting herself killed over on Lick Creek?

No.

Tyler girl got killed in a truck wreck. Heard about it this mornin. Her and her brother both drunk and her killed when they turned the truck over. A young girl layin out dead in a field with whiskey all over her and inside her. I'd hate to meet my maker with whiskey on my breath, wouldn't you?

I get that close I don't expect to have much of a breath left, Tyler said. He couldn't have told you what words he spoke. His mind was full of what she had told him about the dead girl in the field.

Make sport of me if you want to. It ain't me found dead cut all over from a broke whiskey bottle. Nor me that's run off and hid and bein hunted by the sheriff for manslaughter neither.

I got to get on, Tyler said.

Get on where? To find some other house to break into? I reckon not.

Just let me pay for this mess, and I'll get on out of the way.

Oh, you'll pay, all right. I'm still studyin on that one. In good time maybe you'll go. Why do you think a feller would leave his sister in a fix like that and run just worryin about hisself?

I don't know, Tyler said.

The old woman's eyes had turned hard and bitter. Whiskey, she said contemptuously. I wonder when folks'll ever learn that more comes out of a whiskey bottle than card games and loose women.

Something in her vindictive tone made Tyler ask, Was your man a drinker?

Cecil was a Church of Christ preacher, she said, as if one precluded the other.

Anyway, I got to go.

She seemed to have come to some decision. You aim to paint that Delco before you go anywhere, she said.

That what?

That Delco. It don't make the lights anymore, but I want it painted anyway. Things is went down around here without a man on the place. Cecil painted it ever year right up till the year he died. It quit right after that, too. Ain't that peculiar?

I don't even know what one is.

You just before findin out. Sack that stuff back up, and after that Delco's painted you can have it and be gone with ye.

They went down a narrow corridor that smelled of time and solitude. Tyler could see into rooms piled nigh to the ceiling with mounded clothing and stacked newsprint. As if she expected to live forever and had laid by a permanent supply of raiment and reading matter.

She kept prodding him with the gun. Quit that, he said. I can walk without being shoved along with a shotgun.

Stop and study this picture, she told him.

She gestured wallward with the barrel of the shotgun. You might learn something, she said. You might learn ever act you commit moves you one way or the other. Towards Heaven or towards Hell. Hadn't you rather be moving towards Heaven as the other place? Study this picture. If you wind up down there roastin in Hell rollin and tumbling in them hot coals it won't be for lack of bein told.

Like visitors in some curious museum they stood side by side looking at a painting. Faint mottled light from a dingy bedroom window. The picture showed a graveyard. Tombstones capsizing, graves exploding upward, the air full of cemetery dirt. Folks in their graveyard shrouds or funeral silks ascending skyward like startled birds, their arms stretched winglike in supplication or benediction, their faces rapt in the beatific light that hovered over them.

That's the rapture, she said. When the dead awakes and them what's goin goes.

Her voice was touched by a nostalgic yearning, as if she had her ticket in hand and foot already raised to climb on board.

Where do you reckon you'll be on that great getting up morning?

Tyler thought about it. He studied the picture. As far away from this mess as I can get, he said. I reckon I'll just wait till they get up another load.

I know where you'll be, she told him with satisfaction. And you're not goin to like it.

They went out the front door and around to the back of the house. The generator was behind the shed. DELCO, raised letters on the side said. She had found a bucket of paint and an old illcleaned brush. He pried the lid off the paint bucket with the blade of his pocketknife. The paint was turgid and a vile green. A slick, oily scum rode the top of it. He stirred it with a stick. The woman had brought a lawn chair and seated herself to watch with the gun laid across her knees.

You don't need the gun, he said. I'll paint this crazy thing for you, whatever it is, without a shotgun being held on me.

I feel better with it, she said. Desperate folks around here lately, seems like. You never know what'll come bustin out of the woods next.

He dipped the brush into the paint. You better hang onto it then, he said. Because the next fellow out of the woods is a lot more desperate than I am.

He began to paint the generator. Upon contact with the paint the brush had swollen up to twice its size and become virtually unmanageable and it was like trying to paint with a halfgrown housecat.

You got a better brush?

That's the only one I know of, sonny. Just do the best you can.

You want all these little wires and everything painted?

Just paint where Cecil did. Where it was painted before. It wouldn't surprise me if the lights come on and the icebox worked after you get a good coat of paint on it. It's goin to be a comfort havin this thing painted even if they don't, though. You know, I never noticed that grape arbor goin down like it is. That thing's nearly rotten, ain't it?

The grapevines are dead anyway.

They may come out in the spring. I've seen em do it before. I believe we'll just put a good coat of paint on it when we get through with this Delco.

It's about rotted down. Paint won't help that.

He wanted desperately to be gone. He didn't know if she'd shoot or not and he didn't know if she was as crazy as she acted and he halfsuspected she had known all along who he was and was just trying to keep him here. To collect the reward for a manslaughterer perhaps. He had a nightmare vision of Sutter leaping upon him while this old woman forced him at gunpoint to paint everything on the place this vile green.

She was studying the grape arbor musingly. You may be right at that, she said. We took a couple of them old palins out of the barn yonder and braced it first, it'd be better. Can you drive a nail as well as you steal apple pies?

Just about, he said.

I got a hammer and some nails in the house. You reckon I could trust you to go on paintin while I go in the house and get em?

I don't know what you've got to lose besides an unpainted grape arbor. Anyway, I can't outrun buckshot.

You'd be the very fool to try it, though, she said. I believe I'll just take this with me and keep a eye on you out the winder. You use your own judgment about whether you can outrun shot or not. She shouldered the shotgun and trudged heavily toward the house.

He looked at the sun. Pale washedout sun of the winter solstice. It stood at midmorning. He looked back to his work and went on painting until the screendoor slammed to behind her. He made one last stroke and wiped the brush on the rim of the bucket. He put the lid on the bucket and tapped it home with a fist and laid the brush neatly atop it and walked off rapidly toward the walnut grove. He was already in it and moving fast when he heard the creak of the keeperspring and her call, Boy?

He was down the gully recovering the rifle when she called, I won't shoot you. Boy?

He kept on going. She kept on calling Boy fainter and fainter with his progress, and finally he couldn't hear her anymore.

ꙮ

He followed Little Buffalo out of the Harrikin and by midafternoon he was near a road. He could hear an occasional car drone by on the flatlands, and when he began to hear them downshifting to second, he knew he was near the hills leading away from the river. He veered right across a sandbar of silt and gravel. There was a thick fishy smell in the air and in stagnant backwater pools there were rotting carp discarded from someone's trotline.

The sandbar ended and he was in a brake of wild cane grown with tangles of wild grapevines and it was heavy going. When it ended it ended so abruptly he stepped through it like an actor making a curtain call in an untended field and he could see the roadway and a fence winding along beside it on the other side.

The day had warmed pleasantly and the sky when he glanced upward at it was cloudless and very blue. He knew vaguely but not precisely where he was, and he knew Patton's store was somewhere about. He crossed the fence and came out on the blacktop swinging the rifle along by his side. The only car that passed passed oblivious of him, for he'd crouched in a dry gully watching cautiously through a curtain of dry pigweed and then he came out and went on.

Within a mile he could see the hills where the roads converged, and he could make out the gaspumps in front of the store. The field to the right was given over to an enormous graveyard for wrecked automobiles or those deceased from natural causes, and he crossed through the barbed-wire fence and followed a footpath worn between the rows of cars. Perverse sampling of Detroit's wares. Old partsrobbed Hudsons and DeSotos and Studebakers. A black Buick Roadmaster that seemed to have been dropped from some enormous height, so caved and buckled was it. Discarded empty carton death had come in.

At the store he prowled the aisles studying the shelves, trying to decide what to take. He selected tinned Vienna sausages and pork and beans. Little packages of crackers. He bought thick bars of Hershey chocolate and a small tin of snuff just for the tin to keep matches in, and he bought matches. As an afterthought in consideration of bad weather, he bought a lined pair of cotton gloves and a woolen Navy watchcap.

The storekeep was totting all this up on a brown paper bag. Lastly Tyler took a dripping Coke from the icewater in the dopebox and set it on the wooden counter.

I make it four dollars and a nickel. Be a penny more if you aim to take the bottle with you.

I almost forgot. I need a box of .22 long rifles.

The storekeep fetched up the ammunition from beneath the counter. Looks like you might be headin into the Harrikin huntin.

I was thinking about it.

Best be careful less you're used to it. I got lost once in there diggin sang and like to never come out. Went in with the sun shinin and it darkened up and come up a cloud and I didn't know east from west. Barely knowed up from down. They tell you moss grows on the north side of trees, but, hell, back in there it was growin all the way around em. I walked till I thought I'd drop and finally wound up over in the corner of Lawrence County. Not a bit over twenty-five miles from where I thought I was at. And glad to be there, what I mean. Glad to be anywhere it was houses and folks. Be foureighty with the shells.

Tyler handed him a five, pocketed the change.

Your name wouldn't be Tyler by any chance, would it?

He thought about it a minute. What the hell. His fame seemed to be preceding him somehow. Yes, he said.

Thought it might be. Granville Sutter said you'd be in. Told what you looked like. Said tell you he'd see you on the road somewheres.

Thanks, Tyler said. There was a point of cold ice at the nape of his neck, as if someone had touched him gently there with the point of an icepick. When was he in?

Not morn an hour ago. You hurry you might catch him. Or he might be waitin on you. You goin in the Harrikin, Granville's a good un to go with. He knows it, or ort to, much as he's laid out in there hidin from the law.

Well. Thanks for telling me. I'd better be getting on.

Come back, the storekeep said.

The boy passed through the wrecked cars, his purchases in a tow sack slung over his shoulder. Sutter from behind a crumpled Lincoln watched him go. Down the blued length of rifle barrel. He laid a cheek against the smooth walnut. Peered into the scope and aligned the crosshairs behind Tyler's left ear. Tyler seemed very close; Sutter felt he could almost see into the skull and read the thoughts there. Sunlight in the soft blond stubble on Tyler's cheeks.

Bang, he said softly.

Something akin to disappointment touched him. He hadn't thought it would be this easy, had expected more of a contest than the sorry showing Tyler had made. He wanted Tyler to think he was going to make it. To be giddy with victory, the money within grasp, Ackerman's Field a few feet away. Sutter still couldn't believe Tyler's nerve: that he could think he could burn Granville Sutter's house for no more than the price of a match and then go about his business with impunity.

He was at war with himself. A part of him wanted to just kill him now and have done with it. On the other side of the scale, he had nothing else to do and no home to go to, and he was looking any day for more papers to come down. Son of a bitches in courthouses whose sole function was to prepare and serve papers with his name affixed to them.

A sense of the power he held over Tyler washed over him. He was ever the gambler. Fuck it, he decided. He lowered the rifle and just watched Tyler go. Eating his candy bar. Drinking his dope.

I'll get you where folks ain't so thick, he said. If I got you once, I can damn sure get you again. Who knows, I may even let you walk again. If it ain't out of my reach. Like the cat told the mouse.

All day Tyler moved in the woods and all day the winds blew. He moved in a steady shifting of the depths of leaves that roiled and lifted and spun in whirlwinds and all he could hear was the rushing in the trees above him as if he moved through some convergence of all the world's winds.

The perpetual winds grated on his nerves and he hoped they would abate with nightfall but they did not. He went on bearing what he judged was northeast well into the night by what moonlight there was, and he moved through a world that was eerie and strange, all black shadow and silver light. When he wearied he slept in a stumphole covered with dry leaves, and even in his dreams he listened to the creaking of the branches bowering him and he dreamed stormtossed ships on perilous seas. He awoke once and the wind blew still, and he could hear the soft clashing of dry leaves and from somewhere in the night the faroff and faint chimes of belled goats or cattle, and he drew comfort that beyond all this dark there was somewhere a world of lights and men.

In his hushed world of locked doors and drawn shades Breece went dragging the radio across the hardwood floor. Its feet left little skidmarks on the waxed oak. This radio was a huge wooden Crosley console he could barely get his arms around and it was heavier than he'd expected. He ended up with a shoulder against it sliding it toward the double door that opened onto what had become the heart of Breece's home, what he considered the business end of the embalming business, the parlor that held his worktable and pumps and chemicals and all the tools of his trade.

In other more social days Breece had told folks he listened to symphonies and concertos but in truth he had become addicted to a series of soap operas that divided his afternoons into fifteen minute increments. Our Gal Sunday, Young Widder Brown, Stella Dallas. Pepper Young's Family. Tales of women jerked from obscurity into improbable adventures. Young girls from tiny Colorado mining towns who married rich and titled Englishmen, backstage wives who wondered in their more fatalistic moments if there was romance and happiness at the age of thirty-five, and beyond.

This was a baffling world that had become as tactile and real as his day-to-day existence. Yet a comforting limbo where it took forever for anything to be resolved, a vast slowmoving pageantry of incremental crisis, tales of folk who never developed an immunity to amnesia so that they caught it with bewildering regularity, who were constantly being framed and standing trial for murder, folks whose very identities seemed in constant flux because other folks were always stealing their identities and pretending to be them. Doppelgangers posing as wastrel scions of wealthy families rumored long lost in the Mateo Grosso were always turning up for the reading of the wills. Homespun philosophers ruminated and spat and shuffled and passed on shopworn homilies to descendents who didn't want to hear them anyway and were black sheep forever wandering away from the flock.

He propped the doors wide with a hassock and a magazine rack and dragged the radio onto the tiled floor of the workroom. He stood for a moment breathing hard and perspiring almost audibly. He'd had a thought for one of the plastic tabletop radios that would have been more transportable but he'd tried one in the store and didn't care for the tinny tone of it and thought of it as vastly inferior to the rich bass pronouncements and organ music that rolled authoritatively through the velvetcovered speakers of the Crosley. The Crosley's words had the gravity of carved stone handed down ceremoniously from the mountain and a solemnity that dwarfed the tentative whinings of the tabletops. Anyway this room more and more was becoming his Badger's den and he kept moving more of his favorite things into it until it had become living room and bedroom and above all his refuge from the world and its puzzling doings that transpired just outside his walls.

He was no more than inside the room before he halted his radio ministrations and closed the doors behind him. This door had a heavy lock that clicked to in an oiled reassuring manner and a solid deadbolt that he trusted and immediately shoved home. He felt suddenly lighter, cares lifted from him, he felt he could waltz the radio across the room to the wallplug, and humming to himself he slid it across the tile and plugged it in.

He turned it on and wound the dial around for WLAC and when he heard the organ theme music he turned his attention to the girl.

She lay on the table, her arms alongside her torso, hands open and palms up. Reclining so in her enforced and outraged placidity she looked like something you'd offer up from an altar for a dark god's consideration.

He hadn't decided where to keep her. His first thought had been to store her in his most expensive Eternalrest casket and keep her nearby but to Breece eternity was a relative term and he perhaps more than most men was aware of the perishability of the flesh. Already signs of her inherited mortality had been showing up and he'd been hard put to keep them at bay.

What am I going to do with you? he asked her.

She just lay with her sunken eyes and the teasing smirk of her painted hoyden's face with its lacquered cupid's bow mouth. He took up a spray bottle filled with glycerin and rosewater and misted her face so that it glowed as if it had been touched by the faintest of morning dew. The air smelled like spring, like butterflies and fresh green leaves. We'll get you all fixed up, he told her. He stood looking down at her with his chin cupped in a palm and his face furrowed in an attitude of deep concentration. He'd read books on the ancient Egyptian embalmers and necromancers he considered part of his ancestry and already some of her more perishable organs resided in cambric jars awaiting resurrection and with her more delicate female organs he was experimenting with a more pliable and permanent contrivance of plastic and rubber.

Hush now, he told her. Stella Dallas is coming on.

He sat in an armchair listening. His face flickered like roiled waters, reflecting the emotions of the tale, the movement of the drama. Things had been building for days to a crisis stage. Stella and her daughter Lolly were in New York. Lolly had married a rich New Yorker from high society and Stella and her daughter were visiting Lolly's inlaws. Then someone had stolen a priceless Egyptian mummy from a museum and framed Stella for the theft. This created all sorts of interfamilial discord and now Lolly's mother-in-law was trying to get Stella jailed and prosecuted.

But Mommy, Lolly said, surely Mrs. Templeton can't believe you stole her precious mummy.

Someone began to pound on the double doors and Breece's world shifted instantaneously from the New York world of plundered museums to the workroom of his funeral parlor. He looked wildly about. The reassuring austerity of a room painted battleship gray, gray enameled appurtenances and equipment. Yet the pounding went on.

Breece didn't get much walk-in trade but the door opening onto the street was left unlocked during the day so that folks could drop in and make their burial insurance payments or arrange funerals for their dead relatives. But now someone not easily discouraged had wandered in and actually begun to pound on his private door.

Lately he'd begun to let the business slide. He was even thinking about letting it go entirely and going away somewhere with the girl. Let them bury their own dead or let the dead rot and stink above ground until it sucked the carrion crows out of the trees like songbirds. Let all those freed souls burrow toward Hell on their own or scamper up ropeladders dropped from Heaven.

The pounding went on. Hey. Hey, a voice began to call. Hey under-taker man. Hey undertaker man.

Oh God, Breece thought. It's Granville Sutter.

He leapt up and shut off the radio. Oh Lolly, sometimes I just don't know about people, Stella was saying. He draped a sheet he kept handy over the girl and looked about to see if there were clues left about to snare him. No, there was nothing out of place. He unlocked the door and shoul-dered Sutter aside. Sutter was trying to see over Breece into the room but Breece managed to close the door and lock it behind him.

What are you up to, undertaker man?

What?

What are you up to? You're sweatin and you're red as a beet. You look like a kid his daddy caught him jackin off out behind the barn. What are you up to in there?

I was working.

Workin my ass. Workin some kind of devil's business with that Tyler girl'd be my guess.

Poor old Mrs. Hull died. I'm preparing her for burial.

That's a damned shame, Sutter said. About old Mrs. Hull. Although if there's a Mrs. Hull back there or ever was it'd come as a big surprise to me.

What are you doing here?

We had talked about money.

Oh. Yes, I'd forgotten. Well, I picked it up and it's in my office. Just walk this way.

They crossed the room, Sutter behind and miming Breece's ducklike waddle. Breece went behind a desk and opened a drawer. He took out a manilla envelope and laid it before Sutter. This is half, he said. Everything is just the way we discussed it.

Sutter withdrew from the envelope a thick sheaf of bills. He licked a thumb and began to count bills onto another stack. He licked his thumb once for each fresh bill and he moved his lips as he counted.

Impatience flickered across Breece's face. The bank counted it and they were satisfied, he said. I counted it and I was satisfied. It's seventy-five hundred dollars.

Sutter stopped counting. He looked up. You know, Breece, he said, one of the five or six thousand things I don't like about you is that you think you're smart. You think because you went to a college in Memphis and learned how to puncture folk's insides with Pop-Cola bottles you can run a number on me. Forget that. Put that thought away and don't look at it no more. Now the bank counted and they were satisfied. You counted and you were satisfied. That's a load off my mind, that you all were satisfied. But since it's my money, how about if I count it my damn self? I like to be satisfied as well as the next man.

Breece made a tiny gesture of dismissal. Count by all means, he said. If you don't trust me.

There's damn small question about that. I don't trust you worth a shit. And I pity the fool who does.

He went back to counting the small bills. Breece watched him. Lick the thumb, stack the bill, move the lips. Lick the thumb. Breece looked away, out the window. An old grayhaired lady was coming slowly up the sidewalk. Hobbling laboriously along on a walker. Every now and then she'd halt and lean on the walker to rest, her mouth open and gasping for oxygen like a fish suddenly jerked from water to air. Then when she'd caught her breath she'd come on. Breece thought for a fey moment she'd had some premonition and come to sit on his doorstep and wait.

At length Sutter seemed satisfied. He folded the money once and shoved it into a jean pocket and rose to go. Well I'm burnin daylight, he said. I got places to be.

Have you made any progress?

It depends on what you mean by progress. You've seen the result of some of that progress and I expect I could smell her on your fingers if I was a mind to. That playpretty I sent you special delivered in a hearse. That wasn't supposed to be. That dead girl. If anybody was goin to be dead it was supposed to be that mouthy houseburnin brother of hers. Anyway this was supposed to be all about the pictures. Just get a stack of pictures and bring em to you. It went south too quick for me to stop and that dead playpretty is fixin to cost you some more money.

What do you mean?

Maybe I couldn't have her talking. Maybe she had a little breath in her and I had to suck it out. Maybe her neck wasn't twisted just right and I had to retwist it. Maybe I didn't have as much time as I needed to set that wreck up in a way the law would buy. Or go on buyin. Anyway it'll all show up on the bill.

Sutter's air of uncertainty emboldened Breece. Seventy-five hundred dollars seems to buy an awful lot of maybes, he said carefully. I'd like a little more certainty. I explained to you that it's crucial that I get those pictures back.

I'll get your precious pictures. Maybe when I bring em I'll bring that boy so you'll have a matched set of playpretties. Like salt and pepper shakers. How'd that suit you?

Just get those pictures.

Sutter stood up. I'll leave you and poor old Mrs. Hull to finish your business, he said.

When he'd gone Breece still sat in his office chair. Hands palm down on the desk before him. He could see no way to return to the previous scene of domesticity when he and Corrie had been listening to his stories. Winter light crept across the windowglass. He closed his eyes against the images that assailed them. Something that he'd set in motion shambled toward him. He'd been strenuously winding the spring of a device that would ultimately impale him. He didn't know what to do. Sutter was going to become more expensive than he could afford and he was going to run his mouth. Perhaps there was someone he could hire to kill Sutter.

He leaned his face into his hands like one stricken by grief. He envisioned a long line of folks set in motion each one stalking the one set in motion previous but he was all out of exonerated murderers and he didn't know if he could do it himself.

➤

Tyler was wending up a deep hollow that was a funnel for the winds at his back. He moved in a waisthigh maelstrom of blowing leaves and miniature whirlwinds would dart up the hillside in little dervishes as if they had minds if their own. He went past the remains of a whiskey still whose copper had long been plundered and whose barrels showed the axemarks of old violence.

He was following an eerie keening he'd first heard miles back, and he seemed to be nearing its source. At first he'd thought it the wind but it was not the wind. It seemed the highpitched cry of a child or woman but it went on blowing the same mournful note without ceasing or altering, and when he climbed up the mouth of the hollow to higher ground he found it.

The earth here was stony shale and cleft out of the bluelooking limestone was an irregular opening six or eight feet wide. A crude fence had been constructed around it of split rails and old castoff boards wound with barbed wire, but the wood was rotten and insubstantial-looking. Beyond it a stone bluff rose almost vertically and perpendicular to it with a narrow rock doorway between another wall of stone, and studying this Tyler decided the hills must direct the winds and the hollow funnel them across the pit and play it like some mournful harp of the earth.

He approached the opening with caution, stepping across the juryrigged fence and peering down. There was nothing to see. He could hear the keening, but now it seemed to be issuing out of the earth itself, sad and murmurous voices of the damned pleabargaining for their souls. A cold updraft off subterranean waters came like breath from an ancient tomb, and he dreamed inkblack rivers coursing in the stone veins of the earth where chunks of ice black as obsidian clocked through the dark and where whatever arcane creatures lived there were unsighted and at the mercy of the current. He dropped a stone, and it rolled off the sides as it went, fainter and fainter, then nothing, and it went unremarked by the voices that went on and on in their haunting onenote timbre.

Somewhere he could hear the bells of animals and he studied the poor excuse for a fence then rearranged it as best he could and went toward the narrow arch of stone. He paused and then looked all about and knelt onto the earth. There was a flat circular stone at the floor of the arch, and he pried it free and scratched out a hole in the earth. He took out the tin of pictures and placed them in the cavity and covered them with the stone. He rose and passed through the arch, and the hill began to descend and through the trees he could see tended land and a wooden farmhouse leached gray by the weathers.

The house had a shake roof darkening from melting frost and a tall brick chimney whose shadow was told palely in white hoarfrost on the gable opposing. As he watched the house an old man came out and went with a shuffling hobble toward the barn. He watched awhile and saw nothing further, and after a time he eased down through the shadowed morning trees to the house.

❧

By good daylight Bookbinder had fed and watered the goats and turned them into the lot to graze. There were a nanny and her kids missing, and Bookbinder figured to slip down the hollow and find them. These years Bookbinder moved with care and caution. Arthritis had seized his eighty-year-old knees, and on the steeper hillsides he looked not unlike some

gaunt puppet jerked along by an inept or careless puppeteer who'd lost
interest in him.

There had been predawn cold and a rime of frost, but the sun when it
smoked over the horizon burned it away, and after a while the day warmed.
A golden haze like Indian summer hung in the air, and the old man could
feel sweat beginning under the chambray shirt he wore.

He went farther than he'd planned hunting the goats, and after a while
he crossed out on a roadbed so densely packed by traffic nothing would yet
grow there. Idly he followed the road. The sun had ascended and warmed,
and sweat darkened the back of his shirt between his sharp shoulder blades.
He stopped once and with a big Case pocketknife cut himself a walking
stick, and then he went hobbling on. After fifty yards or so more the
roadway ascended, and he could see all there was left of the El Patio Club
beerjoint. He went on up an embankment through sere tilted weeds, then
the weeds fell away and there was the old parking lot of cracked paving
and the four stucco walls still blackened by ancient smoke beyond a row of
Lombardy poplars planted like a curious harp of the winds. Past the walls
halflost in saplings two privies still faintly marked His and Hers.

The parking lot was encysted with ancient bottlecaps, arcane and
extinct brands of beer like words in a foreign language. He hunkered on
the crumbling paving and took out a pipe homecarved from briar root and
stuffed the bowl with roughcut tobacco. He struck a match on a thumbnail
and lit the pipe. He studied the El Patio through the shifting blue smoke.

All so long ago. The old man from his house used to hear the cries of
revelry. Love or what passed for it in these regions, old rivalries brought
to fruition. The music from their dances, like dispatches from a world he'd
forsaken or it him. Cars coming and going at all hours of the night,
fullthroated mufflers breaking on the switchback, motors opening up on
the stretch like racehorses getting their second wind. Laughter sharp and
brittle as broken glass used to drift down through the trees. Laughter from
women now old as he was, or dead, twenty-five forever and ever.

⤳

She came easing into the room with her slippers in her hand. The room dark, all the light there was moonlight, oblique and deceptive through the windowglass. When he spoke, he startled her so she dropped a shoe; then she recovered and her hands were at her hair, taking it down.

I thought I told you to stay away from that place.

Well. Maybe you did. I forget just now.

He could smell whiskey in the room. I meant what I said.

It doesn't matter anyhow. Nobody gets to say what anybody else can do or can't do. Nobody owns anybody else. They turned the slaves loose a long time ago.

Then she'd come in later and she'd come in later and one night she didn't come in at all. Like some wild thing he'd tamed and chanced letting loose and lost a little at a time. He awoke stiff and sore in the rocking chair. As cold and bleak a dawn as he'd ever known washing the windows. He never saw her again. She was a page torn from a calendar, a year folded neatly and laid aside in some place you never look. Her name on his tongue was dry as ashes, bitter as quinine.

⤳

He knocked the pipe out and stood up and approached the building. A blackened and unshapen ruin. It was here she'd taken up with Hankins. Here Hankins had sat on the last day of his life drinking boilermakers and getting up his nerve to come up the hollow and get the bedstead or kill him. He hadn't known it but he was getting up his nerve to die.

He turned away. Old memories had lost the sting of pain and it was the loss of feeling he mourned more than anything else. It was all so long ago and might have been something that happened to somebody else, might have been some old story in a yellowed newspaper.

He went back down into the woods from the other side of the parking lot. There was a footpath here the old man had worn himself down through the years, and he followed it through the woods directly opposing the way he'd followed it a lifetime ago in the dead of a Sunday night, leant slightly with the weight of a five-gallon bucket of kerosene, midnight visitor bearing the gift of fire.

He didn't find the goats that morning and he decided to go out again after dinner. When he got back to the house it was approaching mid-morning and there was a thin young man sitting on the edge of his porch idly drawing patterns in the dirt between his feet with a riflestock.

Hidy, the boy said.

The old man hadn't been surprised in a lot of years and finding company on his front porch didn't surprise him now.

How do, the old man said. Warmin up some, ain't it?

Aren't you Mr. Bookbinder?

I'm Hollis Bookbinder. I ain't never been Mistered too much. Who might you be?

My name's Tyler. I heard your goatbells in the night. You got a lot of them?

They's several. I don't know exactly how many. Ain't run a census on em lately. They a right smart of company.

You seen a man named Granville Sutter come through here?

No. Was I supposed to of?

I don't know. I just wondered.

Was you huntin him?

No. I'm pretty sure he's hunting me, though. Do you know him?

I know him well enough to stay wide of him. That's a right nice rifle you got there.

Thanks. My granddaddy gave it to me.

Winchester lever action with that octagon barrel. You don't see many of em, but what you do generally shoots true.

The old man had climbed the porch steps, and now he opened the screendoor. I ain't had the rest of my mornin coffee. How about you?

I didn't have any at all.

Then I reckon you ready for some. He disappeared into the house, and Tyler could hear the rattle of pans somewhere inside. He looked about. The house was set on the side of a hill, and the yard sloped away into the woods. The shadow of a cloud went across the sunlit treetops like smoke. Tyler couldn't see as far as he would have liked, and he wondered where Sutter was.

The coffee when the old man brought it in a delicate china cup was opaque and dark and so strong it almost required chewing. The boy sipped it cautiously and watched the line of woods where the sun made moving shadows.

Sutter got it in for ye, has he?

I reckon. He tried to kill me.

It ain't none of my business, but what did yins have your fallin out about?

Well. It sort of come up about my sister. We got into it over her. He fell silent and sat staring at the ground, and his face was bleak with some grief he didn't name.

And you took to the deep pineys. I would of thought this was somethin for the law to handle. I was never one to run overquick to em, but they get paid for protectin folks can't protect themselves.

I can protect myself. I just don't want to kill him unless I have to. Besides, I've been to the law. They never paid me any mind. Somebody told me there's a sheriff in Ackerman's Field supposed to be an honest man. Bellwether. You know him?

I know of him. He's got the name of bein a pretty straight law. There's a lot of these laws around here their badge just guarantees they can do their meanness and get away with it.

꩜

The cell door clanged hollowly behind him. He followed the jailer down a steep stairwell to a green room where folk sat about drinking coffee and pretending they were working. A deputy unlocked a locker and took out a pocketknife and a wallet and a cigarette lighter and handed them to him.

Next time you want to bust up a bar, do it in somebody else's county, he said.

Bookbinder was going through his wallet. Now wait a goddamned minute, he said. I had sixty dollars in this billfold.

Everyone was watching him. Bland eyes out of calm faces.

Chief? the deputy said.

A heavyset man behind a desk scratched his sandy head. He rummaged about looking for Bookbinder's papers.

One pocketknife, he read. One Zippo cigarette lighter. One black cowhide wallet. Nothing about contents. You was charged with a public drunk. You sure you had any money left?

I wadn't drunk. And I know goddamned well I had it.

All right, Mr.—he glanced down at the report—Bookbinder. There must of been some kind of a mistake. Wallace, take him back to his cell till all this confusion's cleared up.

Let's go, Wallace said.

Bookbinder didn't move. He seemed to have been struck by some profound revelation. Wait a minute, he said. I believe I left that money in my other britches.

The chief was watching him. His face relaxed. All right, he said. All cleared up. See how easy that was?

꩜

The old man had been silent a time. I never cared much for the law, he finally said. Or the law in this county anyway. They hired one old boy was a deputy and he liked to whup folks with that club he carried. Like to beat a couple of fellers to death, whupped em right up the steps to the hospital. Right near the funeral home. They got on to him about it and it pissed him off. He ask em, what's the use of bein a law if you can't beat nobody up?

Could you tell me the best way to get to Ackerman's Field?

Well. If anybody could, I ort to be able to. I worked them mines back in Overton the biggest part of my life. Now the way I'm goin to tell you ain't the shortest, but it's the easiest. You might as well forget any other way; these old roads wind and twist and sometimes they just peter out. You try to stay on the roads and you'll just circle around and run over yourself. Go due east till you hit the railroad tracks. They growed up, but they still there. It's about twelve or fourteen mile. The tracks run north and south. Go south and you'll come out right in Ackerman's Field.

And that's all there is to it.

The old man set his cup aside and took out his pipe. He grinned. First you got to get to the railroad track, and that ain't no Sunday drive, specially if you ain't used to the Harrikin. Likely you'll come up on Overton. The tracks is right near there.

Overton?

It's just a bunch of buildins now. Nobody left but the ones in the graveyard, and if they could of left, they'd be long gone, too. When Overton went, it went like a June frost. All it was was a minin town, and when the ore run out she just folded up.

Did you live there?

Off and on. My, that was a rough place then. I was bad to drink then, and I used to spend some time in that crossbar hotel they had. I was in there one night they had me locked up with this nigger. Way in the night there was a terrible commotion. Folks hollerin, tryin to break into the jail. I was unused to folks tryin to break in. Thought it went the other way.

They broke down the door and knocked out the sheriff and took his keys. Roughest-lookin bunch of folks I ever run into. Most of em drunker than I was. They had torches, and one of em was carryin a rope. Lord God, I thought. They're goin to hang me for bein drunk.

But it was the nigger. They drug him out and hung him from a big whiteoak. Turned out it was over a whore. They had this albino whore named Wanda, white as if the sun had never shone on her. Hair the color of seagrass twine, and even her eyes looked white. She charged two dollars, and this nigger offered her five, and somebody caught em together, and she swore up and down he forced her.

What did they do to the whore?

Do? They didn't do nothin except keep on givin her two dollars. There was a lot of em in Overton back then. The miners worked the mines and the whores worked the miners and the only ones come out on top was the company bosses.

Tyler rose. All this time he had sat on the edge of the porch seemingly poised for imminent departure, and now he seemed to have come to some decision. Well, I guess I better get on. I got a long way to go.

Well. Best not rush off in the heat of the day. But I reckon you know your business. I wouldn't worry too much about Sutter. Likely he's forgot about you by now and he's drinkin him a cool one somewheres.

There was a fierce intensity in the boy's face. No. He's not forgot. And you better worry about him, too, because he's headed this way, and he'd just as soon kill you as anybody else. There's something the matter with him. When he comes here, just tell him where I went. That won't hurt me, by then I'll be somewhere else. And whatever you do, don't start anything with him. I didn't mean to mix you up in this.

I ain't tellin him jackshit. And you ain't mixed me up in nothing. I reckon I can set on my own front porch and drink a cup of coffee with whoever I want to. But if that stuff about Sutter is so, you need to be anywhere else besides the Harrikin. You need to be out where there's more folks. Witnesses. He won't do nothin if there's a bunch of folks around.

I got to do it. I believe my best chance is to get to Ackerman's Field. Get to Bellwether and tell him the whole story. There's a lawyer there named Schieweiler trying to get Sutter sent off.

Like I said, I reckon you know your business. What I'd do is stay on the edge of the Harrikin, close to the roads, and try to catch a ride. Most anybody would give you a lift into town.

I don't have time. He's too close on me, and I can stay away from him better in the woods. What's that hole down there, back in the woods? Just a big hole in the rocks, makes a whistling racket.

That's what they call the whistlin well. I don't know how it makes that racket it does. Kindly a mournful sound, though, ain't it? I knowed some old boys went down in it one time on a rope ladder. They went down to where a tunnel like branched off the shaft. They went a ways back in the tunnel, but they was leery of the shaft. Said they didn't make enough rope. Said you'd drop a rock off in the main shaft and just grow old waitin for it to hit. Said they wadn't no bottom, but common sense'll tell you ever-thing's got a bottom, howsomever far it may be.

Well. I'll see you, Mr. Bookbinder.

You just remember what I said. Due east. And if you see ary ghost in Overton, ask him does he remember old Hollis Bookbinder.

❧

The day had waned and grown chill before Sutter came. Bookbinder dozed in his rocking chair, an old plaid shawl across his lap, but he slept a cat's troubled sleep, waking at every noise.

Yet when Sutter came there was no noise, just some alteration of the atmosphere so that when the old man's eyes blinked open, Sutter had one foot uplifted in the act of stepping onto the porch, then standing for a moment in awkward indecision, then setting it down in the yard and leaning to stand the scoped rifle against the wall. Beyond him the world had gone sepia with dusk, and twilight's lengthening shadows ran like dark liquid across the packed earth yard to pool in the lower ground of the woods.

Mr. Bookbinder, he said. You recollect me?

The old man nodded. Head clouded by the tatters of some old half-dream. Faint taste of muscadine wine in the back of his mouth.

I'm lookin for a young feller up this way, figured you might of seen him. He was fumbling about his pockets. Withdrew a worn leather wallet and flashed the old man a glimpse of a badge and a card that might have said anything. Or nothing at all. He repocketed it and the old man looked away, and when he looked back at Sutter his own face held a look of almost unspeakable contempt.

You seen him?

I don't know if I have or I ain't. You got ary picture of him?

No. Course to hell I ain't got no picture. You don't need one to make you remember if you've seen a young feller wanderin around.

It's been six or seven by today, Bookbinder said. Some days I get a run on em. I don't know if I've seen the one you're lookin for or not.

Sutter was silent for a time, his mismatched face an emotionless mask. The air grew faintly menacing. Bookbinder thought the face looked as if, while the clay was yet wet, God Almighty had laid a hand to either side of it in a sudden fit of anger and altered it slightly to mark him.

Sutter turned his head and spat into the yard. A black kid goat had come round the corner of the house and approached Sutter's feet. It nuzzled the calf of his leg, and he whirled as if he might kick it then thought better of it, then abruptly bent to scratch its curly head.

I always been a respecter of age, Mr. Bookbinder, but I ain't got time for no jokin around here. You seen that badge. I'm a duly sworn constable of the Sixth District, and you got to cooperate with me.

I don't know if you're a constable or not, Bookbinder said. But I do know one goddamned thing. You're not in the Sixth District. You're goin to have to get further into the Harrikin than this to work that kind of shit. And just say you was a law. That constable shit don't cut no ice with me. Far as I'm concerned you just a trespasser, and you need to get on down the line to where you're welcome.

You a mouthy old son of a bitch, Sutter said easily. To have one foot in the grave and the other in a pile of owlshit. You tired of livin or what? His hand came out of his dungaree pocket with the switchblade knife. He thumbed the button. Bright serpent's tongue of the blade flicking out. With his left hand he grasped the kid's head. He twisted it upward hard. The goat's eyes walled in its head and it bleated softly and it made jerky little motions with its feet on the earth.

I reckon a man lives alone puts a lot of store in his animals. I guess you're right fond of these goats.

They a right smart of company, the old man said again, like a one-size-fits-all answer he kept in stock.

This'n acts like a pet. I bet if I cut its throat it'd make you remember where that boy went.

Or it might make me blow a hole in the middle of you a log truck could drive through.

The goat was trying to escape. It and Sutter making abrupt little dancing motions. Be still, goddamn you, he told it. He looked up. You might if you had a gun, he told Bookbinder.

With his left hand the old man moved the shawl. It slid off his lap soundlessly onto the porch. He was holding trained on Sutter an enormous old dragoon revolver, and its hammer was thumbed back.

It so surprised Sutter that he released his grip on the goat. When it jerked away and fled, Sutter looked down at the knife he was holding. It ain't loaded, he said.

I done a lot of foolish things in my life, Bookbinder said, but I ain't never threatened to kill a man with a empty pistol.

Piece of shit would likely blow up in your face anyhow, Sutter said. I don't believe you've got the balls to shoot it, let alone kill anybody with it.

The old man slowly moved the barrel away from Sutter and aimed it at a locust fencepost. When the hammer fell the concussion was enormous and the top of the post exploded into fistsize chunks of rotten wood and when Sutter looked back from the post the gun was on him again. The old man was watching him with narrowed eyes.

You just crazy enough to do it, Sutter said. Hellfire. I just wanted to talk to you.

The old man didn't say anything, and the gun didn't waver. Sutter closed the knife and pocketed it. I aim to get my rifle, he said. I'll just be on my way.

Just don't let the barrel point my way, Bookbinder said.

Sutter retrieved the rifle. He kept the barrel pointed earthward.

You know I'll get you for this, he said conversationally. You're graveyard dead and don't even know about it yet. I'll come through your window like a cat some hot night and cut your throat where you lay.

You come ahead, Bookbinder said. And they'll be scraping bloody pieces of you off the wall with a goddamned putty knife.

Sutter turned and went. At the yard's edge he hesitated and would say more, but Bookbinder raised the piece and Sutter kept going. The old man didn't lower the gun until Sutter had vanished into the darkening wood. He laid the gun aside. His hands were shaking and he clamped them between his thighs to still them.

❧

Somewhere deep in the Harrikin Tyler began to come upon curious arrangements of sticks strung from trees, lengths of wild cane wired together in designs strange and oblique, some simple and composed of only a few sections, others intricate three-dimensional compositions, and all alike suspended by tiewire and turning slowly in the air like alien wind-chimes or hieroglyphs from some prior language no one knew anymore. Like messages left by some otherworldly traveler who'd gone before him and left these signs in invitation or warning. They became more frequent, a veritable forest of them, asymmetrical and random and somehow sinister.

A dead fox strung head downward from a tree by wire threaded behind the tendons in its legs. He looked at it curiously, then went on beneath the great lowering trees with wind in their upper branches and doves calling from some lost hollow, past ancient utility poles tilted and wireless that bore witness to a civilization that had come tentatively and long since gone. In a bower formed by the roots of a liveoak and sleeping in a bed of moss was a child's doll. It lay in a miniature casket and its cheeks were rouged and shadowed by improbable lashes and upon kneeling to examine it closer he saw woven into the doll's flaxen locks humanlooking hair of a darker shade, and a wood screw had been threaded into the doll's molded navel. He studied it a time in a kind of wonder without touching it, and then he rose and went on.

Some motion drew his eye and he saw a rusted fifty-gallon drum sitting upright beneath a tree and from its concave top a huge great horned owl was watching him. He approached cautiously. The owl watched him with its great liquid eyes, and he saw himself twinned and grotesque leaning toward their depths. The owl's left leg was imprisoned in the clamped jaws of a steel trap and a chain led away over a tree branch where wire secured it. The owl had been trying to escape the trap, for its feathers were bloody, and Tyler could see that the jaws had bitten into the flesh of its leg. The owl closeup looked like some monster from a child's fever dream, but when he reached a tentative hand toward the trap it did not move, just watched him blankly and slightly inquisitively and with enormous patience from beneath its great tufted horns.

He tried to open the jaws of the trap with his hands but could not and finally pried them partway with his pocketknife, then inserted a stick and sprung them enough to free the owl. He backed away, expecting it to fly,

but it just stood favoring its left leg and watching him back, and he went
on. He'd gone a few feet when he heard the concussion of its wings and,
looking up, saw it pass above him with wingspan terrible like some great
prehistoric bird that had outlived its time and now was fleeing this one.

He had been following the tracks of an ironrimmed wagon that had in
turn been following the spectral roadway along the humped back of a long
ridge, then down into bottomland grown with pinoak and poplar and
maple. This bottomland was cleft by some stream nameless to him, and it
seemed pasthaunted, vibratory with the traces of past habitation as if all
that happened here happened still and concurrent with all other events and
just out of his sight and hearing. He passed tiny log cabins mouldering
down into the earth that might or might not have been slave quarters long
ago or the houses of woodsprites or littlefolk and he passed a stone spring-
house. A cooling box for milk and butter had been chiseled out of the solid
limestone, and old waterpipes gone almost entirely to rust were fed here.
Turning in the direction the pipes led, he saw a gently rising slope grown
with cedar and hemlock and beyond and above them the looming bulk of
a ruined mansion.

He went up the slope abstractedly, he'd realized he was turned around,
had angled too far southeast and was in Lawrence County. This had to be
the old Perrie mansion, and he knew it was not in Ackerman County.
There were still miles and miles of wild country to go, and miles to back-
track. He looked upward. The dark bulk towered above him, three stories
of handmade brick with four columns in front. The earth had settled under
one of the end columns and it canted outward at the top. A ruined balcony
dangled precariously from disintegrating masonry. He went inside.

The roof was gone, lost in the fury of a long-ago storm, he could see
a square of mottled sunlight falling down the curving stairway. He turned
in a slow pivot, more impressed by this ruined glory than the foxes and rats
and nightbirds that called it home now.

He went cautiously up a wide stair to a landing and a great hall with rooms opening off it and windowless apertures through which he could see encroaching trees.

Through a window opening he saw a brick outbuilding and a tiny wooden shanty like a witch's house in a fable. The shanty was impaled with a length of stovepipe like a stake driven through its heart and a column of blue woodsmoke rose and dissipated. The house was surrounded by an enormous amount of ricked firewood and there was a blackened washpot sitting on its three legs over a smouldering fire. Even as he watched a woman came into view. She was laboring up a deeply washed gully dragging what appeared to be a great bundle of honeysuckle vines.

By the time he had wended his way through the bullbriars and vines that formed the lawn of the cottage, she had reached the yard and dragged the vines onto the porch. She was sitting in a willow rocker catching her breath. A tiny gnomish woman who'd come no higher than his chest, a dried and fragile elf of indeterminate but advanced age who seemed light and delicate as the fluted bones of birds found in the woods. Dressed all in homedyed black like the sole survivor of some obscure sect she'd outlived here in this lost wood, with foxes for lapdogs and whippoorwills nesting in her henhouse. The porch was well corded with heaterwood, you'd think the old woman had had word of an impending winter of profound intensity.

Hidy, he said.

How do. Get you a seat there.

Tyler seated himself on the edge of the porch with his back braced against a stanchion. He had not realized how tired he was until he stopped to rest. The porch floor was strewn with soft, curling shavings of hickory.

You been making something?

Handles. You come after one?

He wondered at the degree of emergency that would drive him so far in dire need of a handle. No, he said.

I got em from tack hammer handles all the way up to axe handles.

I don't reckon I need one.

She had a pile of sticks two feet or so long laid by the rocking chair, and now she took one up. The stick had a fork on its small end, and she looped a length of honeysuckle vine about the fork and commenced winding the vine into a ball.

I guess you come about a potion then.

A potion? What sort of potion?

She shrugged. Whatever kind it is you need. I get calls for all kinds. She studied him acutely. I figure you for a love potion. One to make some little gal look away from the feller she's with and hook up with you. She cackled dryly, a sound like the rustle of cornhusks. Or look away from you and fix on somebody else. I get calls for both kinds, and I got the herbs and stuff to make em.

Do they work?

Same folks keep comin back.

You got a potion that'll keep a man from killing you?

Her eyes remarked the gun. Looks to me like you totin around a potion'd do that.

I don't want to kill anybody. I just want to keep from getting killed.

I got hexes that'll make him hurt so bad he'll forget he ever saw your face. Tie his guts in a hard knot and draw both ends tight. But you don't look like you've lived long enough to make anybody that mad, though.

I did this fellow.

She looked at whatever it was she was making. She selected a thin brown vine and wrapped the ball then wove the vine through the bottom, then wound the stick and tucked the end under adroitly. She studied it intently as if to see whether it measured up to whatever standard she went by, then laid it aside and began another one.

What are you making now?

Cokeberry trees they call em.

Who calls them?

She shrugged. The man I sell em to. He buys all I make for fifteen

cents apiece. He sells em somewheres. She gestured vaguely, as to indicate
Ackerman's Field, Nashville, the world at large.

He was studying the thing. If it had a use he couldn't divine it. What
on earth do they do with them?

Now there you got me. Maybe they sets em around to look at. Folks
with too much money'll buy anything. Even hexes. You see all this wood
I got? Charlie Peters hauls it to me on a wagon. He thinks I'm a witch put
a hex on his wife. She got a cancer. He started bringin me wood to get me
to take it off.

Did you?

It's a little late for that. She died. He keeps on bringin me wood,
though, cause he thinks I got one on him.

Why would he think you put a hex on his wife?

He shot and killed my dog and she caught a cancer. He seen a connec-
tion there I didn't see. I don't know, maybe the dog done it. I don't know
the answer to everthing in the world.

Could you do that? Hex somebody?

She glanced at him with her berrybright eyes, then at the wood as if
that were answer enough.

All those things made out of cane, hanging from the trees, are they
yours?

She nodded. They to confound my enemies. Somebody start in here to
do me harm'd never make it through em.

Well, I guess I'm all right then. I made it. He thought about asking her
about the doll but then decided not to. What kind of cancer did she have?
Charlie Peters's wife?

Stomach cancer, I heard.

Tell you the truth, I didn't come after anything. I got turned around in
the woods, then I saw the old Perrie place and went up to look at it. I didn't
even know where I was till I saw it.

She laid the cokeberry tree aside and looked at the towering structure.

I been here a long while. My other house blowed away. The harrikin picked it up from around me and carried it off somewhere else. Maybe set it down around somebody didn't have one, I don't know. The world works in funny ways, I don't question it. I took that for a sign and found me another one. Comes a harrikin and gets this one, I'll just find me someplace else. That big house over there they used to have fancy parties. All the high society. Whole yard there growed up in bull nettles used to be a rose garden where the courtin couples'd walk. One night that balcony up yonder was overloaded with folks, and one end of it come out of the brick, and the whole thing swung down like a wheel rollin, and folks was strowed all over like busted dolls with the sawdust leakin out. All them fine parties is done now. I'm still here, though. All them folks in crazyhouses, old folks' homes, cemeteries.

She sat in a contemplative silence. Summer nights you can still hear them parties. People talkin and laughin far off so faint you can't make out what they're sayin. Some warm nights I set out here and listen to their dance music. You believe that?

I didn't come all this way to call you a liar.

She laid the tree aside and dusted honeysuckle leaves from her dress. Come on in the house, she said. It's about time for a bite of supper.

They entered a dark and cloistral gloom. More wood here. A raw odor of its curing. All manner of handles stood about where she'd leant them. As if she were driven to make new all the world's broken tools. A path wound through the wood like a maze and at its end a shadowed leanto kitchen.

He'd thought himself hungry but not so much as he thought. Supper was some type of cold greens boiled without grease or salt, and the bread was unleavened, as if she held to some vow of abstinence. She watched him while he chewed this tasteless mess in silence.

How come this feller wantin to kill you?

An undertaker hired him to, I reckon.

I'm a old woman, but I never knowed undertakin to be so slow they had to kill folks for the business. Folks dyin all the time, it's the way of the world. Help yourself to them greens there.

Tyler finished and swallowed with an effort and pushed his plate aside a fraction of an inch with a thumb. He hoped she didn't try forcing the greens on him and she didn't. She rose and covered the pan with a cloth and set it atop the cookstove, perhaps for another meal.

You want me to tell your fortune?

I reckon not. I'll just play them like they fall.

Life ain't no card game. Be forewarned. I'd not charge you. Usually I get a dollar, but yours I'd do for nothin.

I reckon not.

Let me give you the dollar then.

He laughed nervously. How come you want to tell my fortune?

There's somethin about you. Some folks say more than they know. You say considerable less. There's somethin about you, and I don't know if it's a great good or a great evil.

Well. You being a witch and all, looks like you'd know.

I would if you wadn't blockin it out. You're hidin somethin.

You can't read people, skim through them like books and lay them aside. All the fortune I need to know is how to get to a road. Can you not tell me how to find the railroad tracks?

There was more wickedness in the world than you thought and you've stirred it up and got it on you, ain't ye?

No. This fella that you sell your vines to, does he pick them up? How do you get to the railroad tracks?

I don't. There's a wickedness in this world, and I try to stay clear of it, but this time I think it's come in the door and set down at my table.

I told you I was just lost.

You're lost, all right. Now I wonder if I ain't myself.

He had risen and made ready to go. You could tell me where the road goes.

You said you came in on it. If one way come here and it don't go but two ways, then the other way must be the one you want. Ain't that right?

I never did anything to you that I know of.

There's things in this world better let alone. Things sealed away and not meant to be looked upon. Lines better not crossed, and when you do cross em you got to take what comes.

There's a man going to be looking for me, Tyler said. If he comes here don't let him in.

My enemies gives me plenty of leeway to pass, she said. I don't expect yourn to be any different.

He wound his way back through the dusty maze into the wan winter light. She had followed him to the door as if to ensure that he kept going. He took up the rifle. I'll see you, he said.

She did not reply, and he wound through the nettles past the dark cathedral where the ghosts held sway and back down the slope into the bottomland.

A gaudy Christmas moon candled up out of the pines and watched Sutter above jagged black carvings of scrimshaw trees. His shadow appeared palely beneath his feet like some faint image developing on a photographic plate. He came out of the hollow following his shadow through the slashes of dreaming trees past the ruined mansion with its enormous keep of hoarded silence until he came upon the toy house with its windows blind save the refracted moon and its weathered walls bleached with silver light. Its dark tin roof seemed the very negation of light.

On the porch with fist upraised to pound on the door he thought he heard the furtive pitterpatter of hasty retreating footsteps. Some creature of the night perhaps who'd sensed his presence and struck for deeper timber.

He lowered the poised hand and twisted the doorknob and pushed the door open onto a darkness so profound the house seemed to store nothing save the dark itself. He stepped into the room and vanished, the dark simply took him. He stood invisible beside the framed oblong of moonlight. He stood holding his breath, listening. When he breathed again he could smell the room, stale smoke and kerosene and years of old cookery. The odor of curing wood and tinned mackerel and the sour musty female smell of the old witchwoman herself. Nothing of humanity here, the smell was the smell of some old vixen fox's lair.

Young Tyler, Sutter called. If you're here come on out. I just need to talk to you.

Silence. He tilted out a kitchen match and struck it on a thumbnail. Orange light filled the room, objects leapt out at him, shadows reared and subsided about the walls as if Sutter had suddenly unleashed into the room dozens of his darker selves.

There was a kerosene lamp atop an old sewing machine cabinet and he unglobed and lit it. Warm yellow light banished the shadows and the first thing he saw was the ricked wood. Goddamned if you wasn't expectin a cold spell, he said aloud. His voice sounded harsh and unreal in the silence and it seemed to startle him.

With the light held aloft like a smoking torch he searched the house without expecting to find anyone and his expectations were fulfilled. He peered into cabinets and under beds and he prowled through cardboard boxes. The old witchwoman seemed to possess even less of the world's goods than Sutter did and he deemed himself much the better housekeeper. The back door stood ajar to the night and all there was beyond it were the stygian trees. Long gone ain't she lucky, he sang softly to himself. She's a long gone mama from Tennessee. He shook his head and grinned ruefully to himself and turned back to the kitchen.

He found two tins of sardines and half a box of soda crackers. He pocketed the flat tins and tucked the crackers under an arm. He found a pone of cornbread so hard it seemed some sort of weird fossil or a flat cylinder of petrified wood and when he hurled it against the wall it rang like stone and spun onto the floor unbroken. I bet a man could drive a nail with that son of a bitch, he said. He found a little coffee in a tin and he took that and then he went out.

He paused by the ruined mansion and sat on the stone doorstep and popped the key on a tin of the sardines and opened them. He laid sardines side by side on one cracker and topped them with another making dainty little sandwiches. He ate until he'd finished one tin and then he lit a cigarette and sat smoking. Grinning to himself he imagined the old woman fleeing soundless out the back door and running sylphlike and blind into the bowering trees. Up and gone at just the imminence of his footstep, gone before his upraised foot touched the plank floor.

There may be something to this old fortunetellin business after all, he told the night.

After a while he dozed and he dreamed music and distant revelry and the rising and falling cadences of voices and he came instantly awake but he could still hear them. He'd long known this place for haunted but it did not bother him. All those lost voices, those lost shades drifting from room to room like smoke. He felt he could have entered their conversation without interrupting it, could have fallen easily into their number and gone unnoticed.

❧

When Phelan pushed against the funeral home door it did not open as he'd expected it to and for a moment he just looked at it in perplexity. He pushed again but the door was locked. The few times he'd been here before for the funerals of colleagues and family the door opening onto Walnut Street had always been unlocked during business hours. This permitted public access to the viewing rooms and chapel.

Phelan was wearing his Sunday clothes. Sport coat in a somber plaid and a blue tie loose at the throat and his shoes were shined. He knocked on the door and looked about. Quiet Sunday morning, cold in the air. Down the street a few late worshipers climbed the steps to the Presbyterian church, he caught scraps of subdued children's laughter the wind brought. Phelan noticed that Breece hadn't had the leaves raked lately and they lay about the lawn and in a loose windrow against the house. A garbage can had been overturned and the wind had kited papers into the box-elder hedge.

Yes?

The door had opened no more than three inches. Phelan could see a narrow section of Breece's face and a necktie knotted tight beneath his ponderous chins. Below that a white smock.

My name is Phelan. I want to make an inquiry about Corrie Tyler.

The door didn't open. Perhaps it closed a fraction. What about her?

Phelan didn't know what to make of this. Well, she's dead, he said. I assumed there'd be a funeral.

Of course there'll be a funeral, he said. Arrangements haven't been finalized.

This time the door definitely moved toward the jamb, the slice of Breece narrowed, just one eye and a section of florid nose with its roadmap tracery of burst capillaries.

Phelan was a respectable schoolteacher who paid his bills and was well-thought-of in the community and was accustomed to being welcomed wherever he went but he wasn't welcome here. In fact he'd never felt so unwelcome.

Hold on here a minute, he said. I want to talk about these arrangements.

No response. The eye Phelan could see looked distracted, and Phelan felt for a crazy moment that maybe he'd already left and Breece was just impatiently standing there watching where Phelan had been.

I know both of the Tylers and know the young man rather well, a student of mine. Perhaps it's none of my business, but I'm aware of their financial situation and I doubt there's any insurance. I'd like to help them in some way. I'd like to know what sort of financial arrangements have been made. I thought I'd pay part of them myself and perhaps take up a collection in the community.

It's been taken care of.

Taken care of how?

Just don't worry about it, Mr Phelan. As I said, it's taken care of, nothing for anyone to pay. Nothing for you to be concerned about. As you said yourself, it's really none of your business.

When are the services? I'd like to view the body.

I don't mean to be indelicate, but the body was badly damaged in the accident. Face crushed and so on. Of course it will be a closed casket ceremony.

Something's not right here, Phelan said. I've spoken with people in the sheriff's department and been informed that she was unmarked. In fact, a deputy told me that the broken neck was her only injury and that when they arrived on the scene she looked as serene as a child who'd fallen asleep in that field.

I'm a professional, Mr Phelan. Who do you choose to believe? Don't you think I'd know the condition of a body I'm preparing? At any rate it's a moot point. The body has been claimed. The body is being transported. By an aunt, I believe. Perhaps there'll be some sort of memorial service. You could attend that, of course.

I told you I know this family. Known both of them all their lives, I've taken an interest in their lives, had both of them as students. There's no aunt.

Of course there is. From Michigan or somewhere, one of those upnorth states. Good day, Mr Phelan.

This can't be, Phelan began, but the door had closed with the finality of a coffin lid and he heard the lock tumblers click into place and he was talking to a panel of polished oak.

He knocked and waited but there was only silence from within. After a long while he turned and went down the concrete steps into the wind, hand sliding on the polished steel railing, his face abstracted and uncertain.

He walked on past the cluster of churches. There was singing from within, one hymn segued into another, they were leaning, leaning on the everlasting arm in the sweet by and by. He went on past Kittrel's car lot with its plastic pennants snapping in the stiff wind and turned the corner and went on up the street toward the courthouse. He thought he ought to talk to someone in the sheriff's office but he didn't know who and he didn't know what he'd say if he did.

He was standing peering into the showroom of the MVA motor company at a new Ford he couldn't have told you the color of when a voice spoke behind him.

You shoppin for one of these new Fords, Mr. Phelan?

What? Oh, no, no, I don't need one, Harris.

Fine looking car.

I was just thinking about something and I'm afraid I forgot what I was doing. I'd been up to the funeral parlor asking about that young Tyler woman. I couldn't get any satisfacion at all. Fenton Breece was acting very peculiar.

Peculiar? What would have been peculiar was if he'd been actin some other way.

Let's walk up to the Bellystretcher and talk about this, Phelan said. I don't know why he'd do it but I believe he was lying to me. No, he was lying to me. I've taught school too many years not to know when I'm being lied to.

Well there's one sure way to tell if Fenton Breece was lyin, Harris said. Did you happen to notice if his mouth was movin?

ﻌ

Light altered and the world was a world seen through smoked glass. The somber light diminished and a small bitter rain began to fall out of a pewter sky. A wind arose and drove before it a cloud of small dark sparrows, bedraggled and homeless as refugees, fleeing nowhere with thin, lost cries. Sutter was passing through a stand of enormous cedars and when the rain fell harder he took shelter beneath one, hunkered on the coppercolored needles, his weight on the balls of his feet and the upright rifle in its zippered canvas case, just peering out beneath the lowering branches and watching the world go shimmery and ephemeral in the blowing rain.

When water began to course down on him through the matted branches and the windbrought rain to soak him, he rose with resignation and went on down the cedared sedgefield, his gait wooden and stoic and implacable.

In the lee of the hills lay the vestiges of a road and a concrete tiling where a wetweather stream went beneath it. He went down the weedgrown embankment to the rocky gully and into the tiling. He had to stoop slightly to enter it. It was dry inside, and he figured if it rained all night this was as good a place as any to spend it. The floor of the tiling was thickly grown with virid moss, and the place had a damp but not unpleasant smell. He sat with his back to one wall with his feet straddling the center, though no water had yet entered the mouth of the tiling, and ate a candy bar, then sat smoking, watching his spherical vision of rain and trees and stone like a world seen through the dirty lens of a spyglass.

After a while he slept or thought he slept. He dreamed or dreamed he did. Anymore the line between dreams and reality was ambiguous at best. For years he'd felt madness sniffing his tracks like an unwanted dog he couldn't stay shut of. He'd kick it away and it would whimper and cower down spinelessly and he'd go on, but when he looked back over his shoulder it would be shambling toward him, watching him with wary apprehension but coming on anyway.

An old woman stood before the mouth of the tiling peering in. A raw-boned, floridfaced woman with graybrennel hair sheared straight across as if by the angry blow of an axe. Fierce little eyes like stokeholes to a red rage flaring behind them. A downturned slit of a mouth as if the workings of the world did not quite go to suit her.

She wore a shapeless old gray dress and a ruffled floursack apron: he remembered when she'd made it. He could see the lethal shape of the butcher knife through the thin, worn cloth of the apron.

She stood watching him intently, her hands clasped behind her back.

You come on home now, the rasp of her voice said. It's time to come with me.

No, he told her. No, I believe I'll just hang around here awhile.

Her face didn't change. I don't know what ever made you think you had a choice, she said.

He sat in silence listening to the rain in the trees. Raincrows called from some distant fallow cornfield. All those sounds he remembered out of the years of his life he wanted desperately to hold onto, to prove he was, rags of memory like cut flowers pressed in a Bible.

She stepped into the mouth of the tiling, a moving darkness silhouetted against falling dark. Water was running out of her hair and down her face; the thin gray cotton held the bony shapes of her shoulders. A thin trickle of dirty yellow water pooled in the tiling. She squatted in it without seeming to notice. Raw red ankles in a pair of broken-out men's slippers. A worn and bewenned hand made absentminded pleats in the hem of her dress.

Come on, she said. You'll like it here where I am. You don't have to do anything except what you want to do. Nobody expects anything from you. There ain't no rules, and there ain't no limits to what you can do. Nobody to tell you folks don't do them things. Nothin binds you except the limits of what your mind can think up. Nobody signs papers, swears out warrants. There's things done here nobody would write up anyway the ink would run like flamin gas, the paper would catch and burn. I been keepin a eye on you, and it's time to go right now.

No, he said. I don't want to.

She stood up. When she spoke, a steely threat had entered her voice. You come on. You go right now of your own free will and I won't send em after you.

She stepped out of the tiling into the rain, and the dark rain enveloped her, abrupt and revenantial and absolute.

He leapt up to follow her. His head struck the concrete hard and fireworks flared behind his eyelids. He stood clasping his head in both hands. He staggered out into the rain.

Ma? he called into the night. Nightbirds took up the cry mockingly. He called again and there was a thread of fear woven into his voice and the cankeredpenny taste of it in the back of his mouth.

When he opened his mouth to call again she stepped close behind him and clasped a fist in his hair and jerked his head upward, and the butcher knife, honed to a razor's sharpness, opened a gaping slit in his throat and bright life's blood darker than claret erupted down his shirtfront.

Lying there sleeping on the mossy concrete, his face jerking with the troubled passage of his dreams, he is provisionally still brother to all humankind. He has strayed far from the ways of men but there has always been a kind of twisted logic to his violence. The things he desired and struggled for made a kind of sense. Revenge, avarice, a thirst for power. The things only dreamed by normal men. Their own secret thoughts made carnate and ambulatory. Silver threads, thin and frayed though they be, hold him yet to the ways of the world. Here in the night they part and the ties give one by one and he falls away like some winged predator into another country, dark and unmapped and turbulent, so that he is finally free from all restraint, lost.

꙳

Coming down a long spine of ridge through a forest of dead chestnut Tyler chanced upon a pack of wild dogs or they upon him. They paced him silently from a distance, turning to watch him and check his course, and when he dropped off toward the hollow they adjusted their course simultaneously with his all dogs at once as if they communicated with each other in some manner above or below the comprehension of men. He began to regard them with disquiet and stopped once to check whether the rifle was loaded.

They'd gone wild in the Harrikin. Or their forebears had. These had been born wild as wolves or jackals, and any kind word or touch from man was nothing save a genetic memory if that. They were scruffy, halfstarved, and rabidlooking, and anymore they were only vaguely dogs.

When he made his rough camp by a stream that night, they were with him still. He'd killed a rabbit and he roasted it over firecoals banked in a circle of stones. He ate and tossed the bones beyond the circle of firelight where they were contested with snarls and he could see their green eyes moving about like paired fireflies. When the meat was gone and he'd lain down to sleep with his rifle for bunkmate he could see a circle of their eyes drawn about the fire and in his mind he could see them stretched out, chins on paws, warily studying the fire and this strange god they'd adopted. As if they'd wearied of this wild life of freedom and hoped he could give them back what they'd lost of civilization.

He had none to spare and at best a tenuous grip on what remained. Sometime in the night he could hear them howling down the night howl on howl distant then more distant like descending souls crying from the lower keep of Hades and when he broke camp in the morning they were not to be seen.

What amazed him was that Sutter seemed to know where he'd be before the notion even struck him to go there. He had gone up the bluff because it was the highest hill he could see and he thought from there he might be able to see the railroad tracks.

On the near side the hill steepened gradually. Rocky clumps of wild ivy. He had come out of a long fallow field and commenced a leisurely zigzagging ascent; he was seeing country he hadn't seen before, and he felt like an explorer charting unmapped wilderness. He looked up. Great white outcroppings of limestone like sleeping beasts jutting out of the ivy. At the summit an enormous dome of stone.

He stopped once on a ledge and ate a candy bar. There was a fugitive sun, faint frail warmth. A thin and spectral light upon this aerie. He sat chewing the chocolate and looking back the way he'd come. A bleak and wintry vista of timbered ridges told in dull and somber tones and a series of staggered horizons fading into nightransparency and no sign at all that he'd ever set foot there. Or that anyone else ever had. In all that he surveyed nothing moved save the mindless ballet of branches in the wind.

A few feet higher up the bluff a cave opened up. Small cave, close ceiling, he must go there on hands and knees. He crawled several feet inside, but it narrowed further into a dark hole he'd have to wriggle through, and he had a thought for whatever might lie beyond, he had no idea what. He peered about. The calcified bones of small luckless animals, a bed of moss and windbrought leaves. Some predator's lair. On a narrow shelf of rock lay an arrowhead. He took it down in wonder and crawled back into better light to study it. It was perfect and chipped carefully from some pink stone. It held a delicate tracery of pale blue like bloodveins running beneath its surface. The arrowhead was sharp and wickedlooking and he was struck by the singleness of its purpose. It was created to kill and

beyond that had no reason for its existence. He wondered at the dark hand
that had chipped it so long ago. What had transpired during the clocking
of the seasons since the dark hand had laid it on the ledge till his paler hand
had retrieved it?

He laid it aside and took off his belt and with his pocketknife sliced a
thin thong of cowhide and looped a slipknot about the ears of the arrowhead and tied the amulet about his neck.

As he turned, an angry wasp sang past his head and splatted against the
rock. He whirled in surprise at where it struck the rock and splintered and
there were shards of bright metal like bits of molten slag and he could smell
the corditelike odor of shattered flint. He was scrambling for cover even
before the shot came rolling across the field, going pellmell on elbows and
stomach through the ivy, the rifle cradled under his chin, toward a shel-
tering ledge. A closer shot clipped shreds of ivy and careened off into
space.

He couldn't see anything for a time. Then the light altered with the
passage of the clouds and there was just a ghost of movement in the brush
across the field, and light winked off glass like a heliograph.

A scope, he breathed. The son of a bitch has got a scope. My ass is gone.

He aimed the rifle and waited. He knew there was no point at all in
shooting, he hadn't the range or the velocity. Sutter knew it, too. He came
out of the woods and glanced toward the bluff and angled in an unhurried
lope toward a thin finger of timber bisecting the field. At its edge he
paused and waved and did a curious maniacal dance. Tyler fired and Sutter
waved an arm and stepped into the timber, and a fierce and almost uncon-
trollable panic arose in Tyler: the timber ran all the way to the base of the
bluff, and even now Sutter was probably running tree to tree toward the
bottom of the hill.

He scrambled up and went further up the slope, leant in a crouch, his
feet sliding in the loose shale, trying to keep as much of the bluff as possible between himself and wherever Sutter was now. Rickrack stone made

a makeshift stairway to the summit, an enormous table of windy rock. He'd a mind to go down the other side but what he saw made him light-headed and almost took his breath away. All the world seemed spread out here in a smoky pastoral dreaminess. Vast umber fields rolling gracefully away and tangled bluegray forests and far below the treetops the yellow-green river snaking through the pines. He studied his position critically. There was a ledge jutting out forty or fifty feet below him, and he thought with care he could make that. Beyond it he just didn't know.

He looked back down the front slope. He couldn't see Sutter, and somehow that was worse: he could be anywhere, plastered chameleonlike against the stone creeping toward him. He might lie up here and kill Sutter and he might not. He didn't even know for sure if he *could* kill him. Sutter might even get close enough to do some killing himself before he even saw him. He kept thinking of the pictures. Whatever happened to him, Sutter would never know where the pictures were.

He crept backward crablike to the edge of the table and turned and peered into the abyss again. A few dwarf cedars grown twisted and tortured by the perpetual wind. The hell with it, he thought. If I got to do it, then I got to do it. With the rifle clutched onehanded he began a hunkered halfslide in a hail of small rocks scuttling away before him toward a half-grown cedar. When he reached it he paused a moment, clutching it to him and trying not to look at the dizzying landscape below. It was a long way down and he was already seeing the folly of what he'd done but it was too late now to go back. He slid on before he could delay further and the next sapling he grasped came out of the earth roots and all and he was clutching bothhanded at the limestone for purchase with the rifle clattering away somewhere below him. A wristsize pine he managed to grasp held, and he clung to it a moment in giddy relief. He could feel icy sweat creeping down his ribcage and his heart wouldn't quit pounding. He slid onto the ledge. The rifle had ended cocked stock upward against a boulder and if it was damaged he couldn't tell by looking.

He couldn't have known from above but the bluff fell away under the ledge convex for fifteen or twenty feet then dropped vertically to the riverbank and below him were still the tops of trees. He looked down the front side into windy space and the yellow river was clocking along far enough below him that he didn't want to think about it. He couldn't believe he'd been so stupid: he'd taken the chance of falling to his death to get to a place completely bare of cover that he couldn't get away from.

All he had to do was wait until Sutter appeared on the rim and shoot him. He sat hunkered with the gun in his lap while the day waned. Light gathered in the west above the timbered hills and the sky went red and gold as the rest of the world darkened incrementally as if all the light there was were gathering there and draining off the rim of the world.

He was watching the rim when Sutter appeared: first his hat, then his head and arm and the rifle barrel so quick he wasn't prepared for it, and a bullet rang on stone so near that splintered rock showered his cheek and he could feel blood. He backpedaled wildly away when Sutter fired again and threw up the rifle toward Sutter and when he tried to squeeze the trigger he could not. The trigger was locked in some manner and he stood staring at it as if it had turned in his hands like a serpent. He looked about in horror: there was nowhere at all to hide. He backed against the bluff for a running start and ran to the ledge and kept running, leaping as far as he could into space, brandishing the impotent rifle aloft, and above him he could hear Sutter's wild cry elongated and distorted like a garbled electronic shriek. He turned in midair and there was a graybrown frieze of stone and trees rushing dizzily upward and stark black cedars going shapeless with speed. He hit the water feet first and shot all the way under, turning in the swift current and immediately fighting for the surface. He felt the branches of a submerged tree rake across him and for a moment snare him, then the yellow current sucked him downstream. He was aware of the hot aching in his lungs. He surfaced in an explosion of spray, gasping for air. He was on his back bearing downstream and when he'd wiped the water from his eyes the first thing he saw was the bluff. It was diminishing rapidly but Sutter was silhouetted against the pale sky, fist aloft and dark and motionless as crude sculpture from obsidian. Or yet some baleful god remonstrating with a world he'd created that would not do his bidding.

He drifted downstream as far as he could stand the cold water and where the river shoaled and grew shallow enough he waded out. Like a beast driven to earth by the dogs of hunters he sought deeper woods. From old leached stumps he kicked out of the earth he built an enormous fire and hunkered before it shivering. The fire roared and great showers of sparks went cascading upward but he just piled on more wood. There was a cold measure of comfort in knowing where Sutter was tonight, and unless he was taking the express as Tyler had there was no way he was getting here. Wherever here was. He didn't even suspect where he was. He was deep in the heart of the Harrikin and he was hopelessly and desperately lost and the walls of the night were drawing in about him.

↬

It is true this world holds mysteries you do not want to know. Visions that would steal the very light from your eyes and leave them sightless. The drawer opened on its oiled rollers without a sound. She lay quite composed with her arms at her side. Legs together, eyes open. Breece'd combed and curled her hair in a becoming way she hadn't worn it in life and at her left temple he'd placed a white gardenia. There was another woven into the darker triangle of her maidenhair, and he studied it critically with the eye of an artist and made some small adjustment. Her mouth was slightly open, and he could see the white line of her teeth. Her pale breasts pooled like flowers of melting wax in the cool blue fluorescence. Sweet gutter angel, just far enough past redemption to make it worth his while.

There had been cuts on her forehead and cheek he'd worked on earlier and now he leant and touched them delicately with a forefinger. He unpocketed from the limegreen smock he wore a tube of tinted cream and carefully daubed the wounds. Studied the effect and wiped away a minuscule amount with a tissue and seemed satisfied.

Within a few minutes he had her dressed in black underwear and a pink evening gown, and he caught her up in his arms and went with her to another room. A great amphitheater of a room with sloping ceilings and dark wooden beams and a hardwood floor of oak pegged with cherry. An orchestra played softly from concealed speakers.

He placed her on the divan with a grunt and stood for a moment breathing hard. He watched her. Her head stayed erect for a moment, held by the divan at the back; then it tilted forward and lolled loosely sideways. He leant and straightened it, and it lolled the other way, and he stayed it with a pillow.

He seated himself beside her and clasped her hand. For a time they just sat there listening to the music. He chatted away at her, and her face wore a slightly quizzical look, as if she couldn't quite fathom what he was talking about.

Brandy? he asked her. He got up and from a sideboard brought a bottle of brandy and two snifters. He moved a small table near her knees and set her snifter atop it and sat with his own cupped in his small white hands. After a time he drank it, and then he drank hers as well.

The sourceless music wafted about the room. That's Mahler, he told her. I don't suppose you're familiar with Mahler. His voice gently chided her lack of erudition.

Gustav Mahler was an Austrian composer from around the turn of the century. This is a cycle of songs called the *Kindertotenlieder*. Translated, that means 'Songs of Dead Children.' Don't you think that's a nice touch of irony?

He went on lecturing the dead girl for some time about classical music and various composers and then he seemed stricken by some emotion.

Overcome perhaps by the music or the brandy or her perfumed presence. The room swam, veered like a warping world with its supports suddenly jerked away. He placed her hand on his thigh and when it slid away replaced it. He already had an arm about her shoulders, and now he dropped a hand to cup her breast. He drew her to him with a stricken urgency and buried his face in the soft white curve of her throat. Across his shoulder the dead girl with her unfocused eyes stared out across the great empty room as if she watched something from across a vast gulf of distance or was straining to hear some faint and faroff sound.

❧

The clapboard house sat in a clearing surrounded by dense trees. Unlit, silent. A pale moon clocking through ragged clouds wrought his shadow a twisted dwarf beckoning Tyler on. He didn't know to where. When he came into the yard, the first thing he saw was a German shepherd watchdog chained to a clothesline. The dog was lying at the farthest reach of its tether. Tyler stopped. He stared at the dog in bemused wonder. It was lying in a pool of blood that looked black in the moonlight and its eyes were open and its lips drawn back over its teeth in a perpetual snarl. He stood hesitantly, then glanced toward the dark house and stepped around the dog and up a stoop of stacked rocks and hammered at the door.

Just silence answered him.

I need help, Tyler called.

The voice, when it came, came instantly, muffled but alert. You'll by God need some shortly if you don't get off my porch. Get away from that door.

I'm lost. I just need to talk to you a minute.

I was just sittin here thinkin about blowin a hole in my front door with this shotgun. You standin on the steps there, you liable to get hit.

Tyler stepped to the side of the door. Open up a minute.

There was silence within. A flare of dim light. Then a covert stirring.

The door sprang inward as if under the onslaught of enormous winds and an overalled figure stood above him clutching the door in one hand and a doublebarreled shotgun in the other. Tyler could smell kerosene, and behind the man a yellow light dished and wavered in its globe of glass. The man's face was florid and unshaven and he looked halfdemented. How is it all you crazy son of a bitches always know how to find me? Out of all the people in this round world and half of it covered in trees, why is it you fools keep wanderin up out of the same goddamn woods into my front yard?

Put your gun up. I don't aim to hurt anybody.

Put up yourn. And I shore can't say the same about myself.

Tyler glanced down. He'd forgotten the useless rifle. It don't shoot, he said. I jammed it somehow.

How many of you crazy sons of bitches is it out here?

Tyler considered. Just one, he said.

It's folks has to work for a livin. Has to sleep. All of us can't get by runnin crazy in the woods all night long.

Who else was here? Somebody's killed your watchdog.

No shit.

Granville Sutter's after me. I think he's crazy.

You think he's crazy? I know for a fact he is. I can guarangoddamntee he's crazy as a shithouse mouse and getting farther into the territories all the time. And it's a thousand wonders I ain't layin here dead as my dog is yonder. If Sutter hadn't of had the sense to stay away from the winders, Fenton Breece would be tyin a necktie around his neck.

He aims to kill me if he can.

You need to get the hell on away from here. As long as you're somewhere else I'm thinking he'll be too. I've just about had my bait of this crazy mess.

Who are you?

I'm Sandy Barnett. I know who you are. Sutter told me and that's all I need to know about you.

I'm trying to get to Sheriff Bellwether. Have you got a car?

I got one but it's broke. All I got is a team and wagon.

Take me to Ackerman's Field.

Not likely. I'm a Godfearin man. I ain't messed up with you two and don't plan to be. I know for a fact he shot my dog in cold blood, and no tellin what you done. Diggin up graves and everthing else from what he was ravin. And aside from all that I don't believe this is the night I want blowed off a wagonseat with a 30-06.

Then let me in awhile. I'm about wore out. You want to talk about graverobbing, somebody needs to check out Fenton Breece. He's crazy, sick somehow, the things he's doing to dead folks. Open a few graves and you'll see what I mean.

Tyler could hear him breathing. Wind caught in the glass globe of the lamb and behind Barnett the room seemed to be in motion.

The man did not speak, nor did he move to unblock the door.

All right then. At least show me the way the railroad tracks are.

The man just pointed mutely into the night and when Tyler looked the way he pointed there was only darkness.

That way? Hellfire. That's the way I came.

I can't help that. They've always been there, and unless they moved em they're there still. Now head out. And the next man prowls into my yard tonight they goin to have to drag him out.

He stepped backward, and the door slammed to in Tyler's face. A wooden latch fell with a sound of finality. Through the cracks faint yellow light, remote, tantalizing, inaccessible. Tyler turned and trudged back down the stone steps into the yard. The light was blown out and the windows went secret and still and black and there was only the moonlight foreign and oblique. He went on toward the woods. Halfway across the yard he turned.

How far is it?

Nothing.

How far?

The house seemed vacant, some old place with newspapered walls and caving roof he'd stumbled across in the Harrikin long ago.

Tyler seemed suddenly taken by a fit of rage. He was fairly screaming. Goddamn you, he shouted. I never made these crazy sons of bitches. None of it's my doing. They're just put here for me to contend with. They've killed my sister and tried to kill me, and I don't even know if she's buried or not.

He could feel the wet earth of the yard through his jeans. He'd fallen to his knees. He was almost sobbing. As if in prayer or remonstration with whatever gods held dominion over these territories no one wanted. He kept thinking about Corrie but the face that kept coming to mind was her freckled child's face as if her life had stopped at this innocent point and none of this had yet happened.

He stood for a time waiting for a reply but there was none. Had he been able he'd have brought a bolt of lightning out of the uncaring heavens and blown the house to splinters but as it was it occurred to him what a good target he made in the moonlit clearing and he faded into the woods and struck out for darker timber.

∿

Late in the day he was going through a country showing signs of old commerce. Steep bluffs tended away to treegrown hollows, and the bluffs were riddled with horizontal shafts. Old rusted purposeless machinery like the flung playthings of petulant giants with a bent for the peculiar and the machinery itself in places Tyler couldn't fathom how it got to and the ferriclooking bluffs hung still with rotted scaffolding dangling into space and everywhere the bright orangebrown rocks and split boulders with their layered centers in subtle gradations of earthtones and old rotting conveyors where the ore had gone and on a flattening of one of the ridges a perfectly round building forty or fifty feet tall built of contoured blocks with the roof caved and serving now as floor and the last few feet at the top gaptoothed and asymmetrical, and it was as inexplicable to him as some druidic configuration of stones ten thousand years old.

He skirted a deep quarry, its sides cannelured by marks where the featherdrill had gone. Far below, blacklooking water pooled in the quarry bottom and as he watched a bobcat drank then highfooted back up the sloping side, boulder to boulder with an almost surreal grace and vanished like some creature wholly of the imagination.

He began to come upon the ruins of shanties and silvergray tinroofed shacks fallen and vinecrept and solitary chimneys like sentries left charged with some watch, then forgotten, and after a while in a frail stand of sassafras he came upon a desecrated graveyard. He'd heard of a black cemetery in the heart of the Harrikin pillaged by vandals. It was part of local folklore that blacks were buried with whatever of value they possessed and the thought of such chattels as jewelry and gold pocketwatches had drawn those who'd already gone beyond the pale here to initiate their own tawdry resurrections, and Tyler's own nights with a pick and shovel were not lost upon him. He passed an open grave with sloping rainwashed sides at whose bottom lay a splintered coffin, and reflexively he looked away, but there was a glimpse of a yellowed skull and a funeral suit bleached absolutely colorless by the weathers. This world should know better than to leave an old grandfather staring sightless into the sun with nothing of shelter left to keep him from the rain and predators.

He hurried on through thin tilting tablets of stone with their weary redundancy of script, and all there was to sum up these lives was the two dates so told. He stopped at the edge and stared back at this desolatelooking city of the dead. All these hardscrabble honor graduates from the school of hard knocks. Their lives had been drawn so thin it was one continual struggle just to exist and when death came like the one kept promise they'd ever encountered, their graves were pillaged for watches they'd never owned, jewelry they'd never even aspired to owning. The very air was telluric with all these untold stories but there was no tongue left to tell them, no ear to hear them save his own.

He went on. The land was ascending through thinning timber and he had come upon a town. A town whose thoroughfare was grown with brush and saplings and whose wooden sidewalks were rotting. Old buildings tilted and robbed of windows, with doors standing open as if awaiting commerce. Stores with faded signs for Dr. Pepper, Groves Chill Tonic, 666. He went up a high set of steps to a porch that ran the breadth of the building. When he entered the store he flushed a family of pigeons who fled startled through glassless windows. He'd been hungry all day but whatever tinned foodstuffs had been left here had been looted long ago, and all that remained was a cavernous room with broken shelving and a long counter down one side. An ancient cash register had been broken open and cast aside. A few flyspecked bottles of some darkly coagulant cureall patent medicine still remained, and a hardened and moldy set of horseharness hung from a nail driven into the wall. A cool, dank smell of old rains and drifted leaves and animal dens and the subtle composite smell of time itself, the cancerous work of the shifting seasons.

He prowled about looking for some sort of tool to attempt repair on the rifle, but anything at all that would have served a useful purpose seemed to have been removed. Even boards had been ripped from the walls to repair other dwellings, great poplar and chestnut boards of improbable width.

He went out. Shadows lay long and distorted in the waning day. The sun was fleeing west. Such sparse windowglass as remained burned briefly with orange fire. He went past a log building mouldering into the earth; this building's windows were barred with crisscrossed slabs of hammered iron, and he guessed this must have served as the jail. He thought of Bookbinder. Do you remember old Hollis Bookbinder? he asked the silence. A row of smashed whiskey bottles on a window ledge bore witness to some past hunter's target practice. He went on past the jail down sloping earth, and in a clearing stood a great whiteoak that drew his eye, for this must be where the black had died for impugning the white whore's honor. He didn't see a church or a school or if he did he didn't recognize them. He kept thinking he'd happen upon the railroad tracks but he did not.

A rising wind ruffled the carpet of leaves and with the wind at his back he hurried on. He wanted shut of this place with its air of dissolute ruin and its desecrated dead. A host of voices rode the wind, garbled and indistinguishable, all talking at once and all telling him stories he didn't want to know. Old grievances he couldn't bear. He came upon a stone building open to the sky built across a stream and within a spring. He raked leaves away and waited for the water to clear and drank and when he raised his face the world had darkened.

The sun had not set but clouds blown in from the west had obscured it and a few drops of rain sang in the leaves. He turned and the rain was swinging across the clearing toward him and what lay beyond it went shimmering and translucent as if it were all being erased from existence.

Just at dusk he came upon an old truck, rusted and motorless, down a hillside cocked against a tree. By some miracle all its glasses remained unstoned and its seats intact and he got in and closed the door against the rain and sat wearily staring out the blurred windshield. After a time his eyes closed and he slept with his head laid back against the back of the seat.

It was full dark when he awoke and he was sore and stiff and moonlight was falling through the windshield. He got out. It was clearing and high above him clouds sped eastward in the keep of some enormous wind. They trailed inkblack medusalike tendrils and the moon shuttled in and out of them and appeared to hurtle eastward but never neared the horizon. He walked with his shadow fading in and out with the passage of clouds until at length the clouds were gone and the woods began to burn with eerie silver fire.

He went on and he came to feel that he carried the seed of some dread plague that would lay waste to all before him and behind him and that word of his coming had preceded him so that folks dropped whatever tools they were holding and grasped up their children and fled into the woods with doors left ajar and meals left halfeaten on dining tables.

Then he thought he must have crossed some unmarked border that put him into territories in the land of Nod beyond the pale where folks would shun him for the mark laid on him to show that he'd breeched the boundaries of conduct itself and that he'd passed through doors that had closed softly behind him and only opened from the other side of the pale and that he'd gone down footpaths into wilderness that was forever greener and more rampant and ended up someplace you can't get back from.

He went on eastward looking for some high point he might climb and search for a light. When he found one he climbed it and turned, unwilling to believe all this blackness to the four points of the compass, but all lay sleeplocked and dark as if in all this desolate world he moved through he was the first man awaiting others or the last man left mourning those who had gone before.

❧

For what seemed to him hours he had been following the sound of human voices raised in song and faroff imprecations of fervent faith or rage. He kept angling toward it and ultimately came out on a road. Beyond in a muddy clearing a tent and worshipers thronging out into the chill night. Voices called each to each. Goodnight, brother. God bless you. See you at the meetin tomorrow night.

He stood uncertainly by the wayside with the rifle, which was by now an extension of himself, dangling at his side, searching countenances in the vague dusk and trying to decide who to ask.

A family passed. A short, slouching man and a bonneted woman, then, in descending order, a darkhaired girl and a teenage boy a year or two younger, then another boy younger still.

The man abruptly stopped, and when he did the woman and children as well as if they had walked into an invisible wall or were in some manner all geared together. The man was studying Tyler's face intently and leaning forward in the failing light. Boy, he asked, are you washed in the blood?

Tyler shifted his weight on the balls of his feet. Not him, he was thinking. Man follow his directions, no telling where he might wind up.

I don't reckon, he said.

Say you don't reckon. That means you ain't. If you don't know for sure, then there ain't no use hemmin and hawin about it.

No, then.

Then what are you even doin here then? This ridge is a place for worshipers tonight. No place here for sinners. No stormcellar here for sinners and backsliders to crawl into.

I just heard the singing and followed it. I've been turned around in the woods. I'm lost.

Lost? The face had leant closer yet and wore such a look of beaming benevolence that Tyler had begun to look skittishly about for someone else to ask. Madfolk he had fallen among here and no safety in numbers such as these. The man had proffered his hand, and Tyler shifted the rifle right hand to left and warily shook it. The hand was hot and dry and frantic.

I know all about lost, the benevolent madman was saying. I wrote the book on lost. I was lost myself till Jesus reached down tonight and plucked me out of the slop I was crawlin in and stood me on my own two feet. You can ask Pearl if you doubt what I say.

The bonneted woman was nodding indiscriminate agreement all the while, but the children's faces watching were just the carefully closed and slightly skeptical faces of children and they told him nothing at all. The darkhaired girl was very pretty, and she was staring at him with a nigh-transfixed intensity.

Claude was saved tonight, Pearl said. He was a drunkard for twentyodd year, but tonight he give it all up.

I'm just trying to get to Ackerman's Field, Tyler said. I come from Centre and I've been turned around in the woods.

Lord, you're a long way from home, the man said. But you're closer to Ackerman's Field than you are Centre. You must be plumb wore out and about starved to death.

I just need to get to town. I have to see somebody bad. You don't have a telephone, do you?

Lord, no. They work on wires, don't they, and they ain't never run no wires in here.

I can maybe catch a ride into town from here then.

But the man would not have it so. His hand had clamped Tyler's biceps. His eyes sought Tyler's eyes with a divine fixity as if righting this lost and doubtful sheep would consolidate his pact with whatever had struck him here this night.

You goin with us. You goin to get somethin to eat and a bed to sleep in and you goin into town with us in the mornin. We go of a Saturday. Can't let you wander around here all night, and it wouldn't be Christian to leave you to the varmints.

Tyler made to pull away, but this seemed much the lesser of several evils, and at the mention of food his stomach had twisted with an almost painful writhing. He allowed himself to be tugged along toward whatever they were moving to. All the other revelers had gone as finally as if the night had taken them. The trees were steeped in a murky blue negation of light, and above them and the dark blue suggestion of horizon a moon had risen halfobscured by lavender clouds like a pale cataracted eye watching them.

The man talked as they progressed; he had not ceased. This here is Pearl, he said, gesturing toward the woman. These is Drew and Aaron and this here grown girl or thinks she is is Claudelle.

There was an old pickup truck turned into a sideroad. The truck had a flat bed with sideboards cobbled up out of slabs. It had been black but was a black now that remembered nothing of paint and seemed to draw light and suck it out of sight somewhere beneath its surface.

Nobody said anything, but Tyler guessed he was to ride in the back and climbed onto the tailgate. The two boys followed, and the girl would have as well, but the woman grasped her arm and pulled her toward the cab.

The road they followed was bowered so low with branches that they were forever ducking and ended sitting against the cab. As they progressed light to dark, the moonlight made lace filigrees of moving shadow in the truckbed.

He rested his head against the cold metal of the cab.

The road spooled palely out behind them and shadow took it and it seemed never to have existed, a road formed by the headlights and diminishing in the red glow of the taillights, beyond that just windy space and nothingness save Sutter trying to devise a way to cross it.

What was you huntin? the biggest boy shouted over the roar of the truck. The younger boy was already asleep against Drew's shoulder, eyes closed and lashes shadowed on his pale face.

What?

What was you huntin? Squirrels, rabbits, what?

Bears, Tyler said.

The boy glanced at the rifle Tyler clutched. He leaned to spit through the sideboards at the fleeing road and gave Tyler a cold cat's look. You come armed mighty light for em, he said. Tyler just grinned and didn't say anything. When the truck ceased they were not before some shotgun shack as he had expected they would be but a substantial farmhouse set in the lee of dark hills. Beyond it other buildings that lay in shadow, the bulk of a barn. He could smell woodsmoke from the fire they'd left. The cab doors sprang open and they got out.

Is Aaron done asleep? the woman called.

I reckon. He's laid against me ever since we left.

Hand him down here then, Drew.

Claude was striding toward the porch. At its edge he halted. Boy, where's that wood you was supposed to stack on the porch. There ain't nary a stick up here.

Drew had scrambled down from the truckbed. I clearlight forgot it, getting ready for meetin and all.

You reckon a good kick in the hind end would help you remember? Claude asked, but there was no real force behind his words. He seemed still touched by whatever of brotherhood he'd soaked up at the campmeeting and willing to pass this magnanimity along to those with human failings.

I believe I can remember it without you goin to that trouble, Drew said easily. I'd do it right now, I reckon.

I reckon you will. Take this lost sheep along with you to help. He turned to Tyler. Just follow Drew here. It's down by the barn.

When they had progressed out of what Drew judged to be hearing distance, he said, He's the damnedest feller for stackin wood on the porch I ever seen. Specially as long as I'm doin it.

Tyler didn't say anything. There were no trees to block the moon here, and the barnlot lay told in somber shades of black and silver. The wood was corded under a crude shed of old barn tin nailed on poles, and Tyler started ricking it up on his arms.

It's a wheelbar here somewhere. Saves totin it.

The wheelbarrow was a rickety homemade affair of short boards nailed to cedar poles, and its wheel had once served a cultivator. The wheel was unsure of its moorings and moved when you pushed the wheelbarrow with a fey drunken whimsy of its own.

Was you sure enough lost?

I sure enough was. Still am.

You wadn't huntin bear, though. My guess is you was coon huntin and got turned around and lost your dogs. Did they not ever tree?

If they did I didn't hear them.

Boy, you was lucky to get out alive, wanderin around in there at night. I ever get lost in there, I aim to travel in the daytime and lay up at night. There's all kinds of wells and holes back in there. Mineshafts. I had a uncle, Mama's brother, Clifford Suggs, he went huntin in there Christmas Day in 1945 and he ain't come out till yet. They hunted for him no tellin how long and never even found a track. What do you reckon happened to him?

I don't know.

I bet he's down one of them shafts. Nothin but bones by now, I bet. Clifford was all right. He was one of my favorite uncles, but still and all, I'm glad it's him and not me. Think about dyin like that. Fallin off down one of them things and no way out. Layin there hurt and nothin to eat and them walls too steep to climb. Watchin the daylight and birds flyin over and stuff. It just seems to me somebody ought to be watchin things like that.

Do what?

You know, whoever's in charge of all this. Whoever's supposed to be watchin things, seeing after em. Pa always gets the religion at these tent meetins, but he misplaces it after a few days. Pa always says His eye is on the sparrow, but I reckon He must of looked away a minute when Clifford stepped off in that hole. Don't you ever think about things like that?

Not if I can help it, Tyler said. I'm just like everybody else, trying to get by.

You goin to town with us tomorrow?

I sure am. Don't you think this thing's about loaded?

Heavier we load it the less trips we got to make. Boy, we'll have us a time in town. We'll go to the picture show. You got any money?

A little. Not much time, though. I need to see a man in Ackerman's Field, and then I've got to figure how to get a ride back to Centre.

It don't take long to see a picture show. Last time I went it was Lash LaRue, you ever seen him? We'll find us a couple of them town girls and set up in the balcony and play with their titties, that's what I'm layin off to do.

Drew glanced toward the house. Lamps had been lit now, and warm yellow squares of light defrayed the dark. He lowered his voice to a conspiratorial whisper even though the house and any ear that might be listening lay fifty or sixty yards away.

You ever had any pussy?

Any what? Seems like I've heard of it somewhere, but I can't think what it is.

That's what a girl—oh, shit. Nobody's that lost in the woods. You funnin me again, ain't ye?

Maybe a little.

Anyway, they say these town girls'll flat put it on ye. We give Pa and them the slip tomorrow, we just might find out. But you better watch Claudelle; she's boy-crazy.

Say she is?

Shit yes. You not seen the way she's been watchin you? Like a cat slippin up on a bird. Ma says it's just her age, but it just looks to me like she's come into some kind of a heat. Like cows and such does. She'll light on you like a duck on a junebug. You better watch Pa, though.

Is that right?

It damn sure is. He's done run off three or four with a gun. What do you think about that?

I think if we don't get this wood to the house he's going to have one after us.

All right then, let's go. I just get to talkin and don't never know when to quit. Out here I ain't got nobody to talk to.

Claude waved them to table with an expansive arm. The table had been laid, and Tyler's sweeping eye took in white beans cooked with chunks of ham and a steaming bowl of snowy mashed potatoes and a platter of fried pork chops. Biscuits from the warming closet and what he judged was muscadine jelly and glasses of buttermilk all way round.

It ain't much, but it beats hickory nuts and a claw hammer, Claude said. Just help yourself, boy.

Tyler didn't need asking. Drew was already ladling full his plate, and Tyler was eyeing the level of beans in the pot and spearing pork chops with his fork. The sloe-eyed girl was eyeing him from across the table but he had an eye only for the food and was dishing out mashed potatoes and awaiting the pot of beans.

I like a boy not afraid to help hisself, Pearl said.

Then you bound to pure dee love this feller, Claude said. He makes hisself right at home.

I was about starved out, Tyler said.

Who are you anyway, Lost Sheep? You from over around Centre?

I'm a Tyler. We always lived down on Lick Creek.

Lick Creek? You ain't kin to old Moose Tyler, are you?

That's what folks always called my daddy.

Claude had laid aside his eating utensils and was staring at Tyler in parodic disbelief. Well, I'll be doubledipped in shit, he said. Why, boy, I've held you on my knee a lot of times. Old Moose Tyler's boy.

You watch your mouth at table, Pearl said. Be baptized at a meetin and come straight home and talk that way at the supper table.

'Shit' ain't takin the name of the Lord our God in vain, Claude said. Or wadn't the last time I looked.

It's vulgar talk, Bible or no Bible, and if it don't say in there not to say it, it ort to.

If this ain't the beatinest thing, Claude said in wonder. Of all the people to come up out of the woods and wind up at my table. Boy, I knowed your daddy thirty year or more. He used to make as fine a whiskey as ever run down my throat, and I shore was sorry to hear when he passed on. I've passed out in your house and slept in your front room more times than once.

And a lot more front rooms, too, Pearl said. Not that it's anything to brag about. She was watching Tyler intently, and he felt his social standing had plummeted precipitously, and he was eating incrementally faster as if the red-and-white-checkered tablecloth might suddenly, plate and all, be jerked from beneath his knife and fork.

Didn't you have a sister a little older than you? Pretty little brindle-headed thing with big eyes?

Yes.

Where's she at? Claude grinned. She ain't lost, too, is she?

Tyler's jaws had ceased working. He lowered his fork and sat silent for a moment staring at his plate.

She died, too, he finally said.

Drew was fiddling with the radio. Twirling the dial from one end of the scale to the other. Garbled bits of laughter, music, soap jingles. Applause. Snippets of lives that were so foreign to them they might have come from another country, another planet.

Leave it in one place, Claude said. Put it on WCKY. They might have the Chuck Wagon Gang.

I ain't studyin no Chuck Wagon Gang. I'm tryin to find the Long Ranger.

Claude looked up from the Bible he was poring over. Boy, the Lone Ranger ain't goin to get you into Heaven.

He'd come about as close as the Chuck Wagon Gang, Drew said. But I reckon he must be out of town tonight. I can't even get the station.

Let me see that thing. Claude dialing. The tailend of a gospel song. A voice came on telling about a miraculous photograph that had cured folks of cancer, arthritis, goiters. Whatever they had. Tumors the size of goose eggs miracled into oblivion, malignancies turned benign. A photograph was taken of a rose garden and when developed it showed the softly glowing figure of Christ the King reaching out toward whoever held the photograph. All free for the asking save postage and handling and a small donation.

Drew rose and went out and pulled the door to on the night. Claude built himself a Bull Durham cigarette and sat with the Bible open on his lap, listening to the voices coming out of the radio, his eyes closed. The woman was not about, and Tyler guessed she'd gone to bed. Somewhere in the house a clock was ticking loudly, he couldn't tell where.

He looked toward the kitchen and Claudelle was standing in the door watching him. He looked away out the window at the dark, and when he looked back the door was empty. After a while he rose and went into the kitchen. A cabinet the length of the kitchen held a drysink, and the girl was standing with her back to him washing dishes. Her black hair fell to her waist. At his step the hand holding the dishcloth stopped its motion, and she seemed to be waiting for something. She faced a window, and the lamp mirrored the glass so that Tyler could see himself reaching across her shoulder for the dipper in the water bucket. In the lamplit glass his face looked sharp and predatory. When his arm touched her shoulder, she turned, and when she did they were very close. In the yellow lamplight her face was translucent and poreless as a face carved from marble.

Why don't you just slip up on a body? she asked.

You heard me coming.

I did not.

We won't argue about it. You were waiting for me, though.

Waitin for you to do what?

For the first time her eyes met his. They were darkly fringed with lashes and in the lamplight they looked violet in their depths.

I don't know. This maybe.

He kissed her and she didn't pull away, but she stiffened, and under his mouth her lips were little girl's lips, prim and clenched. He cupped a breast, and she made some murmurous sound, and her mouth opened and a hand still wet with soapy water came up to clasp the back of his neck. Her eyes opened and he knew she was watching the doorway across his shoulder, and he could tell by the look on her face the doorway was empty.

He dropped a hand to her hip, and her pelvis moved involuntarily against him. He slipped the hand between their bodies, and she made some minute adjustment to accommodate it. He cupped her mounded flesh, and she went slack and boneless against him. Her legs parted and her tongue was in his mouth for a moment, and she hugged him hard and suddenly pushed him away.

We'd better quit. Daddy'll be here in a minute.

He's listening to the radio.

That's not all he's listening to, she said.

There's nothing in here for him to hear.

That's exactly what I meant.

He released her reluctantly and stepped away from her. He drug a ladderback chair from the table and turned it backward and sat watching her with his arms crossed over the top slat. All right, let's talk, then.

Okay. You were right, I did want you to come in here. I wanted you to do that, too. I didn't want to quit.

What part? The kiss, or what?

She reddened. I don't know. All of it. The kiss. I never kissed a boy before.

He grinned. Me neither.

A caramelcolored dog had roused itself from the corner where it slept. It looked about for the girl, then trotted over and lay back down with its chin on her foot and lay watching Tyler warily.

Why on earth is that dog wearing earrings?

Ain't that somethin? Claudelle said. I saw this movie star in a book. She was holdin this dog that looked just like Carmie and it was wearin a pair of earrings. I bought these at the dimestore, and Drew pierced her ears for me with a needle.

Well, that's the first one I've ever seen.

It's only the second one I've heard tell of.

Claudelle.

She jumped. What, Daddy?

Wind up them dishes and get in the bed.

All right, Daddy.

Right now.

Where am I supposed to sleep? Tyler whispered.

In the front room, I guess. On the couch. It's all there is.

All right. When everybody's asleep, come in there with me.

Do what?

Come in there with me when they're asleep.

Why would I do that?

Because you want to, Tyler said. Because I want you to. We can sit in there and talk.

She grinned. What else'll we do?

Nothing you don't want to.

I will if I can, she said. If I can stay awake till they're all asleep.

You can if you want to.

You know I want to.

When all the lamps were blown out, the darkness was absolute. He lay in the strange room with the mothball-smelling quilt pulled about his chin and listened to the sounds the house made. Being lost at sea would be like this, Tyler thought. In the stormy dark. There were no walls, no ceiling, no floor. No north or south, nothing a compass could affix to. Nothing save the dark and the wind funneling cold down the hollow and flattening itself against whatever contained him against the night. He thought of Sutter, and then he forced Sutter out of his mind and thought of Claudelle. Her eyes so near his own. Dark, wise, woman's eyes in a child's face. The taste of her mouth, the clean soapscent of her hair. He was utterly weary, and the womblike comfort of the quilt was like a dream. I will wake up in a stumphole with the rain in my face, he thought. Maybe I'll stay another night, he was thinking drowsily. Or two. The food's not half bad. I could just move in and they could adopt me. Marry Claudelle. Have a little log cabin in the woods with a trellis for climbing roses. Claude could give us a cow and a hog for a dowry, and we already have a dog that wears earrings.

After a while it began to rain. Winter lightning bloomed and showed him a rainstreaked window. Inkstained Rorschach trees on the move. Beyond the window the night looked purple. The window vanished and thunder came rumbling down the corridors of the night. The rain came in hard, windy gusts, then subsided to a slow, steady winter drizzle, and he wondered where Sutter was. Under boughs of cedar, hidden with the nightbirds clotted about the branches like malefic fruit, driven to earth like the rest of the beasts of this fabled wood. Crouched in a dry spot beneath the caved roof of an abandoned house, malign revenant among other revenants keeping council. Cursing the rain and biding his time. Or maybe he had just trudged on, as impervious to the vagaries of the weather as stone.

He went to sleep thinking about the girl. Shucking her nightgown over her head, the pale secret bloom of her body. The warmth of it laid against him, breasts pooled against his chest.

But it was not Claudelle but Claude himself who shook him awake at some clockless hour. He came awake slowly as if he were rising in muddy yellow water.

Get up.

Just crawl on in here, Tyler said sleepily.

What? Wake the hell up, boy.

He awoke instantly then, coming halfupraised in bed, eyes sweeping the room, though there was nothing save dark to see, and the voice came again, and in a drunken rush of relief he realized it was not Sutter but Claude.

What is it?

Get up. It's mornin.

He looked about. He couldn't even see a window. It was still raining.

If it's morning why ain't it light?

It's getting light, Claude said inanely.

Where? Tyler wondered.

Claude fell silent though Tyler could hear the steady rasp of his breathing. He seemed to be leant forward in the dark.

What was it you wanted?

You didn't have a little drink hid out, did ye? Down there by where we picked you up?

No. No, I don't even drink.

I just thought bein as you was Moose's boy, you might. I had some, but she's hid it or poured it out, one. I wisht I knowed which. If it's poured out, there's no use lookin, but if it's just hid, I might find it if I go on lookin.

Well. I don't know what to tell you. What does she say?

She's not sayin much one way or another, Claude said.

I thought you quit, anyway.

I did, I did. I just hate havin somethin and not knowin where it's at. I reckon I'll go back to bed.

Tyler lay back on the pillow. Footsteps wandered away in the dark.

He went back to sleep to the windy rain, and when he awoke again, there was gray light at the window and it was raining still. He didn't know if the rain or the light or the voices had awakened him.

If you ain't the beat of all I've ever seen, Pearl was saying. You take the cake. Baptized one night praisin Jesus and up before daylight huntin whiskey. If that ain't the beat.

Claude was trying a reasonable tack. The Bible ain't down on spirits, he said. Why even them old prophets and disciples and suchlike of old was known to take a dram of wine.

They never blowed the grocer money on it, though.

Claude gave up. They would if they had a sourtongued old bitch like you doggin their ever move, he said.

They fell silent save the clatter of pans, the rattle of cutlery. After a while he could smell coffee boiling, and this drew him up out of the warm quilts. It had turned colder during the night, and he could feel drafts in the room, cold air sucking under the door, tinkling the unglazed windowpanes with soft chimes. He checked under the couch for the rifle, then hunkered before the heater tying his boots. As he straightened and held his hands toward the fire, Claude came through the door with a cup of coffee in his hand. In the cold room the coffee seemed to be smoking.

Get you a cup of coffee.

I believe I will. Turned off cold, ain't it? Tyler could see his breath in the cold air.

It'll warm up here directly. It's that north wind. I ever build another house, I'll never build it facin north like I did this one. Get you a cup of coffee. It's done.

He was spooning sugar into a cup when she said, We about out of sugar around here. Best save what's left for them kids' oats. I got to get em some breakfast here directly.

He'd had an uplifted spoonful bound for his cup but returned it to the jar. He'd wondered about cream but figured that might be rationed, too, and started with his coffee back to the front room. She was watching him with bitter eyes, her face stony as a banker's.

What'd I do? he asked, pausing in the doorway.

She didn't answer for a time. When she did, her voice was a hoarse croak. You got him to thinkin about whiskey again.

Tyler guessed that whiskey was never very far from Claude's mind, but he didn't say so. If I did, I never meant to, he said. He went back into the front room, where Claude was standing with his back to the fire.

We still going to town today?

Sure, it's Saturday, ain't it? We got to. We about out of groceries.

She thinks I got you started thinking about liquor.

Don't pay her no mind. I don't need it nohow, I'm shut of it. Givin up drinkin and cussin and startin a new life. I just had me one of them white nights where you can't sleep, and along about three o'clock in the mornin it laid pretty heavy on my mind. I just can't for the life of me think what she could of done with it. I know she ain't thowed it away. That woman's so tight she'll boil coffee grounds till they fade plumb out.

The front door blew open in a gust of wind, and Drew came in. Shut that door, Claude said automatically before the boy was even in the room. It's got a awful raw breath.

You think it's raw here, you ought to try it down by the hogpen, Drew said. His cheeks were red and chapped, and his nose was running, and he kept rubbing his hands together to show how cold it was.

When we goin to town? he asked.

I believe we'll wait till after breakfast.

There was a curtained doorway leading off to a room Tyler hadn't seen, and through this door Claudelle and Aaron came barefoot and sleep-yeyed and aligned themselves before the fire. Why is it so cold? she asked.

It's wintertime, Claude said.

Tyler moved aside to make more room by the heater. Claudelle caught his eye when Claude was looking the other way and shrugged elaborately. I couldn't, she mouthed.

Don't you let Aaron touch that hot stovepipe, Claude told her.

It's ready, Pearl called.

Breakfast was a hasty meal of smoking oatmeal with buttered biscuits and more coffee. Going to town seemed to be on everyone's mind, and there was an undercurrent of restrained excitement. An almost holiday mood that touched everyone save Pearl. Tyler glanced up once from his bowl, and she was watching him with something akin to trepidation, and he wondered what new offense he had committed. She seemed to have concluded that the sooner they were shut of him the better, but the girl had slipped down in her chair and stretched her legs out and imprisoned Tyler's ankles between her own. She went on spoonfeeding Aaron oatmeal as if she didn't know Tyler existed.

Drew finished and pushed his bowl back with a thumb. He drained his coffee cup and set it aside and stood. We best be getting ready, he said. I aim to be there when the show opens. You want me to warm up the truck?

I don't reckon you're runnin this operation just yet, Claude said. I'll say when to get ready. And you ain't goin to no show.

Am too. You done said.

If he goes, I'm goin, Claudelle said.

I said ain't nobody goin. Them shows ain't nothin but shootin and fist-fightin and them gals runnin around with their bosoms hangin out.

I ain't never seen that one, but it sure sounds like a good one, Drew said. You don't recall the name of it, do you?

You ain't goin.

Watch me.

At length they were ready. The girl in a blue-and-white-checked calflength dress Tyler knew she thought of as her town dress. Claude in a white shirt buttoned to the chin and suitpants and brogans blacked with shoepolish. Dressed for town, Drew looked like a diminutive and amateur pimp. He wore a semitransparent nylon seersucker shirt and trousers baggy at the upper legs and pegged sharply at the cuffs. They were a pale limegreen with contrasting stitching of a darker green.

I ordered these special out of Chicago, the boy said. They come mailorder from a place I seen an advertisement for. The Hep Cat. I dug several fenceposts to get the money to buy them britches. I'm savin up now to get me some of them pointytoed shoes.

Claudelle was studying his hair curiously. It was slicked back stiffly in a grotesque pompadour. What on earth has he got on his hair? she asked rhetorically. She leaned to smell. He was at pushing her away. That boy's got a double handful of lard on his hair, she said.

Least I ain't got socks crammed in my brassiere, Drew said viciously. That hadn't sounded right, and he glanced around to see who'd heard. Or wouldn't if I was wearin one, he amended hastily.

Boy, that mouth of yourn needs some tendin to, Claude said. And it's fixin to get it here shortly. You and Lost Sheep here go get that tarpaulin and lash it over them sideboards. Less you wantin to swim to Ackerman's Field.

You could of come up with this before I got ready, Drew said.

Them slickers is on the back porch.

The yard was already filling with water, here and there islands of higher ground crested with dead yellow grass and the tilted husks of last year's weeds, and they progressed island to island to the barn. There was a crude ladder nailed beside a crib door, and Drew skinned up it. I'll thow it down to ye, he called. See if you can find any wire anywhere.

Tyler found several footlong pieces bent and hooked through a logchain secured to the ridgepole and dangling a little over headhigh in the hall of the barn. He stared a moment trying to divine its purpose, but if it had one other than the storing of wire, he couldn't divine it. The folded tarp fell heavily in a dirty slipstream of drifting straw, and several drownedlooking chickens ruffled their feathers and turned quarreling to study Tyler with jaundiced, unblinking eyes, then turned back and stood humpbacked and disconsolate, watching the rain stream off the edge of the tin roof.

Hellfire, Drew said. We're goin to get as wet foolin with this damn tarp as we would ridin to town. You can't get any wetter than wet less you drown.

They trudged out into the rain and unfolded the tarp over the sideboards and pulled it taut and began wiring the eyelets through fence staples driven into the slabs.

We goin to get them town girls? Drew asked.

Bring them on, Tyler grinned. Water was streaming out of his hair and down his face, and he had to be continually wiping it out of his eyes. Drew's hair had risen in sharp, stiff spikes, and greasylooking gray water ran out of it and beaded like oil on his freckled face.

Damned if we ain't a pair of drowned chickens, Tyler said.

What the hell. We goin to town.

When they had warmed and approached a semblance of dry and were aligned expectantly in the truckbed, the truck would not start. The motor whirled, but it would not fire nor hit, and after a few moments the strong odor of raw gas came seeping back under the tarpaulin. He's floodin it, Drew said. You're floodin it, he called through the sideboards. Claude got out and raised the hood with an attendant squawk of protesting rusty hinges and propped it with a stick and stood peering down into its mysteries. One by one they got out and stood with him, watching in commiseration or aiding him with their silent prayers, and when he felt the weight of their eyes, he turned upon them a confident gaptoothed grin.

Likely it ain't much, he said. It ain't never done this before. Likely it'll hit here in a minute. He shoved his hand into the maze of wires and tubing and wiggled a few things at random. There now, he said professionally. He dusted his hands together. Try it, Drew.

Drew got behind the wheel and whirled the motor a few times. More of the same.

Timin may be a little off, he said. He turned the distributor cap an infinitesimal degree. Now try it.

Come *on,* Tyler prayed.

Nothing.

Claude turned upon them all his look of beaming benevolence and then back to the motor, staring at it fiercely as if he would brook no more insubordination, or yet as if he could by the sheer force of his stronger will raise it from the dead like some decrepit mechanical Lazarus and set it on the road to Ackerman's Field.

We'll just let it rest a minute, he said, his manner suggesting that the truck might be merely tired or had perhaps dozed off.

I ain't standin out here in the rain like a fool, Claudelle said. I'm goin in the house.

Then get this chap in the dry, Pearl said.

The girl turned walking away and gave Tyler a sloe-eyed look back over her right shoulder. He stood looking at her retreating back and tried to think of an excuse for going back to the house.

More than likely the distributor cap's just got water inside, he said. If I got a clean, dry rag and dried it out, more than likely she'd crank right up.

Not so much of a fool as he might have liked, the old woman gave him a look transparent with fierce malice, and Claude said, I reckon you been to mechanickin school. The edge of his smile jerked nervously, and his eyes looked harried.

Tyler just stared off to where the woods took the muddy road. The bowed trees stood bent like penitents under the windy rain, and through the blowing water the horizon seemed in tumultuous motion, wavering like a horizon seen through fire, and it seemed to be receding from him.

Likely it'll just get well on its own, he said.

Claude ignored him. Nothin else works we can always push it, he said. Get her rollin down this grade and she'll fire right up like a sewin machine.

This having occurred to him, nothing would do but they must try it right away. With Claude behind the wheel and everyone else, even the old woman, leant with shoulders to the truck, it began to inch forward through the sucking mud to the slope. Tyler pushed with a kind of fevered desperate hope that the truck would start. He felt that his lungs would burst, and funny lights flickered behind his eyes, and his feet were slipsliding wildly in the slick gray muck. The truck rolled silently toward the downgrade.

We got her on a downhill run now, boys, Claude yelled. Halfway down the slope he popped the clutch and the truck slewed sideways when the gears meshed and the wheels threw great contemptuous gouts of mud back toward them, but it did not hit, nor did it the next time when he tried where the slope leveled out and where it ultimately ceased, sulking in the roadbed like some illformed creature with a malefic will of its own. When Claude leapt out he slammed the door so hard glass rattled in its panel, and he kicked the door with a vicious broganned foot and looked wildly about for some weapon to strike it with.

You goddamned eggsuckin son of a bitch, he told the truck. I ain't never in my life seen nothin so aggagoddamnvatin.

We ain't goin, Drew said.

We goin too, Claude said. It's done got me mad now. Let me think a minute.

I'm goin to the house, Pearl said. She was slathered with mud, and anger smouldered and flickered in her eyes. You may as well quit on it. Like you do on everthing else. She started up the slope, skirting the worst of the mud.

Put on a pot of coffee, Claude called after her, but she didn't say if she would or she wouldn't.

Claude opened the truck door and sat with his feet on the runningboard. Sheltered so from the rain he began to build a cigarette but when he raised it to his lips to lick the paper water dripped from his hair onto it and he was left with half a shredded paper in each hand and brown flakes of tobacco strewn over his lap. He sat staring at it not in anger but a kind of bemused stoicism, set upon by all things mechanical and now by the very elements themselves, as if whatever god had plucked him from the midst of sinners was sorely testing his newfound faith.

Claude got out of the truck and dusted the tobacco flakes from his trousers. Boys, there ain't but one thing to do.

Tyler dreaded hearing it, but there seemed no choice. Let's have it, he said.

We're goin to have to push her back up the grade and roll her off again. We'll scotch her and take another bite and work her on up.

Hell, there ain't no way, Tyler said.

Claude ignored him. Drew, you and Lost Sheep go get some big cuts of that heater wood and tote em down here. I aim to warm my hands and see about that coffee. Yins get the wood down here, come on to the house and warm. I believe it's turnin colder.

They went lethargically back up the hill to the barn. Tyler could feel his wet clothes chafing his body. He could hear frogs singing somewhere below the barn where a pond might lie. Rain sang on the tin. Drew began stacking wood in his arms.

Don't overload yourself, Tyler said. There is no earthly way we're going to get that truck back up the hill.

Drew just shook his head and went on stacking his arm full. So bedraggled and mudslathered and absolutely wet he seemed set up as some cautionary symbol of such depths as human misery can descend to. Tyler was touched by a pity for Drew and a sorrow he couldn't put a name to.

Hell, cheer up, Drew. There'll be another day. They're not goin to run out of town girls.

When they had the wood at the foot of the hill, the thought of heat drew them to the house, and they found Claude seated on the couch before the fire, his clothes steaming richly from the heat and a quart jar three-quarters full of a colorless liquid clutched in his lap that he stroked absentmindedly like an alien pet and a fey look of distances in his eyes.

She hid it in the picture box under the Bible, he said in answer to an unasked question. You boys ready to try it up the hill?

We about ready to warm, Drew said. We ain't got no fruitjar. We have to warm from the outside in.

What about that coffee? Tyler said.

She never made none.

Then if we got to do it, let's do it and get it over with.

Loath to lose the jar again, Claude slung it along in his hand and at the peak of the slope stopped and drank and stood studying the grade intently as if he were figuring angles and degrees of inclination and then went on down the hill.

Drew, you the least. Get you a stick of wood ready and me and Lost Sheep'll push it as far we can up the grade, and you scotch it. Then we'll get us another toehold and go again.

They tried, and the truck wouldn't move. You goin to have to help us, he told Drew. Help us roll it and maybe we can hold it till you throw your block under it.

They locked their feet in the mud and leaned into it. The truck moved two or three feet and then no more. Drew threw a whiteoak cut under the wheel, and they released the truck and stood hands on knees breathing hard.

Again. This time no more than a foot. With his breath exploding in his lungs, Tyler stood staring up the muddy slope, and it seemed to stretch to infinity. He turned toward the woods, and the blue horizon lay beckoning like a promise.

One more time, Claude said, but the truck just rocked on its springs and the wheels would not move. No matter how hard they rocked it or lunged against it, it would not roll.

Claude went to his knees in the mud breathing hard. It's went in gear somehow, he said.

Drew looked. No, it ain't.

It ain't going anywhere else, either, Tyler said.

Claude began to curse the truck. There on his knees in the mud swearing he seemed like a penitent praying to a god of blasphemy. After a time he ceased but remained sitting in the mud with the rain channeling through his sparse hair and the eggsized bald spot he'd so carefully combed over bared to the elements.

I got to think, he said. I'm not whupped yet. Go in the house and warm. I'll think of somethin here directly. He raised the bottle aloft to the winter light and drank and set it carefully in the mud, wallowing out a hole with the bottom of the jar to prevent its overturning.

The serried warm gloom of the house. This is the last goddamn time I'm changin clothes today, Drew said. I've got me a good mind to just go back to bed and start all over.

When they came back through the curtained doorway to the front room, Claudelle said, Let me try to find you somethin of Daddy's to put on.

He stood steaming before the fire. There's no need of it, he said. I'd just get them wet. I'm going back out and see if I can help him do whatever it is he thinks of doing to the truck. Did your mama ever make any coffee?

She just shook her head.

When he'd warmed awhile and judged he'd soaked up enough heat to hold him against the cold, he went back out. He met Claude coming up the slope, but Claude didn't speak or otherwise acknowledge his presence. Tyler noticed that the level of liquid in the jar had fallen, and Claude seemed to list slightly as he slogged through the mud. For lack of anything better to do, Tyler followed him to the barn.

By the time he caught up in the hall of the barn Claude had a bridle slung over his arm and was opening the door to a stall off the strawstrewn hall of the barn. Tyler could hear a heavy stamping behind the door. Here, Stannybogus, Claude was calling into the haysmelling dark. A horse's head appeared in the widening crack, and when it did Claude grasped its mane with a fist twisted in it, and the horse tossed its head and Tyler could see it was blind in one eye. He shook his head and went back out into the rain and down the hill to the truck. After some time Claude came stumbling down the grade leading the horse and carrying a board in his free hand. He laid aside the board and hitched the horse to the bumper of the truck and took up the slab and turned to wink at Tyler.

When the board slammed the horse's rump its one good eye walled fearfully and it leapt against the traces with bunched muscles, simultaneously lashing out with its hind legs. Its right hoof caught Claude a glancing blow on the thigh and he collapsed into the mud, thrashing about and trying to rise. The horse had fallen to its knees leaving great raw slashes in the fresh mud and it was frantically trying to regain purchase before the board could fall again. It veered right and left, rolling its good eye to see then lunged again and for an elongated moment the chains held and it stood straining and vibratory with nervous tremors rippling its hide and when the traces broke it lost its footing and fell again.

From the porch the woman was yelling something the wind stole, and Claude was rolling around in the mud clutching his thigh, face contorted in histrionic anguish. Crazed so all over with mud and lightly furred with straw he looked like the luckless victim of some peculiar catastrophe whose survival lay in grave doubt. Graver still, for the woman had left the porch and was approaching with long purposeful strides.

The horse was running in great sliding lopes around the hillside with the singletree randomly banging the ground and each time it did the horse redoubled its speed toward the edge of the woods. They looked good to Tyler, too.

I got to get on, Claude, he said. I'll see you.

Claude just shook his head and wiped his cheek, leaving in the wake of his hand a slash of mud. Boy, I ever need anymore back luck, I aim to look you up and wear you like a charm on a watch fob. You draw misfortune like shit draws flies.

Tyler knelt in the mud before Claude. There's a man looking for me named Granville Sutter, and he may come here. I just don't know. If he does, don't fool with him. Don't even let him in. He's crazy.

You bring the son of a bitch on. After the day I've had and it not over yet, nobody's goin to come on my own land and jerk me around.

Tyler rose and went on up the hill. Meeting the woman, he gave her a wide berth, and she shot him a look of fearful godspeed and he went on to the porch. The girl met him there. She had a folded coat in her arms and a brown paper bag with the top rolled down.

It's Daddy's old army coat. Try not to let him see it.

I think he's got other things on his mind. I guess I better get on.

I guess you had. Mama's pretty mad. I fixed you a little lunch, some bread and jelly was all I could find. And some coffee. I don't reckon you'll have any trouble findin water to make it.

Thanks a lot.

Bring that coat back. It's Daddy's old World War coat, and he wouldn't take nothin for it. You are comin back, ain't you?

You know I am, he said. Even your mama couldn't keep me run off.

I just hope you ain't lyin about it. I wished Daddy hadn't stayed up all night stumblin around. I wished we'd of done it knowin we'd get caught. I've just got a bad feelin I ain't never goin to see you again.

I'll turn up.

No, you won't. Give me somethin of yours to keep.

Do what? He looked about. All there was was the gun.

Anything of yours to remember you by.

He laid the coat and bag down and untied the thong from the arrowhead amulet and handed it to her. She tied it about her throat and tucked the arrowhead into the top of her dress. Her face was touched with an inexplicable sorrow. I don't even know your first name, she said.

It's Kenneth.

Well. Bye, Kenneth. Be careful.

You be careful. If a man shows up around here and asks about me, you head out. If you have to go out a window or whatever. Just stay out of his way.

What in the world are you talkin about?

He picked up the folded coat and the bag and the rifle from against the porch stanchion. It's a long story and you wouldn't believe it anyway. Just do what I asked you. He raised a hand in farewell and went back into the rain.

He angled toward the barn and figured to come out of the hollow back onto the roadbed. He had a thought for the tarp, but he could hear angry voices from the vicinity of the truck. When he had the barn between himself and the house, he unfolded the coat. It was emblazoned with the insignia of old wars long won or lost, and when he wrapped it round him there was room enough for a companion had he had one, but it was thick wool and very warm.

He went through the dripping brush skirting a wetweather stream boiling up from a mossy shrine and up a rocky incline and through a curtain of blackjack onto the road. He trudged on. The rain did not abate. The day drew on gray and somber, and when dusk fell you could not have told the exact moment it did so. The light just faded by immeasurable increments until ultimately he was walking in darkness.

꙳

Sometime in the night he met a horseman. He'd been walking on half asleep, stumbling with a wooden gait, and the horseman was almost upon him before he recognized the sound of steel shoes on the packed earth roadbed. There was a bend in the road ahead and the rider just beyond, and without even thinking he veered off down an embankment and crouched in a thicket of winter huckleberry bushes till the rider should pass. When he passed, he passed above him with the sound of steel on stone and the creak of the saddle, and Tyler could see the smoking breath of the black horse and the rider pale and indistinct like some underimagined protagonist in a fever dream. Horse and rider diminished into the foggy rain, and the mist muffled the slow clop of hoofbeats. There was a sharp pain in his chest and he realized he'd been holding his breath. He exhaled in a pale plume of steam and hunkered there in the winter huckleberries. He was shivering from more than the cold. He fought an almost overpowering urge to flee crazed and directionless into the fog that drifted between the dark boles of the trees. He didn't know if it was Sutter or not, and he didn't know if it was real or he had dreamed it, but he knew that something dread had passed over him in the night and gone on.

He could hear a rush of water toward the hollow that kept increasing in intensity, and he went downhill tree to tree over the slick, soggy leaves. Runoff was massing where the hollow was deepest, and he could hear more than see the churning below him, a vague, dark, turbulent motion and thick, creamlike gouts of foam clocking rapidly downstream.

Loath to return to the road just yet lest the horseman double back, he clambered on around the hillside, going steadily downhill. The carpet of wet leaves thinned to ultimate stony shale, and he could hear his boots on the rocks. His feet felt wooden and strange and he wondered idly if they were frozen. He didn't know how cold it was, but it didn't seem to matter. It was just cold. The earth flattened and widened here and he was moving through halfgrown cedars that loomed suddenly out of the mist like shrouded ghosts, and the water was boiling into a larger body of water and he stopped to get his bearings. He looked up as if to chart from the stars, but the heavens were leaden yet, and out of them the ceaseless rain still fell. Some nameless creek on his right, but he didn't know what creek or even which direction it should be flowing. He went on. On his right hand rose an embankment that came out of the fog and continued on too symmetrical to have just happened, and he clambered up its rickrack sides to the summit, where railroad tracks laid on crossties gleamed palely with a wet phosphorescence through the dead weeds grown through them. One way led to town, but in the dark he wasn't sure which. Down the bank on the other side another shadow loomed anomalous out of the more familiar shadows of trees and stone.

He approached cautiously. If it was a house, it might be inhabited, and folks hereabouts sometimes answered a nighttime summons with a shotgun in hand. It was a house, or at least a building of some kind. A wall with darker rectangles for stonedout windows and a doorless cavity behind a canted stoop. He went in slowly, feeling for missing floorboards with his feet and for the snuffbox of matches with stiff fingers, and whatever tenanted the house this night crossed the floor in nighsoundless scuttling and over the windowsill and into the night. Somewhere in all this dark a startled nightbird rose with a clamor of wings and subsided against a wall with a soft thud. Rose fluttering again.

He dried his hands as best he could on the lining of the coat and lit a match. A low ceiling over his head, loose paper hanging in shreds. On the wall across the ruin of a fireplace. A litter of old newspapers, broken boards. The match went out, and he could hear the rain drumming on the tin roof.

Within a half hour he had a cheery fire going in the fireplace and he was crouched before it feeding it broken pieces of boxing he had ripped off a partition wall. The room was lit with a hellish orange light, and he had the firebox fairly stuffed to the damper with splintered chestnut before he ceased, and he just sat on the hearth for a time basking in the heat. He'd never felt anything better, and he hadn't known such cold as he'd been existed. He'd kept the bag sheltered from the rain as best he could, and now he ate the lunch she'd packed. Thick slabs of yeast bread smeared with butter and jelly. Loose ground coffee in a folded paper tied with flour-sack ravels. He could smell the coffee through the paper, and he had a taste for a cup, but he could find no sort of pan about.

When he had eaten he stripped off his clothes and put the steaming coat back on and buttoned it around him. He leant boards against the brick mantle and hung his trousers and shirt to dry. He went on gathering wood for a while until he had a great pile mounded before the hearth. The chestnut burned fiercely hot, but it was dry as tinder, and there wasn't much last to it.

He gathered a stack of old newspapers to read and sat as close to the hearth as the heat would permit. An eye to the boards cocked against the mantle, he had to be forever turning his clothes lest they scorch. He chewed a handful of the coffee raw, swallowing the bitter essence, and tried to read, but he was utterly weary, and the stories the papers told were strange and surreal, and whole sentences tilted and slid off the page into the fire.

When the clothes were dry, he put them on and restoked the fire one last time, and with a stack of newspapers for a pillow and the coat for a blanket he went to sleep.

His dream was strange and fevered.

He was on a blasted heath where the trees were sparse and dead. Birds he couldn't put a name to clustered their bare branches and called mournfully ahead of him and fell silent at his approach, then resumed when he'd passed as if they'd announce his entry into this sepia world of shades. He moved on a thin skift of snow that a sourceless wind kept setting in motion and settling back and all there was was the white snow and the black skeletal trees.

The weary road he traveled wound gently downhill toward a vague depression in the earth, and he kept trudging on, and after a time he could see another traveler approaching, a black figure seeping across the snowy landscape like a line of ink dripping down the snowy page, and he came to think that across a vast distance he was approaching a mirror image of himself.

When they met, they ceased walking without speaking for a time and hunkered in the frozen roadbed to rest. The man took out a sack of Country Gentleman and rolled himself a cigarette with deft economy of motion and offered the tobacco, then, when it was refused, pocketed it.

Then Tyler knew him.

Why, you're Clifford Suggs, he said. Wait till Claudelle and Drew hear about me running up on you. Drew thinks you were lost down a mineshaft, and they've been hunting you for years.

The man exhaled acrid blue smoke from his nostrils. Beneath the felt hatbrim his shadowed face studying Tyler with a kind of distant amusement.

I don't know who you are or how the story come to you, but you got it turned around backwards. I'm the one been huntin them. They're the ones that's gone.

Tyler was studying his shoes where the snow was compressed into a thin sole of transparent ice and between his feet were little curling strands of grass all seized in tubes of ice and when he looked back up the man's face with the curious illogic of dreams was gone. In its place was a yellowed skull with a few strands of lank, dead hair. Within the skull there was furtive movement. He leant to see. A rat's sharp gray face peered through an eyesocket and all about the eyeholes the bone was chamfered with teethmarks, but the rat would not fit. It withdrew, turning, trying the other eyehole then growing claustrophobic and agitated and turning endless upon itself within the bony confines of the skull but there was no way out.

❧

At some unclocked hour the rain ceased and Sutter was on the move almost immediately, wending his way through the brush which dripped continually in small echoes of rain. He was trying to remember where the house was, and he kept making false starts and recovering and going on, and after a while a wornlooking disc of moon eased out of the broken clouds and hung there like a flare to guide his path.

When he came upon the barn lot it was all shadow and white light and where water stood it gleamed in the moonlight like pooled quicksilver. He stopped here to study the house. It seemed cloaked in sleep. He leant against a stall door to rest and he could hear a horse snuffling in the stable and he could hear the quick disquieted movement of its hooves. It seemed to be turning restlessly about in the stable.

Outside in the barnlot he looked up and the pale moon was directly over him and allencompassing. It appeared to be lowering itself onto the earth and he could make out mountains and ranges of hills and hollows and dark shadowed areas of mystery he judged to be timber and he wondered what manner of beast thrived there and what their lives were like and the need to be there twisted in his heart like an old pain that will not dissipate. As he watched, enormous birds stark and dimensionless as the shadows of birds passed the remote face of the moon, wings beating slow and stately and silent and they were like birds that had once existed but did no more and he could not put a name to them. They were at once familiar and foreign, archetypes from some old childhood dream that was lost to him.

There in the shadows he seemed a darker shadow than those he moved among, some beast composed wholly of the ectoplasm of the night and with some arcane magnetism drawing to itself old angers and discontents and secret and forbidden yearnings freefloating in the humming and electric dark. The sleeping house seemed to be waiting for him, and he went on toward it.

He went on up a muddy grade past an old pickup truck hopelessly mired in the sucking clay, and he didn't even notice it. He was thinking: You better be here. They better hope you are because whatever happens if you ain't will be on your head. He crossed onto the porch and began to hammer on the door.

For a time he could hear nothing. He hammered again as if he'd rouse the dead, and there was an abrupt scuttling of claws across the floor and a fierce yip yip yip of a small dog on the other side of the door. The dog was growling and sounded as if it were tearing the door from its hinges and its barking was wellnigh hysterical.

Shut up, you little son of a bitch, he told it.

A woman's muffled voice said, What on earth? Then, Claude. You wake up, Claude. Then silence, but he could imagine the man swinging his legs off the creaking bed and sitting so for a moment and running a hand through sleeptousled hair, then going to the door.

Shut up, a voice told the dog. You the Lost Sheep back? it asked the door.

Yes, Sutter said, as lost a sheep as ever was.

The door opened onto a musky sleepy dark. Somewhere in the room a match flared. He could smell kerosene, stale whiskey breath, taste the residue of old unspent angers. A lamp was lit and adjusted to a dim yellow glow. Shadows flitted about the walls and ceased.

What the hell? Claude said. He added inanely, It's three o'clock in the mornin, as if perhaps Sutter had merely stopped to inquire the time.

Sutter hadn't waited to be asked in. He was standing in the center of the front room. His clothes were soaked and reeking and he was dripping water onto the rug. A woman had come in, children, the room seemed to be filling up. A ravenhaired girl restrained the dog then took it up in her arms and clutched it protectively to her breast.

How long's he been gone?

Who?

That Tyler boy. You tell me what I want to know and I'll be on my way without anybody gettin hurt.

Just who the goddamn hell do you think you are, mister? You seem to forgot you're on my property. As a matter of fact, you're in my house without bein asked at three o'clock in the mornin.

I'm the fellow that's huntin Tyler, Sutter said. And if you don't tell me damn quick where he's at I'm goin to unbreech you like a shotgun. Now I better hear somethin.

Sutter's hand had found the knife. Its blade lay against his thigh. A forefinger felt its edge. It winked dully in the light. No one save the woman seemed to notice.

She said, Tell him, Claude.

Shut up. I ain't tellin him jackshit. And you ain't neither. I don't care for the ways this feller's got. I don't take orders from ever son of a bitch wanders up out of the woods.

He's went to Ackerman's Field, the woman cried.

Claude's blow was thrown wild but it caught Sutter hard enough to jar him and make blue lights flash behind his eyes. Claude seemed halfdrunk. He was windmilling his arms crazily but a glancing blow jarred Sutter's jaw and Sutter could taste blood in his mouth. Now Claude was listing to the side like a drunken dancing bear and Sutter just stepped inside the flailing arms and hooked the knife deep and jerked upward in an explosion of blood and putrid gasses so hard Claude's feet momentarily cleared the floor. When he withdrew the knife Claude stood disemboweled and looking down at himself with stunned incredulity and trying to put himself back together with both bloody hands.

Some sob or strangled cry jerked Sutter's head around and he stared in momentary confusion. He seemed to have forgotten all these folk. Who they were and where he was and what was his purpose here. They were aligned against the wall like spectators at some perverse bloodsport that had gotten out of hand and when he advanced toward them with the dripping knife he moved upon a wall of stricken eyes.

※

Well, Granville's got a bad name, but he never done nothin to me, a man named Tarkinton said. He opened the door of the coalstove to spit, then slammed it to. Fact was I always sort of liked him. You'd not know it by the name he's got around here, but he didn't like nothin better than playin a joke on somebody. Me and him was sort of runnin mates when we was young. He hadn't been in this part of the country long when we took up together. We used to drink a lot of whiskey, run a lot of women. Trouble was he caught most of the women, and I wound up drinkin the whiskey.

He'd do anything, Granville would. He was crazy about tricks. He didn't like nothin better than to get a big joke on somebody, though even back then they'd get a little out of hand at times. He'd lean a little heavy. He never knowed when to quit. I had this old halfgrown bobcat one time. I got it with the notion of makin a pet out of it, but hell, they wadn't no pet in it. It was bobcat through and through. It was I reckon born mean and determined to stay that way. I had to keep it chained up, Sam, you remember when I had it.

I finally got tired of feedin and waterin it and it watchin me like it was just waitin for a chance to take my head off, and I told Granville one day, I believe I'll just turn this son of a bitch aloose. Take it way out in the woods and let it hunt its own feed and water.

Then this idea hit Granville. He had this big old suitcase, and he got a bottle of paregoric or some kind of dope at the drugstore and he fed that bobcat some in a bowl of milk. It never did go plumb out, just got drowsy enough so's we could get it stuffed down into that suitcase. It was a right tight fit.

He drove out on 48 and pulled off in a logroad and set that suitcase in the middle of the highway. We had a pint we was nippin along on, and we laid out in the bushes to see what would happen.

That old bobcat had done come to itself and it was wanting out bad. That suitcase would growl and jump a little ever now and again and finally it fell over on its side. After a while this car come by. It went by the suitcase and stopped and come backin up real slow. Carload of them Beech Creek boys. This old boy named Wymer got out and grabbed it. He was lookin all around, he figured it'd lost off somebody's truck and they'd be comin back after it. Thought he'd found somethin. He jumped in the car with it, and they hadn't went fifty feet when the brake lights come on and they locked her down and stopped right dead in the middle of the road and all four doors flew open. All hell broke loose, you never heard such squallin and takin on. They run clean off in the bushes in as many directions as they was folks in that car, and they wadn't dodgin nothing, they was just ridin over halfgrown saplins and headin out, and you could hear brush pop a quarter mile off.

Directly this here bobcat eased out just as lightfooted and calm as you please. He looked all around and highfooted it toward the Harrikin and that's the last I ever saw him.

☙

When Tyler reached the first scattered houses of the town a wan sun stood at midmorning over the bare winter trees. A pale band of lighter sky lay above the horizon and the air felt like snow. Where the city limits sign was he halted and sat on a bank watching off toward the spare outposts of commerce as if he were of a mind not to go on. He felt he'd been so long in the Harrikin he'd lost touch with the doings of these more normal folk and the way they'd grouped themselves together here in this outpost with houses leant one atop the other seemed a strange way to live. But at length he unfolded himself and went on, the rifle yoked across his shoulders and forearms dangling.

He was constantly looking about. He was looking for Sutter, and Sutter was the last thing he wanted to see, but he had to look anyway. No one who looked like Sutter and no one with a curious eye for him, and this suited him just fine. He unyoked the rifle and went along swinging it gently at his side.

The first thing he came upon was a restaurant named the Snip, Snap & Bite Café. Nearly empty. A bald man mopping the counter with a rag. Smells of grease and frying bacon and coffee. His mouth watered.

Hey, you can't bring that thing in here.

Do what? He blinked and looked down at the rifle. He'd forgotten it.

Sorry, he said. He went back out onto the sidewalk. He looked all about. He felt strangely dislocated, his vision darkened, the edges seemed to burn. There wasn't anything to do with the gun. He went back in.

It ain't working right anyway.

Oh, all right. Open the bolt and stand it in the corner there by the hat-rack. Just don't club nobody with it.

He commenced with coffee thick with cream and sugar while sunny-side-up eggs and country ham fried. When they came he finished them clean, chasing down the last bit of runny egg yolk with a triangle of but-tered toast. He ordered another side order of toast and pear preserves and more coffee and a glass of orange juice for his thirst. When he ordered this last and finished it and wiped his mouth with a napkin, the counterman was regarding him with something akin to admiration. Tyler himself had begun to feel downright expansive, and a warm sense of wellbeing com-forted him.

Could I bring you somethin else?

I reckon that ought to do me awhile. How much do I owe you?

He paid and pocketed the change. Where's Sheriff Bellwether's office?

In the courthouse basement, less they moved it without tellin me. That's where it's always been.

He got the rifle and went out. He looked up and down the street cautiously, like a man sweating in the last card in a poker hand. Ordinary folk going about their business. Their very ordinariness reassured him. The dull day-to-day routine of life seemed suddenly very dear to him, for it was something he had lost. All these rustic folk with their complacent faces seemed to dwell in the happy-ever-after end of a fable. He took a deep breath and held it a moment. He could feel his heart pounding in his chest. All he had to do was make it a block and a half to the courthouse. A cripple could do that, a blind man tapping with a cane.

Old men like fragile statuary were already set about the courtyard benches for such faint sun as there was. They looked up expectantly as Tyler approached, as if he might do something interesting to break the monotony that yawned before them, but when he didn't and just strode purposefully on, their eyes dismissed him and they went back to the nothing they'd been doing before.

The courthouse was a square twostory brick building. The boy looked up. Windows on the upper floor were barred, and Tyler wished he might see Sutter's face peering down at him. The words COVRT HOVSE were chiseled into a great concrete lintel set above the double door. He turned the corner and there was an iron railing round a set of concrete stairs descending to the basement.

An old grandmotherlike woman sat on a bench like a sentinel guarding a palace door. She wore an anklelength dress and men's brogans broken out at the side and a ratty plaid shawl wound about her ample shoulders. She watched him out of the folds of the pokebonnet she wore tied beneath her long chin and from behind dimestore shades with tortoiseshell frames.

He had a hand on the cold metal railing.

She rose at his arrival as if she'd been awaiting him. Sonny boy, she said. Her voice was an ingratiating whine, and it grated on his nerves like a fingernail dragged across a chalkboard.

He turned. Yes, ma'am?

I need a little help, she said. I sure wish you could do me a little favor.

I'd like to but I'm in an awful hurry. Maybe I could when I get done with the sheriff.

He was on the first step. The steel-reinforced glass door lay in shadowed sanctuary.

It ain't much, she whined. Won't take you but a minute. I'll give you a dollar.

Once more he turned. I really can't. He started down the stairs.

My old man took and died, she said, and I ain't got nobody to do for me but strangers. It's awful to be at the mercy of strangers.

He stopped.

And me about blind on top of it.

She was just not going to let up. All right, he said. What is it you need done?

Not much for a big strong young man like you, she said. Just load a sack of cowfeed in the trunk of my car for me.

She had turned and was hobbling away. Tall old grandmother with broad humped shoulders. Confident of him now, she didn't even look back. He followed.

Where is your car?

Down by the tie yard.

They passed under casual eyes that remarked them without interest. The railroad then and a sulfurous pall of coal smoke and tackier houses with black faces pressed against the glass to mark their progress. Old blownout automobiles enshrined on tieblocks while poisonoak crept their rocker panels. Surly watchdogs watched from chains with cartire anchors, and one chained to a clothesline followed them to the end of its tether with the chain skirling on wire then sat on its haunches and watched them go.

I don't really understand this, the boy said. Would they not load the feed for you where you bought it?

The boy at the store had a bad back, Grandmother said.

Then how the hell did it get to the tieyard? he wondered to himself. He didn't pursue it, for he had come to suspect the workings of the old woman's mind. Perhaps his own as well.

The silence between them deepened as the road they trod narrowed to a footpath bowered by winterbare sumac. He and Grandmother walking in a fairytale wood, but a wrong turn has been taken somewhere, for nothing seems right about any of this. The very light had altered, darkened as if for an early December dusk. Behind them a car took the railroad crossing fast and its mufflers opened up fullthroated then the siren came on, laying wail on fading wail on the belabored countryside. He wondered if it was Bellwether and he'd missed him. There was a leaden weight on his heart.

The silence seemed interminable. To break it he asked her back, What did your man die of?

She didn't hesitate. The syph, she said.

The what? He had skipped a step, he'd misunderstood, his ears were failing him.

The syph, she whined. He come down with it and it drug on and turned into the drizzlin shits and he just wasted away.

He figured somewhere in these territories there was an enormous madhouse whose keeper had thrown up his hands in disgusted defeat and flung wide the portals so these twisted folk could descend like locusts on the countryside.

Why, you're crazy as hell, he told her.

I got to stop and pee, the old woman in the nightmare snickered. You wouldn't sneak a peek at a old lady peein, would you?

I've got all the craziness I need, Tyler said. Carry yours on somewheres else, and you can load your own damn cowfeed.

They had come to a cleared area where stacks of crossties were drying. Beside a tiestack a black Buick Roadmaster sat cocked outward bound, gleaming in the frail sun, luxurious, profoundly out of place.

Tee hee hee, Grandmother said. Grandmother's back had begun to
shake with uncontainable mirth, and she was making sniggering, chortling
sounds, and she was trying to stop, but she couldn't. When she turned, her
face was congested with laughter. She grasped her sides and burst out
laughing, pounding her thighs with her palms. Then instantly the look of
revelation on his face seemed to sober her for a hand snaked out and an
iron grip clamped his throat and a broganned foot kicked the rifle away. It
clattered somewhere behind him. They locked and swayed for a moment
in a broken ballet; then she tripped him and fell across him in parodic
lechery. Brass knucks slammed his temple hard and the world darkened
and tilted on its axis. When it righted itself the face was very close to his
own. The tortoiseshell shades hung by one earpiece and the pokebonnet
was comically askew.

I got you now, you little son of a bitch, Sutter said.

Tyler tried to twist his face away, but Sutter hit him hard in the mouth
and Tyler didn't know anything for a while.

᛫

He awoke to a dull throb in his temple and to music. Singing and some
rhythmic accompaniment. A jouncing over rutted roads and the roar of an
automobile engine.

> *...and I wound up her little ball of yarn,* the voice sang.

A radio then. The Grand Ole Opry perhaps.

> *It was just two weeks from this I went out to take a piss,*
> *And I found myself a burden of great pain,*
> *For it had been to my mishaps I had caught a dose of claps,*
> *And I'll never wind that little ball again.*

Not The Grand Ole Opry then. The voice went on singing. The song
seemed to have an infinite number of verses in an ascending order of

obscenity and the voice seemed to know all of them. Not the Grand Ole
Opry. Then it all came back to him. He remembered Sutter, and it was
Sutter himself singing at the top of his voice with brush slapping the rock-
erpanels rhythmically. This son of a bitch is driving in the *woods,* he
thought in wonder. His face lay against the cold glass of the window, and
he didn't know how close Sutter was watching him, but he chanced
opening one eye and all there was was the dark boles of trees streaking by
on both sides of a logroad snaking into deeper timber.

His jaw hurt and an incisor lay on its side in a position it had never
been before. It hurt when he worried it with his tongue but he couldn't stop
worrying it. He wondered if Sutter had brought the rifle. If he had more
than likely it was in the back seat. Maybe there was a chance he could whirl
suddenly and grab the gun and twist the door handle and just jump. There
was an even better chance that when he whirled for the gun Sutter would
coldcock him with a fist as hard and big as the end of a locust fencepost,
and if there was any way around it, he didn't want hit again. Then he
remembered the gun didn't work anyway, and he debated just jumping. He
thought when the timber thinned sufficiently he'd make a leap for it and
try to land on his feet and just keep on hauling. With an eye toward this,
his right hand crept on his right thigh toward where he knew the
doorhandle was. An inch, no more. Again. Creepmouse, creepmouse.

Don't even think about it, Sutter said. Move it agin and I'll leave you
a bloody stub to jack off with.

He knotted his hand into a fist and it just lay on his thigh.

Sutter went back to singing. *The wreck on the highway. Whiskey and
blood run together, but I didn't hear nobody pray, sweet Jesus, I didn't hear
nobody pray.* He had a tuneless monotone of a voice and the whipping of
the brush did not match this song as well.

Where are we going?

Sutter stopped singing. Far enough so's there ain't no busybodies
around. He resumed singing.

Tyler turned. To his surprise, Sutter still wore the gray dress. He had removed the tortoiseshell specs, but the bonnet was still there, rakishly askew and tied demurely under his horselike chin.

You ought to get that radio fixed.

We'll see how smart your mouth is here directly.

At length the road seemed to just vanish, to fade into heavier and heavier timber, but Sutter seemed not to notice. He was driving over wrist-size saplings that caused the car to lurch sickeningly and the engine to labor harder, and he drove it until he reached a veritable wall of timber with no give to it. When he cut the switch something gave under the hood with a soft whoosh and a rising curtain of steam enveloped the car. Sutter's hands were at untying the bonnet.

Where'd you come by that getup?

Sutter studied him. Folks in this world are always just walkin off somewheres else and providin me with what I need. Do you honestly want to know?

Tyler thought about it. No, he said.

I thought not. Now I looked you over pretty good back there at the tieyard. While you was dozed off. You ain't got no pictures. Now what I want to know is where they are and how we get to em.

Tyler was prodding his tooth with his tongue when it gave with a soft cracking he actually heard inside his skull and his mouth was filling with warm blood. He started to open the door, then thought better of it and leant forward and spat a mouthful of blood into the floorboard between his feet.

Damn, boy, ain't you had no raisin? This car probably belongs to a doctor or a lawyer or somethin.

Tyler sat staring at the tooth. A dull anger seized him. He had been run halfway across three counties by some madman he had done nothing to, barely knew, had only heard rumored. Folks who had befriended him were in peril. Perhaps dead. And now the son of a bitch had knocked out a perfectly good tooth, one that would have served him all his days, one that lay worse than useless in a stringy gout of blood. And. And. And a thought that he had been trying to keep stuffed down into the darkness, that kept skittering out playfully and showing glimpses of itself. His sister was dead.

You remember that day in town when me and you had that talk? Sutter asked.

Yes, he said. It seemed a long time ago, but it was not. He tried to remember everything about the day. The way the light fell, what his sister had been wearing when he came in that night, what de Vries had said about the roof.

You see how all I warned you's come to pass? You see how I tried to tell you right. You see what meanness you've brought on everbody, and all that's happened might never have been. It was your choice, and ever bit of it is on your head. There's people been killed over your stubbornness, and probably more to come. I told you to imagine the worst thing that could happen and it would be.

Tyler didn't say anything. He was staring past the glass. Where the brush ended a sedgefield tumbled steeply downhill in a stony tapestry toward a hollow so deep and distant it looked blue. Above the horizon a hawk dipped and rose on the updrafts of wind with soundless grace, and he wondered how it would feel to be there, to be watching all this through the arrogant yellow eyes of a hawk.

It's just business to me. Just money. But more money than a man makes in ten years, just handed to me all at once in a paper sack. And the only holdup is you.

I'm not going to give them to you. The only man that'll get them from me is Bellwether.

You'll give em to me. Oh, yes. When I'm through with you, you'll be beggin me to take em. You'll say, Please, Mr. Sutter, take these nasty things and be done with em. You'll pray to whatever god it is you hold dear for me to reach out and take em out of your hot little hand. Now get your ass out.

He got out into the cold. A wind with a taste of ice in it was looping up from the hollow, and snowbirds flew among the bare trees foraging.

Fixin to snow, Sutter said, studying the onecolor sky, curious weatherman in grandmother drag. Me and you got to get to them pictures and get the hell out of Dodge before the snow flies.

This last was muffled by the dress being pulled over his head, and this more than anything else showed Tyler the contempt Sutter held him in. The rifle was gone, he was threatless, a small viper with his teeth pulled. He came around the car looking for some form of weapon and not finding one, but Sutter's arms were pinned by the dress, and he leapt upon him flailing with both fists and kicking even before Sutter hit the ground. Sutter was trying to roll away from the kicks and trying to get up and simultaneously trying to get the rest of the dress over his head when Tyler stumbled over a windfall whiteoak branch. Sutter was screaming and cursing in rage as if Tyler was not fighting fair and some some obscure code of ethics had been broached.

You blindsidin son of a bitch, he was saying when Tyler hit him alongside the head with the length of whiteoak. Chunks of rotten wood flew and Sutter fell sidewise. Tyler hit him again. Sutter's head was sliding through the collar of the dress like some malevolent demon being born head foremost, and his nose was bleeding. When I get up you're graveyard dead, he said.

But Tyler would not let him up. By now he was sobbing with rage and frustration and swinging the club as hard as he could. Sutter was on his hands and knees and seemed halfdazed and he kept trying to crawl away but Tyler would not let him. He headed Sutter at the edge of the woods and hit him on the back of the head, and Sutter fell facedown in the leaves and could only rise to his elbows. He had his hands clasped over the back of his head with his elbows still snared in the dress and Tyler was beating him about the fingers and blood was soaking through the hair and running down Sutter's wrists. The branch broke and he looked about for another then took up the longest section of the one he'd had. Sutter was struggling sluggishly like some gross insect halfcrushed. A passerby would have been given pause by these demented-looking strugglers.

Tyler hit him a time or two and then he ceased and just watched Sutter with a dull loathing. He squatted on the earth with the club across his knees. His breath was ragged in his chest and his lungs hurt. He sat like a laborer at rest from some curious task. Goddamn you, why won't you die? he asked.

But Sutter would not die. His face was just something you'd unwrap from bloody butcher's paper and the skin was beaten off his fingers and the backs of his hands, and Tyler realized sickeningly that he was just going to have to go on and on until Sutter's head was crushed to bloody jelly, and he didn't have the heart for it. Sutter was just going to keep trying to get up. He had had no doubt that he would be able, given the chance, to cheerfully kill Sutter with whatever fell to hand, and selfanger brought tears of rage to his eyes.

Why won't you just leave me the hell alone? he asked. Sutter just lay breathing heavily. The whiteoak branch had broken his mouth, and bloody froth bubbled as he breathed.

Maybe by God you'll lay here and die directly, Tyler said.

He threw the stick away and went around the car and got in under the steering wheel. He sat for a time just staring out through the windshield at the woods. He turned the key and the motor turned over sluggishly but would not hit. He kept on until the starter turned slower and slower and ultimately there was only a dry clicking sound. He turned. The gun wasn't in the back but there was a folded blanket and he took it up and got out of the car. The day was turning colder and he draped the blanket about his shoulders like a shawl. He struck out the way they'd come but he walked only a few paces before he stopped. The pictures lay the other way, and by now he felt he'd bought and paid for them. He didn't want to think about how dear the price had been. He went toward deeper timber. It had begun to sleet. The windbrought pellets of ice stung his face and sang off in the leaves like birdshot.

It continued colder and by midafternoon pellets of sleet lay cupped in grails of winter leaves and the ground was beginning to whiten with ice, and he moved through the sleet's soft, steady hissing in the trees. He hoped he was bearing southeast toward Bookbinder's farm but he wondered if he'd been in the Harrikin long enough to have acquired a sense of direction. He suspected that if he possessed a compass it would not point as advertised but at some anomolaic magnetic north of the Harrikin's own.

He topped out on a hill and some alteration in the sound of the trees fetched him up short. He stopped to listen. He couldn't hear the sleet anymore. He looked up and great snowflakes were listing out of the heavens, gray against the pale steely gray of the sky, enormous feathers of snow descending from heights he couldn't reckon, and something of the child he'd been stood in bemused wonder listening to the almostsound in the trees and watching the snow drift down from far and far, falling sheer and plumb in the windless silence.

At the hill's summit he stopped to rest a moment. Beating folks with treelimbs is heavy work, he thought. Looking back the way he'd come below the hillside a flat valley lay spread out, merging into a row of cedars, then a slope began, already whitening, and he couldn't believe what he saw. A man was coming down the slope, tiny and dark and furiously animate against the pale field, a dark malevolent stain bleeding down a Currier & Ives winterscape. A dark shifting cloud of birds came out of the woods. A cardinal arced from tree to tree like a bright drop of blood.

He went on. After a while the snow was deep enough so that he was leaving tracks but it didn't seem to matter. He had come to feel that Sutter trailed him by some means that neither of them understood, some curious duality of their natures that enabled Sutter to intercept his thoughts and anticipate his movements.

By dusk the thickly falling snow had drifted against the dark bottoms of treetrunks and filled shadowy stumpholes and stumps wore hats of pale phosphorescence and he was moving through a world of eerie beauty.

By midafternoon thirty or forty men were grouped loosely about the courthouse steps in Ackerman's Field. They were armed to the last man. Squirrel rifles, shotguns, old pistols brought home from the wars, many with weaponry that would have been more at home on the walls of an antique shop and weaponry designed to slay beasts long extinct. They carried sacks or lunchbuckets, and some of them had thermos bottles of coffee, and a search would have yielded up more than a few halfpints of whiskey. They hunkered or milled about in loose groups talking among themselves and chewing and smoking, and there was about them an air of excitement restrained, the air of men setting off on an adventure whose outcome is very much a matter of conjecture.

After a while a man in neatly pressed khakis came out of the courthouse and stood on the top step facing them. The door closed behind him on its pneumatic closer and the man dropped his cigarette and stepped on it. The high sheriff of Ackerman's Field had pale, nearcolorless eyes and wavy hair going prematurely gray.

Gentlemen, he said.

The door opened and a deputy came out. He as well in khakis. He stood slightly behind Bellwether, and there was something of deference in his manner.

We've got two trucks with sideboards, Bellwether said. There's no point in taking more vehicles than necessary. Deputy Garrison and I will go in the county car, and the Holt brothers will bring you all behind us in their trucks. We've got a bunch of flashlights in the trucks. Everybody make sure you get a light and make sure it works.

What about the state?

For right now they're just manning roadblocks. Every road leading out of Ackerman's Field and every road out of Centre will be secured.

Shit, somebody in the crowd said. Roads ain't nothin to Granville. He can be in Alabama and never come out of the woods cept to steal somethin to eat.

Where we goin? another man called.

Last place we know for sure he was at was Claude Calvert's place. That's where the wagonload of bodies came from. I reckon you all know about that. We can get to there fairly easy with trucks. From there we'll just have to play it by ear.

It's a waste of time, the man said. It's three or four hundred square miles in there. What are we lookin for, clues? Fingerprints? He's long gone from there.

He may well be, Bellwether said. But all the same it's got to be done. You understand this is purely a voluntary thing. Nobody has to come don't want to.

I never said nothin about not goin, the man said, but what about Fenton Breece?

What about him?

What all Sandy told about the way he done them dead folks. About diggin up some graves.

Well, Bellwether said, right now it's first things first. I mean no disrespect for the dead when I say it's the live folks I got to worry about right now.

I hear some folks in Centre got that under control, another said and laughed.

Hey, Bellwether, Old Tippydo over in Centre knows the Harrikin better than anybody else. You sent for him?

Bellwether smiled a small smile. I tried, but it didn't do any good, he said. Tippydo's done been dead two years, and I couldn't find a volunteer to go after him.

❧

Sutter quit worrying about keeping to Tyler's trail for he had divined that he meant to get back to Bookbinder's. That's all right, he told himself. Two fish in a barrel ain't much harder than one fish in a barrel. He was crazed all over with dried blood and his body ached with soreness but he kept pushing himself on through the snow. It was falling harder now and the woods were filling up and it was heavy going, but he knew where he was bound.

Once after dark he stopped to rest and smoke a cigarette, and far off on the hillside he saw a long line of lights moving in a slow curve around the face of the hill. The lights were disembodied and seemingly sourceless. Distant and silent and stately as a wending line of torchbearers making pilgrimage to some obscure god. All in silence as if all this was preordained and speech could neither help nor hinder its outcome. They scattered and regrouped and spread again like a curious ballet of fireflies or St. Elmo's fire roiled and swirling in the depths of the sea. He watched them for a time in bewilderment; then he put out his cigarette in the snow and took up his rifle and went on.

It was some time before it occurred to Sutter that they were looking for him.

❧

That boy was all right. He was kind of curious turned, but to tell you the truth I sort of liked him. He'd speak to you. Not like some of these young fellers thinks the world didn't start till the doctor slapped em on the ass.

There is about these old men who have arranged themselves about the coal stove in Patton's store a curious air of waiting, of time in suspension, as if they had already achieved some remove from the world, the eldest among them awaiting death as calmly as someone waiting on a bus.

Beyond them through the plateglass window it is snowing hard and when cars pass to and fro the sound is muted and cloistral and the lights look blurred and unreal, a dream of carlights.

I notice you keep sayin *was*, another man said. I reckon you done wrote him off, then.

When he run crossways of Sutter I reckon he wrote hisself off. I always thought of that myself as one of the more unpleasant ways you commit suicide.

The old man shook his head. You can say what you want to about him, but if I was able I'd be out there with Bellwether and them scouring the woods.

Leastways some good will come of this. Sutter's done it this time. The son of a bitch is finally gone way over the line.

A man named Junior Raymer was whittling something unrecognizable but vaguely obscene from soft red cedar. He sat on his upended Coke crate a time studying his creation then he rose and opened the stove door and tossed it inside. He stirred the fire with the poker and showers of sparks cascaded outward. He spat into them then slammed the door.

Don't you bet on it, he said. He's rolled through the cracks before, and he's fixin to do it again. You mark my words. He'll be gone like a lost ball in the high weeds.

Talkin about that Tyler boy, the old man said, they must be more to him than meets the eye. Some said that schoolteacher of his worked around and got him a scholarship in a college. Up to Knoxville, they said.

He'll work, Junior agreed. That's more than anybody could ever have said about old Moose. Less you count totin sacks of sugar up them hollers back in there. He'd do that. That boy come up hard, him and his sister, too. I used to drink some back when they was little, and I used to lay drunk out there.

Raymer took out a pipe and began to tamp it with roughcut apple-smelling tobacco. Someone got up to peer out the window at the snow blanketing the road. The day had waned and the glass had gone a surreal and unearthly gray against whose cold slick surface flakes list and slide with the faintest of ghostsounds and beyond them there is a faint and sourceless fluorescence.

Raymer struck a match on the side of the potbellied heater and lit his pipe. You know, they used to have cockfights in the Harrikin back then. Moose, he fooled with it some. Raised some of them game roosters. Anything there was money in and the work took out of you'd find Moose in it somehow, and don't nothing draw loafers and lowlifes like a cockfight will. Moose had him one he was real proud of. It was silvercolored and had these little coldlookin eyes like a damn cottonmouth moccasin. It didn't look like no chicken I ever seen. It looked like some kind of a weapon.

Anyhow, this boy y'all speakin of was about seven years old. He had this lit old dominecker rooster he raised from a chick. It used to foller him around the way a dog would. That Sunday Moose was about drunk and the boy's rooster done somethin to piss him off. Messed the porch, I reckon. Young Tyler seen the way things was headin and grabbed that rooster up and hugged it to him. He made to run off, and Moose grabbed him and jerked that rooster away from him. He looked around and spied that silver chicken and set the dominecker down in front of it. He grabbed em and rubbed their heads together, and that game jumped straight up and hung the dominecker through the head and that quick it was deadern hell. It was the beat of anything I ever seen. His own boy's pet. That boy was takin on and talkin to that dead chicken, and I learnt somethin right then and there. I was learnin it late, but I reckon that's better than never. There's folks you just don't need. You're better off without em. Your life is just a little better because they ain't in it. Moose was the first I cut loose, but I cut him clean and I never went out there no more.

॰

When the phone rang Fenton Breece answered it in tones of sepulchral dignity, but there did not seem to be anyone there or, more properly, anyone with anything to say, for all he could hear was a labored catarrhal breathing. This went on for a few seconds and then there was a mechanical click when the phone was hung up, and he thought, They know I'm here.

He was sitting at his desk. He was wearing a burgundy silk lounging robe and matching houseshoes and silverrimmed reading glasses on a cord about his neck. He put aside the funeral director's journal he'd been reading when the phone interrupted and opened the drawer of the desk and took out a German Luger he'd taken to carrying of late. He laid the weapon on the ink blotter before him and sat studying it: there was something sinister about its symmetry, something lethal in its craftsmanship. Something efficient, but he'd read somewhere the Germans were like that: when the death factories were running fulltilt three shifts a day, they'd had cost efficiency reports on the systematic extinction of the Jewish people figured to the last mark. His father had told him once he'd taken the pistol from an officer in the Luftwaffe, but Breece had always figured he'd just bought it like he did everything else.

Past the window the street was a blur of blowing snow, and a vague anger touched him. He ought to be feeling cozy and Badgerlike with the exquisite feeling of being snowed in and the world snowed out, but he was not. He ought to be sitting before the fire with the Tyler girl against his shoulder and a demitasse of Cognac in his hand and soft music adding ambience to the room, but he was not that either. He was drifting in the icechoked backwaters of paranoia, and he could feel them, cold and black, rising about his upper thighs. He'd been navigating these perilous seas for some time, and every knock was a man in khakis with a warrant in his hand, every phone call the IRS auditing him for the last twenty-five years, every letter in the mailbox a note saying FLEE, ALL IS DISCOVERED. I've just got to put it out of my mind, he thought. Either that or I've got to do something.

He adjusted the reading glasses back on his nose, and he had read two paragraphs when someone began to pound on the front door. He rose. He hesitated and then remembered the slick streets: it's been a bad wreck, two or three dead, he told himself comfortingly. But he took up the Luger anyway and shoved it into the pocket of his dressing gown before he went to answer the door.

The oak door was latched with a security chain that he left in place, opening the door a scant three inches.

A motley crew indeed. Twelve or fifteen felthatted and overalled men bundled against the cold assembled with the stoop full and more aligned tense and silent about them. Young or old, they all had in common the set anger in their faces and the utter implacability of their manner. Jaws knotted with lumps of chewing tobacco, and they all seemed to be armed, some clutching rifles and others just sticks, and he thought he saw a ballbat or two. The foremost, who seemed the leader, opened his mouth to speak, and for an insane moment Breece thought he might break into song, for save the fierce outrage of their eyes, they looked not unlike perverse and rustic carolers come to herald the yuletide.

He didn't know from where the strength to speak came, but it did. I'll be right with you, he said brightly. He smiled, gestured toward the robe. I'm not dressed to receive company.

He slammed the door to and threw the deadbolt and went in an awkward fat man's run through the foyer and lounge; behind him he heard the impact of shoulders slamming against the door. He went down a hall into the back. He locked that door behind him and ran past gleaming tables bloodgrooved like the sacrificial tables of ancient pagans and past bizarre tubeappended contraptions like the props to a madman's dreams and through one last door to the garage bay where the hearse sat waiting. He pushed a red button mounted on the wall and the bay door rose electrically to the snow blowing slantwise in the streetlamps. He climbed hastily into the hearse and cranked the engine and had already rolled four or five feet when he abruptly slammed on the brakes and cut the switch. He pounded

his forehead hard with a fist. Sweet Jesus, he said. He clambered back out
and went back into the embalming area.

He'd taken to carrying the girl with him to work and driving her home
at night, and she was here today. He uncovered her where she napped on
the couch and caught her up, half-carrying and half-dragging her toward
the hearse. It was hard going for she was slack and lolled loosely and he
was breathing hard. Hurry, hurry, he kept telling her. He opened the door
on the passenger side and shoved her in. Her head swung bonelessly and
she sat erect a moment then her upper torso dropped and she slid onto the
steering wheel. The door slammed hard on her ankle. Jesus, baby, he said,
contrite. I'm so sorry. He tried to move the foot but each time he moved it
it slid back before he could get the door closed.

Goddamn it, he screamed at her. What the hell's the matter with you?
Can't you see I'm in a hurry here? Can't you do anything for yourself?
Can you not do so simple a thing as pick up your foot?

He left with the tires smoking bluely and her ankle still dangling from
the door, steering lefthanded and holding her about the shoulders with his
right. When the hearse hit the icy pavement it slewed sickeningly broad-
side but miraculously pointed the way he intended going, and he floored
the accelerator and shot past the front of the funeral home. He glanced
toward it. They had the door battered down until it hung crazily on one
hinge, and their heads all turned as one when he streaked past, and they
were running yelling to their cars.

He ran the stop sign at the intersection but he had to brake to make the
left turn at the next block and when he did he could see already a faint wash
of light approaching through the snow. He kept fumbling for the windshield wipers. He chanced releasing her long enough to steady the wheel
with his right hand and turn on the lights and windshield wipers and grab
her again before she slid out the flapping door.

Coming off the Centre hill he was going over seventy miles an hour
and snow was coming so hard he could barely see the road. Telephone

poles were coming like pickets in a fence when the dead girl suddenly folded forward into the steering wheel. When he jerked her back the steering wheel cocked and the hearse went drifting across the ice in a caterwauling of protesting rubber. It went over the embankment in a sudden eerie silence save the small explosions of sumac branches splintering then struck a utility pole. There was a simultaneous sound of splintering pine he felt in his solar plexus and folding wrenching metal and all the glass going and tortured wire pulled tight as a catapult, then the swinging upper half of the utility pole, sharp end first, slammed into and through the hood.

He leapt out into the brush and immediately pitched forward onto the earth. Something was wrong with his left leg, it accordioned somehow beneath him and he could not rise. He crawled around the front through a frozen field of last year's cornstalks and to the other side and grasped the dead girl and pulled her out into the snow. Already he could see the play of lights and hear men yelling, and the first of them were slamming cardoors and starting down the embankment. Above the hearse two electrical wires were touching and shorting out, and they kept snapping and sending arcs of bright blue fire off into the night. He locked his left elbow about her throat and began to drag her into the frozen field.

Breece had never done much physical work as he had the wherewithal to hire everything done and he'd had no idea crawling brokenlegged across frozen cornrows dragging a dead girl entailed so much physical exertion. Could he have hired this done he would have in a flash but he could not. He made it perhaps forty or fifty feet into the field, not knowing where he was going, for he was fleeing from not to: then the men ran yelling out of the brush into the field.

Breece remembered the gun. He could feel it cold against his belly where the robe twisted beneath him. He released the girl and withdrew the gun and sat holding it uncertainly for a moment, then holding the gun bothhanded he took the barrel tentatively into his mouth. It was smooth and cold but somehow not unpleasant. There was a faint taste of acrid gunpowder, gun oil, old violence.

You stop right there, he told them around the gun barrel. You come any closer and I'll blow my head off.

They hesitated, more dumbfounded than intimidated: they'd expected to be shot at but here he was crouched in the blowing snow with the pistol in his mouth threatening to do what they'd traveled so hard and fast this night to do themselves.

The foremost man halted before Breece and leant forward with his hands on his overalled knees. He had a florid face and washedout outraged eyes, and Breece knew he'd seen him somewhere before, perhaps the Bellystretcher. You go ahead, you worthless son of a bitch, the man said. And save me the fifteen cents it would cost to bust a cap on you.

I'll do it in a second, Breece thought. I'll count to five and then I'll do it. Ten.

Abruptly the fat man straightened and kicked the gun viciously away. Breece felt teeth break away in his jaw, felt bits of them on his tongue like shards of broken glass, and when the pistol went it tore out the right corner of his mouth and blood welled and dripped off his chin into the snow.

They'd been trying not to look at the girl but now they had to. Lord God, one of them said. They stood before this strange pair of lovers in a sort of perverse awe, aspirants before some strange god they couldn't even begin to fathom how to worship.

One of them had retrieved the pistol and inspected it. Hey, a Luger, he said. He shoved it into his hip pocket. What are we goin to do with him? he asked the redfaced man.

Breece was whimpering softly, like a puppy outside a door whimpering in the cold.

Just whatever, the fat man said. Do any fuckin thing you want to as long as I don't have to touch him.

He knelt before the dead girl and adjusted her upper clothing then pulled the gown down over her naked hips. Jesus Lord, he breathed. There was real pain in his face, and tenderness in his touch.

Two of the men hauled Breece erect and dragged him toward the road like some loathsome weight that must yet be borne. They went into the thick brush and started up the embankment. He turned his neck to see his hearse one last time. Gleaming there in the snow there was something surreal and eerily beautiful about it, he thought. With the blue fire arcing above it and the splintered cross of pine driven into the motor it looked like some halfmetallic nightmare beast that could only be slain by impalement, sinister, profoundly alien.

～

Tyler came down a long sloping grade too smooth to have been created by nature. The slopes were grown with the dark bulks of cypress and after a while by the dim glow of the snow he could see that it led to a declivity in the earth, an enormous lunarlike crater filling with snow and scattered about its epicenter the wrecks of abandoned machinery like prehistoric beasts flashfrozen by some bizarre reversal of the earth's poles. The boom of an enormous longnecked crane rose bleakly into the invisible sky above him and its dangling steel cable seemed at some point to just appear out of nothingness, unknowable like some source of escape lowered to him and could he but climb it he wondered where he'd be, some bowered bedchamber where Rapunzel lay in wait or Jacl's land where giants smelled blood and spoke in thunder.

He felt absolutely alone, and here in the snowy dark the barrier that keeps back cognizance of events past and future seemed to fade. What had been and harbingers of what was to be lay down like lovers and archaic machinery still belabored a weary earth already under sentence. A vindictive fate stalked him while still in the musky cribs and just beyond the spectrum of his sight an albino whore plied her craft and the very air was electric with old violence, pregnant with more yet to come. He went on through the dreamlike snow passing within four upright supports of some towering structure above him that he couldn't see. He looked up but all there was past the drifting snow was an unshapen bulk black against the paler black of the heavens and he could hear a door clanging shut, metal on metal, then creaking in a wind he could hear but couldn't feel and slamming to again. An iron ladder began six feet or so from the ground and ascended into the snowy dark and vanished. He stood looking at it as if in consideration. Clasped the bottom rung tentatively, then released it. The hell with that, he said. He pulled the collar of the coat tighter about his throat and went on, skirting a lakelike pool of water gathered in the pit of the crater with a thought for what life might thrive there and on up past an ancient bulldozer halfburied in a rockslide and all these artifacts of prior life. Ascending now and nearing the rim of the crater he began to feel the wind and to hear it in the trees. He looked to the four points of the compass hoping for some lightening of the horizon, but if horizons existed he found no evidence of it. All he could see was billowing white and inkslash boles of trees. He went on, and he seemed to carry with him a tight pocket of fierce wind and whirling snow like some hapless miscreant cursed by the weathers.

All I got to do is stay on a straight path, he thought. Bound to come off this son of a bitch sooner or later. If I don't freeze first, he added.

He had a real fear of this. His feet already felt wooden and digitless as hooves, and since coming into the wind his ears and nose were stinging, and he felt about the purloined coat for something to wind about his face, but there was nothing. So he pulled the woolen collar higher about his face. He thought of old man Bookbinder. The capable air of selfpossession there'd been about him. All he'd found of sanity in these made and hellish territories. He knew it lay southwest, and he'd started that way in the light, but now he just didn't know. He wondered what time it was. Then he wondered why it mattered. How far to the edge of this place civilization hadn't trickled down to yet and how far to daylight.

Sutter was descending into a hollow that seemed to go down forever, and he couldn't even see the bottom of it. When he stopped to rest a minute he was utterly weary. I'll catch my breath and then I'll go on and kill the little fucker, he promised himself. He knelt in the snow and rested his back against the smooth trunk of a beech and closed his eyes. He could feel snowflakes matting in his lashes and melting and running down his face like tears.

He must have slept, for a dream came to him like an old friend whose face he recognized but could not put a name to.

He dreamed he was in Flint County, Alabama, and it was an early morning in June. He was young. The flesh of his arm was hard and corded with youth, and studying the arm by the warm light of the sun the fine hair there gleamed like thin wires of copper against his tanned flesh.

He was walking down a roadway so thickly accumulated with dust it rose like talcum with his footsteps and subsided into the vines that latticed the sides of the road, and he could smell the evocative scent of honeysuckle.

His father had sent him after the cow and he was driving it back up from the pasture. It walked ahead of him chewing ruminatively and its hide flexed spasmodically from time to time dislodging cowflies.

The road wound to his railfenced yard, and the old log house still sat at the mouth of the hollow, and faint smoke from the breakfast fire, but a woman he didn't know was hanging out clothes in the backyard. Dark from the hollow bled into the twilight. He drove the cow around the corner of the house, and the woman turned to look at him. She had a clothespin in her mouth and a wing of hair had fallen across her forehead and she blew it out of her eyes. Sutter could not think of anything to say. He did not know the woman and he had no inkling of what she might be doing hanging out wash in his backyard.

What do you want? she asked him after a time.

I just brought the cow, he said. His voice was a rusty and disused croak. He seemed not to have spoken for years.

Well. She seemed confused. We don't even have a cow, she said. Why'd you bring a cow.

It's our cow, he said. I brought her to milk. Where they at?

Where's who at?

Mama and Daddy.

I don't know no mama and daddy. If you mean mine, they long dead.

No. No, mine. John and Lucy Dell Sutter. We live here.

Not for some time you ain't. We live here. My man and me. And Lord yes, I've heard of John and Lucy Dell Sutter. But they've been dead a long time. Years and years ago. Any kids they had would be old and feeble or likely dead theirselves.

This can't be, Sutter said. Where is he, your man? Maybe he'd know.

He'll be comin up the road there directly, but he won't be able to make heads or tails out of such a tale as you're tellin either.

He went back past the house. His reflection in the window glass sun-dappled light to dark and back again. It was full dusk now, nightbirds were already calling. He went down the road and it went into thick greenery that shimmered as if it had not achieved total reality, its edges vibrated and faded and reappeared.

After a while the woods began to descend and to darken and a hush fell over the birds and the quality of the light altered. A great sadness touched him. He saw that he was passing bucolic sideroads he had also passed in life that were closed to him now and he saw that had he taken any one of them all this would have been different.

He went on. After a while he could hear a man whistling and then the man himself appeared around a turn in the road, a thin gangling man all garbed in black with a scythe yoked across his shoulders. His face was shadowed by the shroud he affected but there was a dread familiarity about the way he walked Sutter couldn't put a finger on, and he did not know whether the figure was ghost or antecedent or reflection of himself or harbinger of a doom yet to be.

❧

You would have thought he would die. It would have been so easy. All he had to do was lie there and let the snow cover him and come spring some hunter come across his resting bones, but something in him would not have it so. Something that would not freeze and was contemptuous of the weathers stirred in him hotly, and when he tried to open his eyes they were frozen shut. He'd dozed with a hand clamped to each armpit for the warmth, and he melted the ice in his lashes with warm fingers and made to rise. Snow had fallen upon him and melted and refrozen in a delicate caul of ice, and when he rose it splintered in myriad soundless clashes and he brushed it away and went on.

❧

Tyler judged it long past midnight when he finally admitted to himself that he was lost. There was nothing to distinguish left from right, forward from back. The terrain had flattened; he moved through some obscure and nameless bottomland. He thought he might eventually come upon a stream and follow it to either source or destination. At last hills began to rise on each side, and he was in a long, curving hollow, and he began to hear a curious, familiar sound: a mournful highpitched keening, sourceless and bansheelike, and he knew instantly where he was. He felt almost faint with relief.

He went on up the hollow, moving more confidently now, seeing in his memory the lay of the land and the oblong fault in the earth and the stone arch with its narrow passageway, his exit from a nightmare. He could almost see the old man's house in the lee of the hills, gleaming in a grail of sunlight, the shades darkening from melting frost.

In the spinning dervish of snow the curious harp went on playing its eerie onenote song, sides mounding whitely, flakes drifting into the dark abyss, falling and falling he wondered how far. He kicked the snow from the flat stone and lifted it aside and scratched the tobacco tin out of the earth and shoved it into the pocket of the overcoat. He went on into the channel between the rocks, then stopped abruptly and stood staring speculatively at the pit. Thinking perhaps of the old man sleeping. Dreaming an old man's troubled dreams. Let an old man sleep, he thought. Some core of stubbornness hardened in him. You've got to play the hand that they deal you. And the ante's never as high for the other fellow when you shove your coins across nor is the pot as large as when you yourself drag it in. After the last card comes down all you've got is yourself.

Working hurriedly, he began to dismantle the makeshift fence. Years seemed to have passed since he'd constructed it. He laid the rotten boards and deadfall branches across the narrow side of the pit six or eight inches apart. When he peered down once the snowflakes were vanishing as if they were being drawn into the black maw of the earth. When he had the opening covered save the dark cracks between the boards, he began to carry great armloads of snowy leaves and brush and spread them carefully and return for more, and all the while the falling snow was obscuring his work and the harp's voice grew fainter and fainter. Ultimately the hole seemed not to exist, a thin skim of white already covering it. When the harp ceased the world went silent with it save the soft hush of the snowflakes in the trees.

He was satisfied, but he kept dragging up more wood, and he found the work warmed him. Into the lee of the rocks he dragged treetops and great slabs of lightningstruck whiteoak and thin silver husks of chestnut stumps and windblown branches, mounding it all till he thought he'd rival the old witchwoman at the Perrie place. When he'd dragged all he could find for a considerable circular distance around the chasm, he set about building a fire. Tinder was hard to come by but on the sheltered side of the bluff he pulled handfuls of wiry, curling grass and such bits of moss as weren't iced over, and he began to break the fine branches to length. In a natural hollow of the rock he piled tinder and a handful of the smallest sticks then fumbled out his snuffbox of matches and struck one. Cupping the feeble light in his hands he lit the tinder. By the orange glow his face was sharp and intent. The grass caught and burned in bright fluxing wires of fire. He fed it sticks and bits of moss and then larger branches. The fire in its stone bowl dished and wavered in the wind. He piled on more wood and waited for it to catch, crouched before it with his freezing hands outspread like some Neanderthal lost in the almost sexual wonder of heat. The fire rose, then roared and popped with the wind pumping up the hollow like a bellows. The flames fired the bluff orange and ebony shadows writhed across it fleeing windward as souls in torment are said to do and he just hunkered there for a time letting the heat soak into him.

When he'd warmed awhile and felt several degrees more human, he got up and piled on wood until he'd relocated this woodpile atop the fire and within an hour he had an enormous bonfire roaring fullthroated up the natural flue of the rocks with showers of sparks cascading upward into the snow like antisnow and a standing tongue of flame burning away in the night like an enormous candle. There was a spreading black circle where the snow was retreating from the fire, and he laid a fencepost within it and spread the coat over it as a makeshift but passable sleeping Tyler and went back into the stone arch to wait. There was no room to sit in the narrow passageway but it was relatively dry here and the bluff deflected the wind so ultimately he drowsed in exhaustion neither standing nor sitting, weary body bent to the contours of the stone.

Perhaps he wasn't coming. Perhaps he hadn't even seen the fire, though Tyler didn't know how that could be. Anyone abroad this night, however doubtful that might be, was going to see this fire. Maybe he had already come to Bookbinder's. Crept into the old man's lair and cut his throat where he lay. Perhaps he lay this moment in the old man's bed, the old man's goldrimmed glasses astride the blade of his nose and nightcap drawn down about his ears and his body burrowed beneath Bookbinder's bloodsoaked covers like an enormous mole, a spurious Bookbinder awaiting Tyler's arrival, teeth locked in a smarmy grin, the better to eat you with.

When Sutter came there was no sound save the wind. No rattling stones, nothing whatsoever to foretell his arrival, the upper body just loomed above the shelf of rock and at first he wasn't sure there was anyone there, then the wind intensified and the fire flared and Sutter was climbing onto the table of stone slowly, ever so slowly, coming on implacably like the protagonist of a nightmare escaping whatever bonds separate dreams from reality. Hunkered now. Silently taking up the rifle. Coming erect painfully slowly, as if even the popping of kneejoints might awaken the sleeping Tyler. He stood leant forward studying the coat, and then he looked all about. Tyler was thinking the coat did not much resemble a sleeping human. Sutter turned about like a beast to catch whatever scent the night might bring. Rifle at the ready. Some old primal caution seemed in force here, he seemed to divine by some subtle alteration in the terrain or the atmosphere that the glade was just quit by another.

Come on, goddamn you, Tyler thought. Come on up these stairs. Take another drink and just put your foot on the next step. The door's unlocked and this time I'm ready for you.

Sutter looked to the left. To the right. Crouched and with the rifle held before his midsection he stepped forward onto the juryrigged chasm and when he did the earth twisted and went from beneath him like a gallows trapdoor and he flung the rifle, clawing wildly for purchase.

The rifle was gone but Sutter himself seemed to defy gravity or perhaps the depths had decided they wanted no part of him for he clung desperately to a length of pole that had lodged beneath his armpits and his eyes were intent on the lip of the stone nearest him as if nothing else in the world existed. He hung on the pole as if resting until his strength came back. He was opening and closing his mouth in great gulps of icy air. Finally his eyes locked on Tyler's.

Boy, he said. His breaths were coming in ragged gasps. Tyler could see ice frozen in his hair and eyebrows. Cold, Sutter said. Feathery snowflakes were cascading past him into the earth and they lay in his hair without melting.

Tyler was looking about for a weapon. He took up a length of lumber and stood holding it.

Listen, Sutter said. There's money in my pocket. Better than seven thousand dollars. You can have it, just let me get over to you where you can give me a hand.

Tyler waited with the board clutched like a ball bat.

She ain't dead, Sutter said. When them doctors come they brought her to. All she was was knocked out. And if you hadn't took to the deep pineys we'd of all had a big laugh about it. Likely she ain't even got a headache by now.

You're a goddamned liar, Tyler said. She was dead before I left her and Fenton Breece has got her somewhere.

This money's in my right front pocket. I can feel it burnin my leg. It's yourn if you want it. We can get a lot more out of that crazy undertaker.

He extended a hand, and Tyler stood a moment in indecision. Sutter seemed to sense this lack of resolve and hunched himself along the length of pole.

Tyler suddenly swung the board. It struck Sutter's outstretched hand so hard Sutter swung like a pendulum, the pole swaying. He shook his head and came on anyway, his eyes closed and face lowered onto his arms to evade the flailing plank. When Sutter finally looked up his eyes looked far away as if whatever lived behind them were shrinking, getting so tiny you could hardly see it, and blood was running into his eyes.

Tyler was halfcrying. He swung the board again and Sutter's head jerked sidewise and he slipped and caught by his hands with the pole bouncing up and down and Tyler was sobbing raggedly then and beating at just the hands, the flesh peeling away whitely like the flesh of a corpse and the knuckles beaten to shreds of flesh and bone, and finally he threw away the board and kicked the end of the pole dementedly until the pole slipped past the stone edge and tilted and vanished from sight with Sutter's hands still locked desperately about it.

Tyler stood leaning, peering into the chasm cautiously, halfthinking Sutter might be clinging to the stone walls like a spider, refusing to acknowledge even the laws of gravity and physics, but he was not. There was only the mocking dark drawing off the light and snowflakes sifting down into silence.

He began to kick the rest of the lumber and poles into the hole and all the while the pastoral snow was sifting down and when he'd finished the lips of the crevice were already whitening and the earth had resumed its eerie keening.

He sat dully before the fire. He seemed touched by a kind of numbness. He took out the tin of pictures and opened it and sat looking at them dispassionately. He began to feed the pictures to the fire. Halfcrazy he thought the fire might not even take them, but it did. Their edges curled and darkened and the perverse images bubbled then burned with little blue flames. He burned them one by one, staring at them as emotionlessly as the camera's eye had. One by one they went to a pale gray ash that rose on the updrafts, and they were as clean and pure now as the falling snow that obscured them.

❧

A soulless and unpromising dawn had broken before the motley band of volunteers reached the whistling well. Their number was much diminished by laggards and dropouts and they were redeyed and weary and had been wandering hopelessly lost throughout the night and they were scratched from briars and branches and had fallen more times than they cared to think about. Their feet were wet and nighfrozen and their dungarees seized thighhigh with leggings of ice, and few among them were happy.

The fire had burned to a smouldering mound of ash. A driving snow still fell and these folk clambered calfdeep through it to hunker before the smoking ash. Son of a bitch, one of them said. That's the story of this whole damn mess. You get there right after they left or just before they get there. Who do you reckon it was here?

Bellwether didn't say anything. He was looking about, but everything save the mounded ash was pristine white with trackless snow. Bellwether was nonetheless studying the glade as though there were a tale to be told here could he but decipher it. A few bedraggledlooking birds were looking about forlornly for food.

Old man Bookbinder's place is right down the ridge, the man said. He might of seen somethin.

Maybe, Bellwether said.

Want to go down there and see? Bet it's warm. And it's just possible old man Bookbinder might own a coffee pot.

It sounds better than bein poked in the eye with a stick, Bellwether said.

The men rose. Their breath plumed palely. One of them stood looking warily down into the pit. He didn't get too close. Hell of a thing to be just out here open in the woods, he said. Without a fence around it or nothin. A man could damn sure get his ticket punched he didn't watch where he was goin.

Bellwether looked down. Yes, he could, he said.

Tyler came out of the pines just after good day and went down the slope cautiously for the snow now wore a coat of clear ice and he'd lost count of the times he'd fallen. The woods behind him lay seized in a white surreal glaze, and he'd moved through a continuous gauntlet of tree branches breaking and tops splitting off with sounds like random and sporadic gunfire. Once in the night he'd been on a road and come upon a highvoltage wire trees had broken down. All alone there in the dark the wire was leaping and writhing serpentlike, spitting arcs of blue fire against the fluorescent snow like some forerunning tendril crept up from Hell. There was an alien beauty to the dancing blue wire and he gave it a wide berth and went on.

He looked gaunted and thin, the flesh drawn tight over the sharp cheekbones, the eyes just smoky bores in his grim face. He came down the slope sliding cedar to cedar.

When he reached the point where he'd last left the Breece house there was no house there and he stood for a moment in stunned wonder. Secretly he'd have doubted the ability of fire to negate this symbol of copious wealth but the evidence lay all about him. Enormous piles of unidentifiable rubble all cloaked alike in ice. So much. Tens of thousands of fallen bricks and the charred remains of appliances and rising dizzyingly out of the ashes a brick chimney and high in the air the third-floor fireplace hearth suspended like a fireplace for a curious race of giant folk or aerie for the birds to quitclaim. Atop the chimney some dark bird already crouched uncertainly as if it had no other place to be, then lifted itself with slow strokes of the wings and was gone. Tyler looked about. Trees had shrouded the house and the near side of them was blackened and burned away. The shrouding trees looked like the container the fire had come in.

He sat down and laid a hand to the ashes but the ashes as well wore a film of ice. He stood up and made to go, but like the bird he seemed to have no other place to be and he squatted in the epicenter of this holocaust like its sole grim survivor and when he'd rested for a time he rose and went on.

When he went out it was a Saturday and he didn't know how many days had passed since Sutter had taken him for a walk down by the tie yard nor did he want to sort through these past days to get a count on them. The weather moderated and what snow remained lay in dirty melting skifts. The road too was muddy and he kept skirting the deeper areas of mud with a thought for the new shoes he wore. He carried a tan suitcase and it as well was newlooking and cheap. A pickup went by once but didn't stop, and Tyler took to the ditch to avoid the tireslung sluice of muddy water. Two large handpainted signs adorned the side of the truck proclaiming JESUS JESUS, but to Tyler it just looked like some old farmer making his Saturday pilgrimage to town.

Where the dirt road intersected the highway there was a tiny clapboard church climb with rose briars set back in the corner the roads made and a graveyard with toilers at work, and he saw that the dead were still being replevied from the earth. He glanced once, then turned away, striding on toward the blacktop. Before he reached it a voice halted him.

One old man, two young. The old man watched, and the other two, sons perhaps, flailed at the earth with pick and shovel. It was the old man who'd hailed him and the old man himself coming gingerly through the nettles. One of the younger men stood shovel in hand watching him go and he called Pa once but the old man just went on.

Tyler stood awkwardly holding the suitcase and scanning down the wavering blacktop for traffic.

Ain't this a hell of a mess? the old man asked. Old man with a caved and ravaged face, illfitting discolored teeth.

What?

All this mess. Granville Sutter killin that family back in the Harrikin and slippin through all them laws to Alabama or wherever. Crazy undertakers buryin men and women together and such. Did you ever hear of such crazy goins-on?

Tyler said he never had.

And the son of a bitch still alive in a hospital for lunatics in Memphis. Had a dead girl with him, I heard. Least they finally got her in the ground so's she can rest. Who knows what all he's done ain't come to light yet. Son of a bich layin up eatin three meals a day and sleepin good at night. He ever gets out of that asylum and comes back around here, somebody'll put him out of his misery. I may do it myself if my health holds up. If I'm gone these boys here will. We diggin up Martha to see if anything's wrong. We supposed to let the state do it, but the way I see it, it ain't none of the state's business.

Tyler turned to look. All these latterday Lazaruses, all these tawdry homemade resurrections. One of the young men fixed him with a cold cat's look and turned his face and spat then went back to work. Tyler turned to go, but the old man knotted his fingers in the fabric of Tyler's coatsleeve and stayed him.

I think we owe em that, don't you? All we can do for em. I know I'd hate to meet em up yonder and have to explain why they was done so shoddy. Ain't that the way you think?

What Tyler really thought was that the dead were so absolutely beyond anything the living might do for them it was almost past comprehension and he had no commitment to meet anyone anywhere. He feared that beyond the quilted gray satin of the undertaker's keep there was only a world of mystery that bypassed the comprehension of men and did not even take them into consideration. A world of utter darkness and the profoundest of silences.

Yet he said none of this. The old man carried death on his breath like a harbinger of the grave and his grip on Tyler's arm was fierce and clawlike.

Yes, Tyler said, that's the way I always thought.

Yet if there was only the three score and ten allotted, that seemed to him no small thing, and it seemed not unfair. He'd used up little of his, and the world was wide and its possibilities infinite, and all it took to get there was a highway that was free for the taking.

On the slope the two men had ceased their labors and stood peering into the earth. Pa? one of them called.

Tyler turned away from the sudden pain in the old man's eyes and pulled gently from his grasp and went on to the crossroads. He thought of the old man looking into a face he'd resigned himself to never seeing again in this world. He set the suitcase in a dry spot and seated himself on it and took off one of his new shoes and sat contemplatively rubbing his heel until faroff down the blacktop there was the sound of tires on macadam then the car itself wavering and ephemeral then gaining solidity in a rush.

A black Buick Roadmaster, he didn't even have to thumb it. It stopped and sat idling, and he took up the suitcase and peered through the window-glass and a curious trick of the light behind him rendered the glass opaque and mirrored so that instead of the driver of the car he saw only his own reflection leaning toward itself, and in this altered light it was a new Tyler, older, perhaps wiser, more versed in the reckless ways of a reckless world, as if in some way he had hitched a ride with a more sinister self, ten years down the line.

He opened the door and got in.